THE HAUNTING
ON THE OLD
GRAVEL PIT ROAD

LACYNDA MATHES

World Castle Publishing, LLC
Pensacola, Florida
Copyright © 2025 Lacynda Mathes
Hardback ISBN: 9798291797341
Paperback ISBN: 9798891264380
eBook ISBN: 9798891264397
First Edition World Castle Publishing, LLC, August 19, 2025
http://www.worldcastlepublishing.com
Licensing Notes
Cover: Cover Designs by Karen
Editor: Karen Fuller

Dear Reader,

Thank you for your continued support.

This book is the follow-up to *Ravens' Roost Farm* and features the same characters, focusing on Mike Poole and Jillian Fox this time around. Joe and Bethany are there, too. But this is Mike's story, not Joe's.

I dedicate this novel to my sister, Tammy Jean Deakes. I love you. I miss you.

As always, I wish to thank my best friend, Liz Welker, for her tireless help and ever-present ear as a sounding board for the stories that occupy my imagination. Thanks, also, to my husband, David, for helping me with my research and to comprehend what I learn.

LJM

PROLOGUE

Oak Grove, Virginia
August 1989

Sixteen-year-old Jenny Wade could watch Gordon Chisholm all day, every day. He was what every boy should be: smart, funny, good-looking, athletic, artistic...you name it, he was good at it. The quarterback of Washington and Lee High School's Varsity Football Team, the Eagles, and a senior, Gordon, was every girl's dream, but he was *her* boyfriend, hers and hers alone.

Gordon's family was firmly rooted in the community. They had owned this land since before the Revolutionary War. The current house was a Sears house built in 1942 by Elmer Pruce, Gordon's grandfather, for his bride-to-be, Violet Gardner. Additionally, Violet had grown up on the neighboring farm, Ravens' Roost, so Gordon's roots on this particular country lane ran as deep as the gravel pit that burrowed into the hill back behind the farmhouse.

Jenny, on the other hand, was a newcomer. Her family had moved to the community when she was 4. She had grown up in Placid Bay Estates, a housing development on property that had once belonged to another branch of the Gardner family and to the Poole family. Jenny's house was a prefabricated ranch built in the early 1970s.

She spent every free moment with Gordon, and today was no different. She had ridden her bike over to the Pruces' house immediately after breakfast. At that moment, she was watching Gordon change the oil in his Trans Am. He pulled the oil plug, and the dirty oil poured down his face. He sputtered, cursed, and laughed his fool head off. He shoved the bucket under the black stream as he moved out of the way.

Jenny, sitting on a gray-with-age cedar picnic table older than her house, under one of the many oaks in the yard, covered her mouth with both hands to stifle her laugh as he emerged from under the car covered in black oil.

"I wouldn't laugh if I were you," he threatened, giving chase to her as she jumped up and ran down the gentle slope of the yard to the dirt lane that ran between the Pruce's property and the Gardner's field. The corn was so tall that Ravens' Roost wasn't even visible from the road through the stalks. She turned left and ran up the hill toward the gravel pit.

As the fencing around the abandoned quarry came into view, Jenny drew up short. Gordon halted his chase and stopped short beside her. "Damn it!" he spat. The gravel pit was deep and full of brown water. It was a dangerous place and not open to the public, but kids from Placid Bay often snuck into the fenced area and swam in the treacherous pool that formed inside the manmade hole. They'd jump in from the top of the pit. The water depth was impossible to gauge and, depending on the rainfall, could be shallow or deep. There had been little rainfall over the last three months.

A group of 8 or so kids had snuck in through the gate and were gathered at the edge inside the fenced area. Pam Poole, 12, who lived on Arbor Farm, a property that had been swallowed up by Placid Bay Estates, but that pre-existed the housing development by more than a hundred years, stood on the precipice.

"Pamela Jean!" Gordon yelled. "Don't you dare jump!"

She looked defiantly toward Gordon. Her golden blonde hair was blowing in the late summer breeze. Jenny felt a rush of jealousy towards the girl. Why should Gordon call her name with such familiarity? Jenny reminded herself that Pam was a Poole after all. His family and hers were probably related. Pam took a rebellious step closer to the edge and looked down into the gravel pit. She screamed in utter terror.

CHAPTER 1

Oak Grove, VA
April 11, 2025

Jillian Fox stared at the car in the driveway. Lyle had promised not to be at the house so that she could pick up the things the judge had decreed to be hers. She'd agreed to leave the keys when she was done. She had her cousins, Hank and Bobby Wade, with her to help move the furniture pieces, but they weren't about to deal with Lyle. They were only begrudgingly helping as it was. She sighed heavily.

"You said he wouldn't be here, Jill," Hank called to her from inside his pickup truck.

"That's what he told me, Hank," she huffed.

The marriage had been a huge mistake. She'd never loved Lyle. He'd been a panacea for how she felt about Mike Poole. Actually, every man, other than Mike, had been a panacea for Mike. She'd spent half of her life now loving him, but trying to love anybody else. It was tiring.

Jillian had been a wild child. She was the product of a broken home. Her parents, Gordon and Jenny Chisholm, had separated when she was three and divorced when she was 8. Her father had never remarried and lived in California. Her mother had remarried Dr. Maxim Johnson when Jillian was 10. She had grown up with a stepsister. Kristin was one year older than she was and was the perfect one. Jillian was never able to live up to her mother's and stepfather's expectations and was always in trouble, whereas Kristin could do no wrong.

Oak Grove was a close-knit community. Everybody knew everybody. Jillian had known Mike and his twin brother all her life. She hadn't thought Mike was anything special as a child. In fact, when she was 6, at recess, he had sent a *Hot Wheels* car racing down a track. It jumped the track and flew through the air, striking Jillian in the face. She got a black eye and thoroughly disliked Mike Poole for the next several years. And then, when she was 16 and labeled as the crazy girl in school, while Mike was 17 and the popular football hero, he'd suddenly asked her out. He looked at her and smiled, and that was it. There was only room for Mike in her heart after that.

Unfortunately, neither her mother nor her stepfather liked Mike. Max had forbidden Jillian to date Mike, without any explanation, but Jillian had a thing about authority. She despised it. She did exactly what she wanted.

What she had wanted was Mike. She loved Mike. She was in love with Mike, and even now, as she was trying to retrieve her belongings from the wreckage of her second marriage 13 years later, she had to admit she was still in love with him. No matter how many times she pushed him away, she would always return to Mike, and he always took her back.

Her second marriage had ended at Christmas, when her daughter, Missy, had been trapped in a collapsed barn, and Lyle chose that opportunity to leave. But it had truthfully ended the January before, less than a year into the marriage, when Jillian had gotten two angel wings tattooed on her chest just below her clavicles. During the argument that ensued, Lyle pointed out that Mike's name was Michael Gabriel. Not that Lyle was wrong; the angel wings were a step too far.

She didn't care. Lyle had hit her. She wanted him to leave. She wanted to fail. What's more, she wanted to go back to Mike.

Mike and Jillian's problems began and ended with her. She was simply not good enough for Mike...not that he felt that way. It was her. All her.

Right from the start, Mike had been the golden god, and she had been just barely hanging on. He had the grades, the looks, the football scholarship to Ole Miss…She, on the other hand, struggled to get passing grades and was always fighting. Plus, her family was a mess. Her mother was domineering. Her stepfather was…well, suffice it to say, she hated him. But when she was with Mike, none of that mattered.

It wasn't like Mike's family was any less complicated, though. His parents were old…really old. His sister, Pam, was 15 years older than him and Kenny. It was a dirty little secret that his "parents" were really his grandparents and that his "sister" was his mother. Everybody knew it. Nobody said it out loud. And honestly, in this day and age, nobody cared, except Mike's "parents." They were very conservative.

Mike deferred his scholarship for a year when his "father" passed away just before his high school graduation, and then his brother, Kenny, joined the Marines. It had been a shock to the family, especially Pam, their "sister." Mike felt he needed to be home until things stabilized.

Jillian had been so excited, but her mother told her that Mike would give up his scholarship altogether for her, and then he'd regret it. That's where the problem began. That nagging little fear took root, and Jillian couldn't let it happen. When her mother and stepfather suggested she go out on a date with Rich Lowe, the son of a friend of her stepfather, she'd reluctantly agreed. Mike found out, and they fought. They never officially broke up, but Jillian started seeing Rich. Then she missed her period. She told Mike it was Rich's baby, which broke his heart and ensured his leaving.

Her marriage to Rich Lowe had lasted 5 years. Her daughter, Missy Michelle, was a beautiful blonde angel. Both she and Rich were brunettes. When her father, visiting from

California for Missy's fifth birthday, noted that Missy was the picture of Pam Poole at that age, it all fell apart.

She still insisted that Missy was Rich's daughter, but Rich doubted it. He agreed to pay child support and not seek a paternity test, but the marriage was over. He wanted a divorce. Feeling a complete failure, she had found herself on Mike's doorstep with Missy in tow. He'd taken them in.

It was the beginning of a terrible trend. She'd inevitably hurt Mike and leave. Then she'd start dating someone else, move in, break up, end up back with Mike, and start the cycle all over again. But no matter how badly she hurt him, Mike always took her back…every single time.

Each time she left him, he'd asked why she was breaking it off this time. She'd given him the same old platitude, "It's not you, it's me." But in this case, it was the literal truth. Mike was a deputy with a master's degree. She had her high school diploma, but only just. He was a pillar of the community. She was a clerk at the Stop In. He was an Adonis. She was…a single mother with too many tattoos and piercings. It boiled down to his being passed over for a promotion that should have been his…lead investigator. No one was more qualified. And still, because he was involved with her, the promotion had gone to Tom Palmer, who did have more seniority, it was true, but who had far less education and had solved fewer cases.

Jillian's stepfather, Max Johnson, who by then was a Virginia House of Delegates member, District 67, confided that her reputation certainly hurt Mike's chances when he had applied. When Mike was passed over, she knew Max had been right, and she did what was best for Mike, no matter how much it hurt her. She only wished it hadn't hurt Mike.

This time, she'd married the panacea. That had been a mistake. Lyle was abusive and jealous. But she reasoned that marrying him would make it harder to leave him, and therefore easier to stay away from Mike.

She'd done her utmost to do that, and then Christmas Eve 2024, the Stop In, where she worked, was robbed.

She had stared down the barrel of the pistol and tried to breathe.

"Put all the money in a bag!" the man had screamed at her. She had thought she might pass out, but, shaking and fighting back tears, she had grabbed a bag from below the counter and opened the register. She had grabbed all the cash from the bins and from under them. It wasn't more than a few hundred dollars. She had hoped the man would be satisfied with that, though. The rest was in the floor safe, and she had not been able to open that. She had shoved it all into the bag. "Put all the Marlboros in there, too!" he had demanded. She had pulled all the packs and both cases that were on the shelves behind her and shoved them into the bag with the cash. She had thrust the bag at him. He had laughed wickedly and lifted the gun. She had screamed and ducked as he shot out the camera behind her and over her head. Then he was gone.

She had stayed squatting behind the counter with both hands over her mouth for what seemed an eternity. Still sobbing, she had slowly stood on her shaking legs and reached for the phone to call 911.

Within minutes, two Westmoreland County Sheriff's Department cruisers had come speeding into the Stop In parking lot. She had burst into tears when she saw *him*. He had run toward her. Even though she was married to Lyle Fox, she had flung herself into Mike's open arms. Those arms had closed around her like a protective force field. She had clung to him and let out all that fear. He just let her.

A month later, she got the angel wing tattoos.

And she was facing the hard part of splitting with Lyle now. He was being a complete douchebag.

She knocked on the door.

Lyle opened it and tossed out three trash bags.

"There's your crap. Leave the key and get lost!" he yelled, slamming the door.

She pounded on the door as her cousins left her there alone.

————

Mike Poole had loved the Pruce farmhouse for years. It was a Sears house, the Elsmore, a prairie style, 2-bedroom, 1-bathroom house with a full basement. Elmer and Violet Pruce, married after the end of World War II, had managed to raise their family of 6 kids and then later their grandson, Gordon Chisholm, in the small home. They had converted the attic into an upstairs bedroom and had added a dormer and window over the covered front porch. When the property went up for sale, Mike jumped on it.

His good friends, Joe and Bethany Gardner, lived on the property adjacent to his, separated only by the old gravel pit road, a dirt lane really, that ran between his yard and Joe's field.

Today, Joe was helping Mike bushwhack the yard. Elmer had passed away 7 years ago, and the yard had returned to nature. The property had been maintained by his heir, Gordon Chisholm, but he lived in California now, so he had paid others for upkeep, and the house had been the focus. Needless to say, Mike and Joe had their work cut out for them. They labored all morning, and they had managed to clear enough that the house was once again visible from the road.

"Jesus," Mike said, wiping his brow. "This is a mess. What do you think? I'm just going to have to rototill the whole yard. Should I reseed…or put down sod?"

"Do you have sod in your budget?" Joe asked, taking a long drink from his water bottle.

"Hmmmm. It'll be tight, but I think it will be better than

seeding. Certainly, faster," he laughed.

"That it would be," Joe chuckled. "And easier for you, what with your black thumb."

"Yeah, it's a good thing I went into law enforcement instead of farming," Mike agreed.

They returned to work.

It was about half an hour later that a Westmoreland County Sheriff's Department cruiser went past at a high speed with its sirens blaring and lights flashing. It passed first Mike's new property and then Ravens' Roost, Joe and Bethany's property. It continued down the road toward the Veterinarian's clinic and Harris Lane.

Joe glared at it, and then he looked at Mike. He signaled for Mike to cut the bushwhacker's engine. Mike turned it off.

"Jillian is moving her stuff out of the house today," Joe called.

"She's what? By herself? Without the police there?"

Joe nodded.

Mike still loved Jillian. They were ill-fated, and it never worked out. He had exerted a great deal of effort over the last few months, since Bethany and Jillian had become such great friends, in avoiding being around Joe when Jillian was around. He always ended up heartbroken, and he knew he should just stay away, especially since she was still married. He knew she'd come back to him. She always did.

Over Christmas, after Jillian's daughter had been trapped in Joe's collapsed barn, things between Jillian and her husband, Lyle, had finally come to their inevitable end. Their marriage had only lasted two years. Lyle was an angry drunk, and, though he didn't drink often, it was too often, given he'd beat the crap out of Jillian every time. He and Mike had come to blows over it as well. Shortly after she'd married Lyle, he got drunk. Jillian had come out looking for him. He beat the crap out of her right there in the bar, where Mike, off duty, had happened to be out enjoying a beer himself. He'd stepped in. Mike had only wanted to protect Jillian, but he'd only made matters worse, since Lyle then assumed she and Mike were…intimate. They hadn't been since after she'd broken up with Bruce, her previous boyfriend, a year before marrying Lyle.

Jillian's way of dealing with the tension between her and Mike was to throw herself into toxic relationships. Mike's was to avoid relationships altogether…until Jillian's relationships crashed and burned, and she ended up on his doorstep. Thus far, she had avoided the last part of the equation, though the divorce was just final last week. Lyle was violent with more and more frequency recently, had tried as hard as he could to fleece her in the divorce, and had succeeded.

Seeing the cruiser heading toward the house she had lived in with that jackass, Mike gave into his protective urges and ran to his truck.

Joe, ever a good friend, jumped in beside him. Mike pulled out of the driveway at breakneck speed and barreled down the road after the cruiser. The cruiser had indeed been heading to the small house that Jillian and Lyle had been renting.

———————

Originally, Jillian had stayed, and Lyle had left with his girlfriend, Brittney Baxter, a woman more than a decade younger than him. However, Lyle was nothing if not vindictive. He demanded that the lease be given to him in the divorce. And since he had a lawyer, and Jillian did not, she had been forced to relinquish the home to him and Brittney. She had no choice but to go to her mother's and stepfather's, a situation she despised. Lyle had set the date for her to get her things, but now it seemed he'd decided that he wasn't going to let that happen. She should have brought the police with her, but Lyle had promised he'd not be there. She had finally managed to push her way inside, court order in hand, but she had no one to help move her stuff, and everything she touched, Lyle snatched away.

He was refusing to allow her to take her television and furniture. Hell, that bitch Brittney was actually wearing one of Jillian's shirts, her good pearl earrings, and one of her necklaces. In fact, her entire jewelry box was not even in the bedroom, having been hidden somewhere.

She tried to take Missy's PS5, and Lyle punched her in the face. It was the first time he'd ever hit her sober. When Jillian pushed Lyle away from her, Brittney jumped on her, punching and pulling her hair.

Jillian didn't know who called the police; Hank and Bobby, maybe, she assumed. Deputy Aaron Muse arrived and pulled Brittney off Jillian, as Mike Poole, off duty, and his friend, Joe Gardner, pulled in behind Aaron's cruiser. They stood in the doorway behind the deputy as Lyle opened the door.

"I want her out of my house," Lyle demanded.

"I have a court order to get my things. You agreed to it," she cried. She wiped the blood away from her busted lip.

Mike took one look at Jillian and lunged. Joe held him back, though.

"Get your stuff, Jillian," Aaron said.

"They hid my jewelry box, she's wearing some of my jewelry and my clothes, and they won't let me take my furniture or my daughter's PS5," she explained.

"Scumbag," Mike muttered, brushing off Joe.

Jillian handed the court order to Deputy Muse. He looked at it and then at Lyle and Brittney. "Take everything off that belongs to Mrs. Fox, Ma'am, and let her take her stuff. You two going to help with the furniture?" he asked Joe and Mike.

"Yeah," Mike replied. "That's what the truck's for."

Aaron nodded. "Just the stuff on the list, Gentlemen," he said, winking.

The two men had her stuff loaded on Mike's truck in no time. They even got her jewelry and clothes off the skinny little bitch.

She wasn't sure what to think. Her brain told her to stay as far away from Mike Poole as she could. All she ever did was hurt him. But her heart…and libido…only saw the man she'd ever truly loved. He was a strapping 6'1", not quite the giant Joe was, but still…tall…and God, so handsome. His sandy blond hair, thick and luscious, was cut above his ears, but still long enough on top that it had great style. His square jaw, straight nose, and even his earlobes were so incredibly appealing. That was just above his incredibly broad shoulders. Everything below them was…sex on a stick.

As he and Joe loaded her sofa, the last item on her list, onto the truck, she walked toward him. He climbed out of the back of the truck just as she reached him. Her bottom lip was swollen, but she no longer felt it. She grabbed his shirt in both fists and pulled him to her. She kissed him.

Aaron sighed. Joe shook his head. "Great. This again," Joe said, sighing.

"Tell me about it," Aaron mumbled.

Mike's arms enveloped her, and she didn't hear anything else. Instead, as they kissed, she prayed. *God, let me have this. Please. We can't be happy without each other. Let us be happy together. Please. This time, let us be happy.*

———

Jenny pulled into the driveway of Ravens' Roost. She had to admit, the place looked great. Six months ago, the place looked… haunted. That was the best way to describe it. And now, it was a well-kept, pleasant-looking home. Joe had married the girl to whom Melanie Horton had left the property. Apparently, they had been in an ongoing relationship for many years. Rumor had it that he was the father of her children. And they were expecting another. Further, and of interest to Jenny, Bethany Gardner was Jillian's new best friend. Her daughter and Joe's wife were nearly inseparable. And Jenny was looking for her daughter.

She switched off the ignition. She checked her lipstick in the visor mirror and climbed out. She walked up to the front porch of the old, freshly painted, white farmhouse and rang the doorbell.

The child who opened the door, a girl, confirmed the rumors. She was the spitting image of Joe Gardner.

"Hello, Sweetheart. My name is Jenny Johnson. I'm Jillian's mama. Is she here, perhaps?" she asked, smiling at the girl.

"Hi, Mrs. Johnson. I'm Meghan Alice Gardner. No, Jillian isn't here. But do you want to talk to Mommy and Daddy?"

"Could I?" Jenny asked. The girl was a charmer. She smiled for real.

"Mommy! Daddy!" the girl yelled. "Jillian's mama wants to talk to you."

"Jesus!" Joe's voice came from somewhere in the house.

"What?" a woman's voice responded.

There was a dining room to her left just inside the foyer. And from what must be the kitchen, Joe emerged, wiping his hands on a tea towel as he strode through the dining room toward Jenny. The woman, her baby bump just starting to show, followed him. "What, Joe?"

"Go home, Jenny," he said to the woman at the door.

"I'm looking for Jillian. She was supposed to get her stuff from the house today, and she hasn't come home," Jenny pleaded.

"She got it," he said.

"Seriously, Joe. I've been trying to call her all afternoon. It goes straight to voicemail," she said, grabbing his arm.

He pinched the bridge of his nose and shook his head. "She's fine."

"Where is she?" Bethany asked.

"Oh, God," Jenny huffed, finally understanding. Jillian was with *him*.

"She's 31 years old. You can't keep them apart. And he's a good man...unlike the gems you've pushed her to marry. Stay out of it, Jenny."

"Who?" Bethany asked earnestly.

"Mike," he answered her.

"Mike? Really?" she asked. Had Jillian really not told Bethany? Maybe there was hope to keep her away from Mike Poole after all...if she hadn't told her best friend about him.

"Yeah...since high school," he replied. "Anytime her life falls apart, she ends up back with Mike."

"They...love each other?" Bethany asked.

"Hah. Yeah. Deeply," Joe said.

Jenny turned on her heel and trudged back to her car. No. This wasn't going to happen again. She'd never approve of Mike Poole. He was...too much like Gordon. Hell, he'd even bought Gordon's childhood home.

Jenny hated the place. Things happened there that deeply disturbed her. She wasn't going to leave Jillian there. She got back behind her wheel, backed out of the driveway, and spun her tires on the street as she headed toward the old gravel pit road.

She turned her car into the driveway of the house where she'd first fallen in love. How ironic that she was here to thwart love. She looked up at that attic window...and her heart filled with dread. Terror gripped her.

She took several deep breaths and worked up the courage to get out of the car. Immediately, she could swear she felt the cold, damp hand of Jacob Tilly slowly finger-walking up her spine. She shook off the feeling and climbed the steps. She pounded on the door with her clenched fist.

Jillian opened the door, wearing one of Mike's shirts...and nothing else.

"I'm not leaving, Mama," she said.

CHAPTER 2

Jillian loved her mother. The truth was that the only reason she hadn't married Mike to begin with was her mother. Jenny Johnson was fundamentally opposed to Jillian and Mike. Jillian was not sure why that was. When they had been teenagers, Jenny had claimed Mike was too wild and had introduced her daughter to Rich Lowe, the son of a friend of Max's. Rich was older than Jillian. He was a business student at Randolph-Macon College.

That's how she came to break Mike's heart the first time. Mike had received a football scholarship to the University of Mississippi. With his leaving looming, Jillian had given in to the pressure exerted on her by her family. She hadn't told Mike. When he found out she had gone on a few dates with another guy, they fought. When she found out she was pregnant, she told Mike it was Rich's baby. The truth was she didn't really know if Rich or Mike was Missy's father.

When Rich had learned that he might not be Missy's father 5 years later, it had ended her marriage. He did not demand a paternity test and agreed to pay child support. It was one of the few kindnesses he'd shown her. He had hardly been faithful himself. He just wanted out.

Mike had graduated and returned home, having joined the sheriff's department. She ran right back to him. And he took her back.

She had intended to tell him her suspicions about Missy then, but her mother once again started pushing for her to date somebody else. And this time, her family didn't fight fair. Her stepfather pointed out her many indiscretions that threatened

Mike's budding career with her own wild behavior. She left him again…to protect him from her.

But she just couldn't stay away. With every break-up, she found herself on his doorstep. And in between, she behaved more and more erratically, guaranteeing she'd break his heart again to protect him from herself. It was a vicious cycle.

This time, she was determined to not give in to her inferiority complex's negative whispers. She wanted Mike. Mike wanted her. She had matured enough to understand that her wild behavior was not criminal and not as big a threat to his career as she had been led to believe previously, especially since he'd laughed when she told him and explained to her in great detail why Tom Palmer was more qualified for the job. He'd never expected to get it.

When her mother knocked, she was prepared to tell her to kick rocks.

"I'm not leaving," she said as she closed the door in her mother's face.

Mike wrapped his arms around her waist from behind, kissing her neck below the ear.

"Good job, Babe. Now…all you have to do is mean it," he whispered against her skin.

"I mean it. I really do, Mike. You're all I ever wanted. I swear," she whimpered, turning to face him and kissing his soft lips.

A knock sounded on the door. She pulled away from him and swung open the door angrily. "Seriously, Mama!" she yelled. Only it wasn't her mama. Bethany stood there instead. Joe was behind her, leaning against the porch post, looking off towards the Grand Event Center across the street. "Oh…Bethany, Joe," she said in a calmer tone. "Come in."

———

Bethany sat down on the bed as Jillian pulled on a pair of

jeans. "Why didn't you ever tell me? I'd have understood, Jill," she insisted.

Jillian gave a haughty laugh and sat beside her. "I know you would have, Honey. Probably better than anyone else in this world. It…it hurt to talk about, Bethy. It's such a miserable tale. I always hurt him."

"Why would you do that?" Bethany asked, taking her hand.

"Because I'm stupid," Jillian sobbed. "My family convinced me I was bad for him." She stared at the floor.

"Well, that's ridiculous!" Bethany said, hugging her. "I think the two of you make perfect sense together." She started laughing.

"What's so damn funny?" Jillian asked.

"I was trying to convince Joe to set you up with Mike," Bethany guffawed.

Jillian chuckled twice and then started to laugh.

"That would have been a hard sell to Joe," she said, laying her head on Bethany's shoulder. "He isn't a fan of our being together."

"Jill, Joe is the one who told Mike about your moving your stuff," Bethany explained. "He's…concerned…true. But he knows what love is."

"I'm not walking away this time," Jill asserted. "I'm going to marry him, Bethany. I was your maid of honor 5 months ago. Feel like returning the favor?"

"When?"

"Tomorrow…Can I borrow your dress?"

———

"You're certain?" Joe asked.

"I always have been," Mike chortled.

"True," Joe acquiesced.

Mike took out a cigarette and stuck it into his mouth. He

looked at Joe and offered him one. "Nah, I don't smoke. I haven't since high school. Stuck one in backwards after I set it down to climb a fence…and that ended that bad habit," Joe laughed.

"Yeah, I quit, too, until that ghost threw that pitcher across the kitchen in your house. I haven't been able to re-quit since, I'm afraid." He referred to a strange occurrence in Joe's house a few months back that he couldn't explain. Joe could, but it wasn't believable. It really had been a ghost.

"There are ghosts here, too, you know," Joe teased, sitting beside Mike on the porch steps.

"Yeah, I know the stories. The kid who broke his neck diving into the gravel pit. The Civil War soldiers out by Mattox Creek. The Lady in gray out at the Pruce Homestead. I've been here two weeks, and no pitchers have flown across the room," he laughed. Mike took a long drag off the cigarette.

"I just don't want you to get hurt again, Mike. I…I love Jillian. She's great. I'm not so sure she's great for you." Joe stared straight ahead at the dogwood they'd left when they bushwhacked earlier in the day. It was a gorgeous tree, full of glorious pink blooms.

"Joe, when Greg tricked Bethany into getting a protective order against you, you backed off, but did you give up?"

Joe shook his head slowly. "Point taken." He smiled wryly and slapped Mike on the back.

They sat quietly for a moment.

"Joe," Mike said after the long pause. "I think Missy's mine." Joe breathed in through his nose and then exhaled. "I've thought so for a long while, now."

Joe nodded. "What do you want to know?"

"How'd Ryan take it? The news that you're his father, not Greg?"

"Well Greg was a sociopath who tortured and raped his mother, so he was okay with it. Rich is a pompous ass, but he's not…um, Greg," Joe laughed. "I don't know how Missy is gonna react. I can tell you, she's a great kid, but that's all I got. What does Jillian say?"

"She hasn't said anything…at all…" Mike admitted.

"I'll take on Pam for you if you want. I'll back you up, but if you're going to marry her, you might want to talk about that first."

Mike took another drag and exhaled a cloud of smoke. "I love her. No matter what. My sister…she'll just have to deal with it."

Joe chuckled. "Pam will understand more than you think she will, Mike." Sister, his foot.

He sighed. "Yeah, I know." He smiled warily. "I'm not stupid, Joe."

Joe laughed outright. "I know that. You're the one with the degree from Ole Miss."

Bethany and Jillian came out of the front door. Joe stood. "Let's let them talk, Babe," he offered.

"Please stay!" Mike and Jillian said in unison.

Joe focused on that dogwood. "Are you sure?" he asked. This was a private conversation. It was true that he and Bethany could offer insight and support, having had a similar conversation themselves, but still, they had done it privately. He sat back down.

"Yeah. I need a witness," Jillian joked, sitting on the porch swing.

Joe smiled and nodded. Bethany sat beside Jillian and took her hand.

The four of them sat there for what seemed like several minutes.

Finally, Mike seemed to have worked up the courage. "M…M…Missy?" he stammered. "Whose child is she? Mine or Rich's?"

"I honestly don't know," Jillian answered. "I've always wanted her to be…yours. I…I see you in her…but I can't be certain. Does it matter?"

"No," he said, shaking his head.

Jillian started to laugh. "All those diapers, outfits, toys, books, groceries…the laptop, the PS5, the iPad, the iPhone…they all appeared on our doorstep. Anytime she needed or wanted something. There it was. I always credited my mama. It was you."

Mike folded his hands together in front of him, his elbows on his knees. He stared at his hands. "Yeah. It was me."

"How would you know?" she asked, laying her hand on her chest.

"Um…Kristin told me."

"Kristin? Kristin Johnson? My uptight bitch stepsister?" Jillian exclaimed.

Mike laughed. "Uptight, I'll give you. But she's not really a bitch, Jill. She cares about you…and Missy."

"Kristin Johnson? The woman who has a crush on Joe?" Bethany interjected.

Mike grinned. "One of them, yes."

"Stop that," Joe said, shoving his friend's shoulder.

"So, what do we do about Missy?" Jillian asked.

"I'd like to know either way," Mike said. "It doesn't matter to me. I love you both anyway, but if she's my daughter…I want to know that. What's her blood type?"

"What?" Jillian asked.

"Her blood type?" Mike repeated.

"Oh…I know that…from the accident at Christmas. It's O+," she said confidently.

"Yours?" he asked.

"Um, I donated blood at the hospital after the accident. It's B+," she replied.

"Did Rich?"

"Yeah, he did."

"Do you know his blood type?" Mike pushed.

"Um, hold on." She stood and walked over to Mike's truck. She found a box of documents and rummaged through the papers inside until she found documents from Missy's hospital stay overnight after being trapped in a collapsed barn. "AB-," she announced, holding up a document.

"Oh, shit," Joe exclaimed. Then he clasped both hands over his mouth.

"What? What does that mean?" Jillian asked.

"That there is no way Rich is Missy's father, but it's possible I am. I'm A-." Mike said, shaking his head. "How much child support has he paid, Jillian?"

"$68 a month," she replied.

"Sixty-eight...! Why so little?" Mike sputtered in anger.

"Max said it was best. That he wouldn't contest paternity and would give me $68 a month, and that was better than nothing."

"Jesus, Jillian. You should have gotten a test. Either he or I would have ended up paying the proper amount...way more than $68 a month...That's the bare minimum by law. For somebody with no income! And it would have been me."

"Ha. Gotcha. His blood type eliminates him, doesn't it?"

Mike nodded.

"And yours...obviously doesn't...since there were only two possibilities," she reasoned. "And as an oncologist, Max would know that."

Mike smiled and pointed at his nose.

"$6,528," he calculated in his head quickly.

"There goes the sod budget," Joe chuckled. "How will you ever survive?" He laughed.

"Yeah. I've got it. I've been setting aside $1,000 a month in an IRA to cover child support for the last 9 years or so...but I can cover sixty-five hundred with a check."

"Nine years? I've only been divorced from Rich for 8," Jillian wondered out loud.

"I came home and saw her," he said, smiling lovingly. Jillian smiled back at him.

———

Kristin Johnson sat cross-legged on her sofa, working on her lesson plan for Monday. It didn't matter that it was Friday. She had no plans for the weekend.

The house was too quiet. She was having trouble concentrating. She looked around the empty great room and sighed. She was 32 years old, soon to be 33, and she didn't even have a pet to share her home with. And it was a nice house. It was just so empty.

She gave up on the lesson plan. It was already done before she'd started, anyway. She had just been looking for something to do. She set it aside, uncrossed her legs, and stood. She stretched and went to the kitchen.

She wasn't really hungry yet, but she grabbed a bottle of water from the fridge. She cracked it open and took a swig, leaning against the counter. There was nothing that needed doing in here either. She looked at her reflection in the stainless steel of the fridge door.

She wasn't unattractive. She pulled out the tight, high ponytail her long, dark brown hair was always in and let her hair cascade down her back and over her shoulders. Her features instantly softened. She was almost pretty, she decided as she looked at herself.

The doorbell rang, and she sighed before going to answer it.

She opened the front door to her stepmother.

"Oh, Kristin, she's done it again," Jenny wailed, pushing past her without waiting to be invited inside.

"Who's done what again?" Kristin asked, closing the door. Jenny strode angrily to the sofa and tossed her purse down on it. She turned to look at Kristin.

"Oh, sweetheart, your hair," she criticized before continuing. "Who do you think? Jillian's gone back to Mike Poole. I swear, that girl."

"She's a full-grown woman, Jenny, not a girl, and everyone knew she would. He's even set up a room for Missy in his new house already. I don't understand the problem. He's really good to her. They love each other," Kristin replied, as she quickly put her hair back into the ponytail.

"He's not right for Jillian," Jenny insisted. "I know that you're friends with him, but surely you can understand why he isn't a good match for her."

"Not really," she retorted. The truth was, Mike was more than a friend. Their relationship wasn't romantic, but Mike had always been there for Kristin whenever she needed him, and she had likewise been there for him. It had always been that way from childhood. She loved the Poole boys like family.

Jenny moaned about Mike for twenty minutes before she left. Kristin began to miss the loneliness she'd been experiencing before Jenny had arrived. Mike wasn't anything like Jenny believed him to be, but it did no good to argue with her about it. She believed what she believed.

As she closed the door behind Jenny when the woman finally left, she breathed a sigh of relief. "Good for them," she said to the now-empty house. "God, let them make it work this time. They both deserve to be happy."

As she watched the news, Mike texted her. "Hey. Getting married tomorrow. Please be there."

She texted back, "You sure Jillian will be okay with that?"

"She knows you are important to me. And she loves you. You two just need to talk it out," he replied moments later.

"Will Joe and his wife be there? She might not like that I'm there." Kristin had pursued Joe Gardner for years. She had proclaimed to anyone who would listen that she would only be Joe's woman. Joe had other ideas. The truth was, she was happy for him. She hadn't really been hurt all that badly.

"He will. You can't avoid them forever."

"You know I'll do anything for you…even suffer the vitriol of Joe's new wife. I'll be there," she responded after a moment's reflection. Who cared if she was a little uncomfortable? Mike wanted her to be there. He had done more for her than she could ever repay. She closed her eyes as the tears came, thinking about her baby again, the baby she gave away, the baby no one knew about except Mike, who'd helped her through it.

———

Pam set the garlic bread on the table beside the spaghetti dish.

"Kenny, dinner!" she called.

He bounded into the kitchen like a big kid. "Hmmm. I love your spaghetti," he announced, sitting in his regular seat across from hers.

"Ah, thanks," she said, taking her seat. She adored both of her boys, but Mike was independent. Kenny…well, he'd been severely wounded in Afghanistan, and the traumatic brain injury had left him dependent upon her. She was so thankful that he was alive. She needed him as much as he needed her. She knew that.

She served him a plateful of spaghetti. He took a forkful and slurped a long noodle into his mouth, sauce splattering on his face. They both laughed. She reached across to wipe his mouth, and he playfully evaded her. They laughed harder.

"Have you thought about my moving to Heritage Gardens?" he asked.

Lately, he'd been wanting to move into the assisted living

where her Aunt Bertie lived. She was the one resisting. She'd go crazy without him around. God, he couldn't leave her. She'd have nobody to share moments like this with. She hated being alone.

"I don't think it's a good idea," she said firmly. What if something happened to him and she wasn't with him?

He looked dejectedly at his plate. "You don't think I can do anything," he mumbled.

"That's not true," she argued. "But what if you have a seizure? I...just think we should talk to your neurologist first."

"Whatever," he huffed. They finished the meal in silence.

After they had eaten and she'd done the dishes, she took a moment on the back patio while Kenny played a video game. She looked up at the clouds and drank a beer.

There had been a few moments in her life when she'd felt intense emotional turmoil. This really shouldn't be one of them. He just wanted a little autonomy. It shouldn't compare to when he'd been severely wounded and lay in a coma for 4 months... or when, over the next two and a half years, he struggled to relearn to do everything. That had been the hardest thing she had ever suffered through, harder than the turmoil of becoming a mother to twins at 15 or even of getting pregnant through non-consensual means. She hadn't been raped exactly, but she'd been manipulated and groomed until she had consented. Was it harder even than finding Jacob Tilly's body when she was 12?

She closed her eyes. That was a tough one. That had scarred her...enough that she became vulnerable to the grooming that would come later. "It's okay, Pamela Jean. It's okay," Gordon had whispered to her, hugging her close, much to Jenny Wade's ire. But it wasn't okay, not for Jacob Tilly. To this day, she could still see him, lying naked, twisted and broken, in that puddle of shallow water above the deeper cuts into the earth.

CHAPTER 3

Joe and Mike unloaded Jillian's belongings from the truck. Her newer things replaced some of Mike's things in the house. The rest they moved to the basement.

The second bedroom, Jillian discovered, had been decorated in purple and silver, Missy's favorite color combination. All her things were moved in there. Mike really had been preparing for them. He had just been waiting for Jillian.

After they had finished, they got into Mike's truck, since Bethany and Joe had walked over, to drive back to Ravens' Roost. A month or so ago, Joe had purchased a late-model minivan for Bethany. She loved the old Caddy that Melanie Horton, Joe's cousin and friend, had bequeathed to her, and he didn't want her to have to give it up, but with a baby on the way, and three children, they needed a people hauler. Bethany got the minivan, and Joe got the kids into it. Jillian got in with Bethany. Joe rode with Mike.

They drove to Westmoreland Shores, a housing development about halfway between Mattox Creek Bridge and Colonial Beach, a small town near the community of Oak Grove.

Max and Jenny Johnson resided in a large mid-century ranch with an in-ground pool. Dr. Maxim Johnson, an oncologist and state delegate, was cutting his own grass, with an overly large and expensive lawn mower for the size of his yard, when the two vehicles pulled into the concrete driveway.

"You grew up here?" Bethany asked. Jillian understood the question. It had been asked by all of her friends ever since her mother had married Max. The house certainly wasn't as grand as the houses in Connecticut, where Bethany had previously lived, but still, something about it screamed money. Her person did not.

"Yeah. Me and Kristin," Jillian acknowledged. "I got pregnant and married out of high school. Kristin went to Radford University, then later St. Francis University in Pennsylvania for her master's degree, and became a teacher. She's never married. I'm starting marriage number 3," Jillian said, smiling sadly.

Bethany thought back to her one-time meeting Kristin Johnson. She had seemed a deeply unhappy woman. That had been just before Christmas. The Johnsons may have had money, but they'd sure screwed up their daughters.

"Where does Kristin live now?" Bethany asked.

Jillian pointed to an A-frame alpine house back the way they'd come in and down an adjacent road. "Max and Mama bought it for her when she got her master's."

"But they didn't buy a house for you?"

"I told you, Honey, I'm a real black sheep," she chuckled.

Missy came running out of the front door. Jillian opened the minivan door and got out, standing in the open space behind the door. "Go get your stuff, Baby. We're goin' home," she called.

Behind the van, Mike and Joe both got out of the truck. Max stopped mowing and cut the tractor's engine. He climbed off and rushed forward. "No, you don't! I'll call the police."

"I am the police," Mike mumbled. Then he screwed on a smile and stepped forward. "Dr. Johnson, do you think you have any recourse but to hand over my daughter? I've seen the blood typing from December. There's no way she's Rich's. So, either go back to mowin', or help her get her stuff," he said, coolly, calmly, while smiling.

"Y…you understand blood typing?" Dr. Johnson stuttered.

"I have a bachelor's degree in criminal justice from Ole Miss and a master's degree in forensic science from VCU. Yes, I understand how blood types work."

Jenny came out and grabbed Missy's shoulder from behind. Standing on the stoop, she proclaimed, "She isn't your daughter! She's normal!"

Mike blinked several times, shook his head, and said, "Huh?"

"She's normal! She's not some inbred, retard…like…"

"Kenny?" Mike asked, incredulously. "Kenny's not retarded. And that's a horrible word. He suffered a traumatic brain injury in Afghanistan. He was 'normal' before that. You… bitch."

"He's not retarded? He wasn't born that way?"

"I dated Jillian throughout high school. You thought he was retarded? He was an honor student!"

"I…I didn't know him," Jenny admitted. "But still, you're Jillian's cousin," she insisted.

"Um. No. I'm not," he retorted.

"Her father is Gordon Chisholm," Jenny said, as if that made her point.

"I know," he replied, furrowing his brow. "I'm not related to Gordon…closely, anyway. He's a Pruce. I'm a Poole. Our families settled here at about the same time, but we're not related. I mean maybe 150-200 years ago."

"You're related."

"Um, no…" he explained. "I think maybe by marriage… but not by blood."

Jenny looked confused. "You're not related?"

"Do you think I'd marry my cousin?" he asked.

She turned to look at her husband. "You said that Jillian couldn't be with Mike Poole because of genetic reasons. I believed you."

"Holy shit," Jillian exclaimed. "Half my life…because you didn't understand his genealogy? Mama!"

"Deputy Poole is my father?" Missy finally interjected.

"Yeah. I named you Missy because he was away at Ole Miss. The University of Mississippi. And Michelle...because it's French for Michael. Get your stuff, Baby."

Missy turned to walk into the house.

"That's why you named her Missy?" Jenny pondered. "I...I still don't like that house..." she sobbed. "Terrible things happen there."

"Don't be ridiculous," Jillian scoffed.

Missy re-emerged from the house with her bag. She ran to Mike and threw her arms around his waist tightly, closed her eyes, and laid her head against his chest. She started to cry. "You're really my daddy? Cuz you've always been the best daddy. I always wanted you to stay."

"I've never gone anywhere, Missy," Mike told her, hugging her back.

"I know," she said. "That's why you're the best! Plus, Mama's always happy when you're together and sad when you're not."

———

Missy stood in her new room. It was perfect. She had always hoped that Mike was her dad. He was so much better than Rich. She supposed that Rich had tried, but he was way more devoted to his new family. He'd been grateful to get away with as little child support as he could. Now that made perfect sense. Rich knew. He had to. Now that she knew, she wondered why he'd bothered to pay anything.

Mike, it seemed, really knew her. He'd prepared a room for her in his house in her favorite colors with posters of her favorite singer, Taylor Swift. But best of all, Molly sat on her bed. Molly was her American Girl Doll that Mike had bought her when she was just 8, when he and her mama had been together between Adam and Bruce. Bruce had told her mama to leave the doll, and her mama had done what he asked. She didn't know Mike had kept her. The last time he and her mama had been together before Lyle, that asshat, had only been for a few weeks, and she hadn't seen the doll. She walked slowly to the bed and picked her up. "Hi, Molly," she said through her tears. She hugged the doll to her chest. She sat on the four-poster bed with a sweet canopy and gazed around her room in wonderment.

Her gaze landed on a picture, framed and hung on the wall above her desk. It was a picture she'd drawn herself and given to Mike when she was 5. It was drawn on pink construction paper with crayons. Her stick figure mother had brown hair to her stick figure shoulders and wore a purple dress. Mike had a big yellow star on his brown deputy's uniform over his stick figure chest and a big cowboy-style hat. And Missy…she was between them, her stick figure hands holding onto one of each of theirs. They stood under a big tree, and a big rainbow arched over their heads.

Missy smiled, lay back on her bed, and kicked her feet excitedly, still hugging her doll.

She took out her phone and FaceTimed her friend, Carly. "Hey, Carly! Look at my room!" she squealed, turning the camera and sweeping the room. She turned the camera back to herself. "Isn't it cool?"

"Your mama found a new house?" Carly asked, nodding.

"We moved back in with Mike," she announced. "He's my real daddy."

"Ha! I knew it. Didn't I say that years ago, Doug?" Carly's mama's voice came from the phone as she walked behind Carly on the FaceTime app. "And of course, she moved back in with Mike Poole. No big surprise there."

Carly sighed. "I can't even pretend she's talking about something else," she laughed.

The image on the screen in Missy's hand turned to snow.

She dropped her phone. For a split second, she'd seen a boy, about her age, dripping wet with pale white skin and saucer-like black eyes. Then the screen went back to snow again, and then back to Carly. She was still laughing about her mother's eavesdropping like nothing had happened at all.

Missy tried to catch her breath. "That was weird, Carly," she gasped. "I just saw a ghost in my phone!"

"Really? That's fire!" Carly giggled.

———

Jillian climbed into bed. Mike had fallen asleep while she was in the bath. She ran her index finger down his nose to his perfect lips and stifled a giggle by biting her own lip. He smiled and opened his eyes. "Hey," he said.

"How long did you practice that opening?" she asked.

"Hours," he replied, pulling her into his arms. She snuggled under the cover against him, laying her head on his chest. He kissed her temple and sighed contentedly. "I'm glad you're back, Baby. I've missed you."

"Hmmmm. I've missed you, too. More than you'll ever know. I was so stupid to listen to Mama and Max. I should have listened to Kristin. But I just…can't stand her," she said, laughing.

"Kristin isn't that bad. She just tries too hard," Mike said.

"Yeah. That's true. Especially when it comes to Joe. She's still in mourning."

"Poor woman. He only has eyes for Bethany," Mike agreed, nuzzling his chin against the top of Jillian's head. "I have off tomorrow, but I have shifts on Sunday through Wednesday nights. I'm sorry I can't give you a honeymoon right away. But I'll put in for vacation in July. Maybe the three of us can go to Ocean City, Maryland. Maybe with Joe and Bethany and the kids, if you like."

"Sounds like fun," she agreed, her eyes feeling heavy. She let them close and drifted off to sleep in Mike's embrace. Jillian was home.

It was around 3 am that the 4-wheel-drive truck roared into the driveway. Its floodlights were aimed at the bedroom window. Its horn blared three times. Jillian sat bolt upright in bed.

Mike was already out of bed and racked his weapon as she stared incredulously at him. He appeared fearless. "Stay here," he said sternly.

He walked out the door. Jillian stood and hurried to the bedroom door. Missy appeared at her door. The two of them instinctively huddled together in the hallway as Mike strode bravely, unwaveringly, toward the front door.

Big Billy Walsh's voice rang out from outside, "I warned you, Jillian! Get your cop ass out here, Mike Poole! Time to pay the price for disregarding the boss's wishes." Oh, God! Big Billy. She'd forgotten the threat he'd made after she got the angel wings. He was a friend of Lyle's. She'd dismissed it as an idle threat.

It was in February. He'd come into the Stop In when she was working a night shift. The store was empty except for her. He had gone to the snack aisle. He walked slowly toward the checkout counter, wearing a crazy grin on his face. Like the Joker, she'd thought at the time. He'd put a pack of gum on the counter. When she reached for it to ring it up, he'd grabbed her wrist and twisted it. "Stay away from Mike Poole, bitch. Or don't. I'd love to kill a cop if you don't," he'd sneered.

"Want the gum or not?" she had asked.

"Sure, why not?" he'd retorted, releasing her. She rang him up. He had paid and left. She hadn't given it another thought.

Mike tossed down his weapon and took a BB gun from the cabinet. He pumped it up 5 times.

Mike flung the door open, pointed his air rifle, and pulled the trigger three times. The floodlights flashed out. He pulled the trigger twice more. Glass shattered. He lowered the gun. "That's a warning, Billy. Get the hell off my lawn, or I'll make it so that not even Joe can resurrect that heap."

"Stop!" Big Billy Walsh yelped. "Why you gotta act like that, Mike? The boss just said to put a scare in her. We weren't really gonna hurt you!"

Mike huffed. "Like you could, punk. Get out of here."

Jillian stared in disbelief. Mike never needed her protection. Not from her. Not from Big Billy. He had only ever needed her.

CHAPTER 4

Mike awoke to the sun shining through the window and a knock on the door. Jillian, facing away from him, groaned and pulled the blanket over her pretty head. He smiled and smacked her ass. "Rise and shine, Peaches," he teased.

"'Peaches'?" she queried.

He just grinned.

She rolled her eyes. "That Eat Some Peaches song, right?"

He laughed.

She smiled wickedly. "Not that I minded." He growled and grabbed her around the waist. She squealed and laughed as he held her down under him and kissed her neck.

But the knock at the door persisted.

"Damn," he huffed, rolling off her and lying on his back.

"Mikey!" came his brother's voice.

He stood and walked to the window, which from the porch was to the left of the front door. He opened the window and leaned his head out. "Hey, Kenny. Watcha doin'?"

"Oh. There you are. Are you still sleepin'? Pam said I could come spend the day with you. She really wanted me to come over. Are you fightin' with Pam?"

Jillian stuck her head out the window beside Mike's. "Hi, Kenny. You want some breakfast?"

"Oh. Hi, Jillie. I guess you are fightin' with Pam, then, huh, Mike?"

"No. I'm not fightin' with her, Kenny. It'll be fine," Mike laughed.

Kenny grinned. "Are you happy?"

"Yep," Mike answered.

"Then it will be okay," Kenny agreed.

"So, Pam just left you on my porch...our porch?" Mike asked his fraternal twin.

Kenny turned around. "Oh dang, she's gone. I guess she did."

"Well, come on in, then," Mike said, stepping back from the window.

"Through the window?" Kenny chuckled.

"Why not?" Jillian said, grinning at Kenny.

Kenny had suffered a traumatic brain injury in 2016 in Afghanistan while serving in the Marines. He had always been a little different...a little socially awkward. Now he seemed more childlike. He suffered headaches and mood swings as well as severe anxiety on occasions. But he was the kindest person alive, despite his struggles. The fact that he could walk and talk at all was a miracle.

Kenny's guardian angel had been none other than Joe Gardner, Mike's good friend. They had served together in the same unit. Joe had thrown himself on top of Kenny after he'd been wounded when the IED had exploded, flipping the truck Kenny had been driving. He had protected Kenny from insurgents' gunfire until they were rescued. He suffered injuries himself, though not as severe.

Kenny giggled and took the few steps from the door to the window. Jillian moved back. Kenny climbed through. He stood straight and turned to Jillian. "Hi, Jillie," he said, grinning.

"Hi, Kenny," she said to him, smiling.

He grasped both her shoulders, pulled her toward him, and hugged her. "What's for breakfast?" he asked, holding her tightly.

Mike burst out laughing.

"Cereal," she said.

"Bethany gives me pancakes, eggs, and bacon."

"Yeah, I love her, but I'm not doing that," Jillian snickered. "Go knock on her door."

"I like Frosted Flakes," he announced, releasing her.

"We got 'em," Mike interjected. "Now get out so we can get dressed. You know your way to the kitchen."

———

Kenny filled his bowl with cereal and milk and grabbed a spoon before heading into the living room, where he promptly sat cross-legged on the hardwood floor in front of the TV. He reached over to the coffee table, grabbing the remote. He selected Hulu and started watching *Resident Alien*. He was stuffing his face with cereal and laughing at the Sheriff and Deputy when Mike stepped into the room wearing a black suit and tie. He was holding a blue suit and tie on a hanger. Kenny looked up at his brother. "Why you dressed up?" he asked.

"Just put on the suit, Kenny," Mike replied, winking.

"Are we goin' to church or somethin'?"

Then Missy came into the living room, too, and she was wearing a dress. Missy hardly ever wore a dress. "Isn't it Saturday?" Kenny asked again, becoming slightly agitated.

"It's okay, Kenny," Mike said, doing his best to calm him.

When Jillian came into the room wearing Bethany's wedding dress and carrying a bouquet of wildflowers, he started to understand. "Are you getting married, Mike?" Kenny asked, tears in his eyes. "You can't do that without me!" He was agitated again, panicking.

Mike knelt on one knee in front of him. "Kenny, I'm not doing it without you, Buddy. That's why I want you to put on the suit," Mike replied earnestly, lovingly. "I wouldn't do that, Kenny."

Kenny took a jagged breath. "You promise?"

"I promise. You're my brother. You're my Best Man. I

need you there," Mike assured him.

Kenny tried to breathe. He slowly regained his composure. He looked back into his brother's eyes. "What about Pam?" he asked, noting that Mike had not moved. He just patiently waited for Kenny to catch up.

"Pam knows. She'll either come…or she won't," Mike said.

"But she's our…ma…"

"I know. I didn't know you knew, but I know," Mike replied.

"…ma," Kenny finished.

Mike just nodded.

"Don't you want her there?" Kenny asked, near tears again.

"Yes, but her absence won't stop me. I've made up my mind. Okay?" Mike asked him.

Kenny picked up his cereal bowl in both hands and held it out to Missy. She took it from him. He uncrossed his legs and held his hand out to his brother. "Okay," he said.

Mike smiled, stood, and clasped Kenny's hand, pulling him up. He thrust the suit at Kenny. "Can I get dressed in your bedroom? Your bathroom is too small."

"As you like," Mike agreed.

Kenny adored his brother. And he knew without a doubt Mike adored him. No one had more patience with him. Not even Pam. He took the suit and headed off to change.

He heard the knock. He heard Joe Gardner greet Mike. Joe and Mike were best friends through school. Then he heard Dex Lawson's voice.

Dex had served in the Marines with Kenny and Joe. Dex and Joe had taken care of Kenny. It was like having three brothers instead of just one, though only his twin truly understood him. Joe and Dex came closer to doing so than any other men on the face of this earth, having lived through hell with him.

Kenny was always smaller than the other three. He just barely met the Marine Corps requirements for weight for his height, and the strength and endurance requirements had been difficult, but he'd met them. Kenny was proud to be a Marine. And he'd been a good one. He'd done his duty with pride. He'd done it well.

Kenny smiled. This was going to be a good day.

———

Jillian smoothed down the front of the dress. She usually showed off her tattoos with pride, but she was struggling with the wings below her clavicles today. "Do I look slutty?" she asked as the door opened, expecting Bethany.

"No. Not at all," her stepsister Kristin answered. "You're beautiful, Jillie. You always have been."

Jillian smiled. "Hi, Kristin. I didn't know you were here."

"Do you not want me here?" Kristin asked, coming inside the bedroom and closing the door behind her. She was buttoned up like always. Her hair was pulled back in the usual ponytail. She wore a cardigan 2 sizes too big over a dress with a high collar, that climbed her neck like thistles. Her shoes were sensible. She looked like a librarian.

Jillian sighed. "That's not what I meant, Kristin."

Kristin nodded. Jillian and Kristin had always suffered from misunderstanding and miscommunication with one another. It was like they couldn't speak the same language, even though they were. Jillian certainly found it frustrating. She wondered what Kristin really thought about her.

"I'm sorry, Kristin. I can be overly critical of you," she said.

"Yeah. And the other way around," Kristin agreed, smiling. "Just to be clear…you're okay with my being here?"

Jillian burst out laughing. "Yeah, I'm okay with your being here, you dork. Are Mama and Max here?"

"Jenny is. Not Daddy," Kristin answered. "But man. She's jumpy, Jill."

"What do you mean?"

"I mean, she jumps over every little noise. Kenny Poole dropped a mug by her, and she nearly jumped out of her skin," Kristin answered. "I think this house freaks her out a little."

"Why? This is a great house. Did you look around?" Jillian asked.

"Yeah. It's nice, Jillian. Mike's done well."

"He's great," Jillian said, blushing. "I can't believe he still loves me."

Kristin picked up Jillian's brush. "Sit," she said. Jillian obeyed, and Kristin ran the brush through her hair. "I was going to offer to French braid it, but I think it's pretty down…free… fun…like you. Plus, you've gotten it cut again. I think it's too short." She paused, looking Jillian in the eyes in the mirror. "He'll love you until he dies, and maybe even beyond that. I'm 32 years old, nearly 33, Jill, and I've never been loved like that."

Jillian reached up and stilled the hand brushing her hair. "Kristin, you put all your focus on a man who never had any interest. It's not because you're unlovable. It's because he was in love with someone else. And I know you didn't know that. Nobody did. But you're great. You need to focus on a man who sees *that*," she said. Kristin smiled and leaned to hug Jillian around the neck from behind.

"Hmmm. What's that perfume? You smell like…Lily of the Valley," Kristin said.

"I…I'm not wearing perfume. I thought the Lily of the Valley was…you."

"No. Coco…as usual. That's weird."

———

Mike paced nervously. He had no doubts about Jillian. He had loved her since he was 17 and she was 16. Loved her.

It was not a crush. It was eternal love, fated, meant to be. He'd just been too passive. He had thought that if he let her go, she'd come back. And she always did…eventually. But the truth was, she was worth fighting for. They were worth fighting for. He was determined not to just let her leave anymore. He'd fight to keep her from leaving this time. He'd go through counseling. He'd go through hell if it came to it. But he was nervous. Not because of Jillian…but because Pam wasn't there yet.

Pam was 15, almost 16 years older than Mike and Kenny. Doris Poole had been 52 when the twins were born; Frank Poole had been 59. Mike had put things together when he was 9 or so. But he'd never told Kenny, who had always been more emotionally fragile than Mike. Doris had passed away 4 years ago…and Frank had died when they were still in high school. Pam had practically raised them, as she should have, but she had never publicly admitted to being their mother. They only called her "Mama" in emotionally charged moments and in private. Everybody knew. Nobody ever said anything.

Until today, Mike had thought Kenny believed the lie. How long had his brother known the truth? Would Pam finally admit it?

But mostly, he wanted Pam to be there for his wedding. She was, after all, his mother. She had always claimed she liked Jillian. He was confused by her absence.

It wasn't like they had a lot of people there, and she could blend into the crowd. There were Kristin and Jenny Johnson, Kenny, Joe and Bethany, and their kids, Mr. Morgan to officiate, and Dex Lawson had come from Fredericksburg to help with Kenny's anxiety. That was it. Where the hell had she gone?

Jillian reached out and took his hand mid-turn at the end of the front porch. She smiled. He sighed. "I don't know where she is. She isn't answering her phone," he said, worry in his voice.

"She'll be here," Jillian whispered.

He closed his eyes and took a breath.

Sure enough, twenty minutes later, Pam pulled into the driveway with Aunt Bertie, her father's older sister, in the passenger seat of her car. She smiled and waved as she got out of the car. Mike hurried to hug her and help Aunt Bertie, now 93, out of the car and across the uneven ground to the porch.

Joe helped Mike get her up the stairs and through the front door.

Aunt Bertie took a seat in Jillian's new leather armchair in the living room and beamed at the two men. She patted Mike's hand and winked. She nodded at Joe. "I've always liked that Gardner boy," she affirmed. "He's a lot like old Zach was, only he drinks less."

Joe burst out laughing. "Zach was a heavy drinker then?"

"Zach Gardner was an old man when I was a child. He worked hard all his life. He was riddled with arthritis and bursitis. He drank to dull the pain he was in. If the government hadn't convinced him that marijuana was from the devil, he'd probably have partaken of it, too." The old woman cackled. She winked again. "I sure the heck do."

Mike heard Jillian choke on her giggles while Jenny told her to hush.

"You got any edibles, Jillian?" the old woman hollered across the room.

"No ma'am," Jillian responded, burying her face in her mother's shoulder.

"You want one?"

"Oh, my God," Mike said, exasperated.

"I've got less than an ounce, Mr. Law and Order," Aunt Bertie scoffed.

Jillian lost it and had to leave the room.

Pam sat down on the sofa and buried her head in her hands.

At 12:30 pm, on April 12, 2025, Michael Gabriel Poole was at long last joined in matrimony to his one true love, Jillian Marie Chisholm. His brother, Kenneth Anthony Poole, and her best friend, Bethany Elaine Gardner, stood as witnesses as Mr. Filmore Morgan, a justice of the court, officiated in the presence of their daughter Missy Michelle Lowe, Joe Gardner, Jenny Johnson, Kristin Johnson, Pamela Jean Poole, Alberta Frances Poole, Dexter Lawson, and the Gardner kids; Jessup, Ryan, and Meghan.

They ordered pizza for lunch, and Bethany had brought a sheet cake from Hall's Grocery.

Jillian's mother did not stay for lunch. She kissed her daughter and granddaughter on the cheeks, begrudgingly shook Mike's hand, and practically sprinted to her SUV, looking over her shoulder at the attic window as she left.

Mike, having walked her out, followed her hurried glance and noted that the curtain had moved. One of the kids must have climbed to the attic room. "Jillian," he called into the house from the front door. "Make sure the kids stay out of that attic room. I haven't been through anything up there yet."

"Um, okay," she called back. "They're all in the living room, but I'll tell 'em."

He stopped and shook his head. He had visions of a pitcher flinging itself off the counter and into a wall at Joe Gardner's house a few months back. No, he decided. There was an explanation for the curtain moving. He made his way through the kitchen to the stairs in the mudroom by the back door.

The stairs creaked under his weight. At the top, he found the light switch. Only the center of the attic was tall enough to stand upright. When the Pruces had converted it from storage to a bedroom in the 50s or 60s, they had walled in the sides at about 5 feet from floor to roofline, leaving sliding doors to access the space for storage. The result was a long, narrow room with a window at each end.

At some point after the kids had moved out, they'd resorted to using the converted bedroom just as storage again. The space was full of boxes and furniture Gordon had left when they'd closed the sale. He had communicated that it was mostly junk now, with a few good antiques, but Mike could do whatever he wished with the items.

Mike expected the attic to smell musty and dusty. Instead, inexplicably, it smelled of Lily of the Valley. He made his way toward the front window. Halfway there, the lightbulb in the overhead light blew. Fortunately, the windows provided enough light. The curtain moved again.

Mike became aware of a slight buzzing noise.

That's when he saw the old oscillating fan, probably from the 20s or 30s, given it had no protective cage around the blades. It was on. Somebody had been up here.

He turned it off and unplugged it. Finding it too dangerous to keep in the house if the kids were going to sneak up here to play, he grabbed it off the table it was sitting on and carried it back downstairs.

He took it out the back door and into the garage behind the house. Joe followed him outside.

"What on earth?" Joe asked, pointing at the old fan.

"Ah, somebody's been playing in the attic. It was blowing the curtain. Freaked Jenny out. I thought I'd better bring it out here and take it apart to scrap it. Too dangerous with no cage," Mike answered.

CHAPTER 5

The day was spent in celebration.

As evening approached, Kenny, who was often uncomfortable in groups of people, even people he knew and loved, found himself in need of some space.

He had been feeling the anxiety building for a few hours. He started to combat it by removing the tie at around 1. By 3, he had changed out of the suit and back into his jeans and T-shirt. By 5, he was feeling jumpy, and rather than snap at people, he chose to get some air. The spring air had just enough bite to it that he shivered as he stepped out onto the front porch.

Kristin Johnson was Jillian's stepsister and Mike's friend. She had always been Kenny's friend, too, but Kristin had a big crush on Joe. She didn't like Bethany. Kenny adored Bethany. That colored Kenny's perception of Kristin. He had been avoiding her as much as possible.

So, he was surprised when the door opened, and Kristin stepped outside and held out a zip-up hoodie to him. "It's a little brisk now," she said softly. "I won't invade your space, Kenny. But I thought you might feel cold," she explained when he stared at her.

"Oh. Okay. Thank you," he sputtered, taking the offered jacket.

She turned to go back inside. He reached out and grabbed her arm. "Why don't you like Bethany?" he asked.

"Oh, I...I don't dislike Bethany. I don't really know her. She seems...fine," she replied. He shook his head. He'd offended her. He couldn't just talk to people. He had to make them uncomfortable. He smacked himself. "Oh, no. Kenny, no," she exclaimed, stepping toward him and grabbing his hand. "Why did you do that? Don't do that," she whispered.

"I made you uncomfortable," he cried.

"No. No, you didn't," she replied. Then she laughed. "I'll let you in on a secret, Kenny. I'm always uncomfortable… around…people…adults, at least. I'm great with kids, but adults…they make me feel like I can't fit inside my own skin… or like I've got a million ants crawling on my arms and legs."

Kenny snickered. "Really?"

"Really. I brought you a jacket so I could get some air myself," she giggled.

He nodded, grinning and slipping on the jacket. "Thank you. You…can stay if you want." He was glad she didn't dislike Bethany. He really liked Kristin. He always had. He didn't like not being her friend anymore.

"Are you sure? You don't mind?" she asked.

He leaned forward. "You wanna sit on the swing with me? It's fun…but Mike doesn't like it if it hits the house, so we have to swing gently," he offered.

Kristin laughed. "I'd like that, actually," she replied, and the two of them sat on the porch swing together.

———

Pam watched Kristin and Kenny from inside. She kept looking at them over her shoulder every few minutes. She was twitchy about their sitting together and having a conversation. Mike could see it in her face and her body language. It confirmed a suspicion. He kissed his wife's cheek and moved to sit next to his…mother.

"Jesus, Pam. Max Johnson? He's 19 years older than you… and Kristin is the same age as us. That means…his wife was pregnant at the same time…" he whispered.

"Why do you have to be a detective?" she moaned. "Do

you think she knows?"

Mike was silent for a moment. "No," he lied after a long pause, "but Max does." That part was the truth.

Her eyes grew large, and she gripped the arm of the sofa tightly. "Really? He does? How long has he known? How do you know he knows?"

"Um…okay…in order. Yes, really. He does know. He's known for a long time, and that's why he always undermined Jillian and me. And I know because…I can…see…it…the way he acts around me."

"Oh, God," Pam groaned. "Every time Kristin's around you guys, I'm a nervous wreck, someone will figure out she's your sister. Is that why Max is so adamant that you not be with Jillian, because people might put that together?"

"Aunt Kristin is your sister?" Missy gasped loudly. Loudly enough that the room fell silent, and everyone turned to look at them. Kristin and Kenny, outside the open living room window, turned slowly in unison with their mouths agape. Dex jumped up from where he sat near the piano and rushed toward the door.

"I got him! That's why I'm here!" he exclaimed, as he jogged out of the room.

Mike blinked at Missy. Pam shook her head. "Honey, we were whispering for a reason," Mike said, taking her hand.

Missy's eyes filled with tears. "I'm sorry, Daddy!" she said, pouting.

He laughed, kissed her hand, and pulled her to him, hugging her. "It's okay. It was an accident."

Pam looked up sharply. "Daddy?"

"Shut up…*Mama*," he replied.

"Fair enough," she chuckled.

"So…do I call you Aunt Pam or Grandma?" Missy asked after a moment.

"Do *not* call me 'grandma,'" Pam laughed. "But Aunt Pam

isn't right either," she admitted. "Pam-ma?" she snickered.

Missy laughed hysterically. "Pam-ma! I love it!" The girl flung herself at Pam and wrapped her arms around Pam's neck.

———

Having heard Missy's exclamation, Kenny and Kristin turned to look at each other. Kenny started to hyperventilate. Kristin had no time to be surprised. "Woah!" she yelped. "Kenny, it's okay. Breathe." And she demonstrated by breathing in through her nose and out through her mouth. She nodded at him, holding his gaze. She breathed in through her nose again with Kenny and out through her mouth. She didn't even notice she was gripping him by the shoulders until Dex Lawson knelt in front of the swing and pulled Kenny out of her grasp, turning him to face him instead.

"Hey, Kenny. You okay, Bud?" he asked.

Apparently, Kenny was still dumbstruck, but he nodded vigorously. Kristin blinked back her own tears. Then Dex Lawson winked at her. She blushed as he laid his right hand on her knee. "How about you, pretty lady? You okay?"

She, likewise, nodded. She'd known. Somehow, she'd felt it all along. Still, hearing it out loud, while sitting beside Kenny, had been jarring.

"How about the three of us take a nice, calming walk? Then we can come back and you two can talk to Mike and Pam." He stood and smiled. He offered his hand to Kristin. Her heart leapt to her throat. But she had spent the last 6 years chasing Joe Gardner. She told herself to calm down. He was just being nice. He smiled as she took his hand.

"You guys sure you want me to come?" Kenny asked, astutely. Then he snorted. Dex gave him a gentle shove and a stern look.

Kenny guffawed. "Dex likes you, Kristin," he spouted, laughing. "He's a mad flirt, but he only flirts when he means it."

"Jesus, Kenny," Dex exclaimed, shaking his head.

Kristin giggled. Dex blushed. He was a good-looking guy, with a gorgeous medium brown complexion, deep brown eyes, and luxurious, long lashes. She noticed the silvery white scar on the back of his hand. She involuntarily ran her thumb across it.

"That was me being a stupid kid…a bar fight. I don't behave that way anymore. My pops tore me a new one," he said, smiling.

"Sorry. I…I didn't mean to be rude."

"You weren't." He grinned.

"Yeah," Kenny chuckled. "I'm definitely a third wheel. But Dex…be nice. Apparently, she's my sister. I might not be able to take you, but Mikey can." He playfully shoved Dex's shoulder and jumped up, running back inside the house.

Dex sat down beside Kristin. She smiled brightly. She did not let go of his hand.

———

Joe looked adoringly at his wife's expanding belly. He smiled. Mike handed him a cold beer and sat beside him. "Isn't she beautiful?" Joe asked, grinning like a lovesick fool.

"Yeah, she's a knockout, Man," Mike chuckled.

"So…You decided to marry Jillian last January?"

"What makes you think it was in January of last year?" Mike asked his friend.

"That's when she got the angel wings tattoos below her clavicles…which are very nice by the way," Joe snickered.

"Hmmmm. The wings or what's below her clavicles?" Mike teased.

"Shut up," Joe laughed.

"Yeah. I knew it wouldn't be long when she got the wings. It was like she tattooed my name on her chest," Mike chortled.

"It's true," Jillian said, sitting on his lap. "Of course, it wasn't his literal name. My actual name is on his waist above his hip."

"Oh, is it?" Joe laughed.

"I have a tattoo," Bethany interrupted.

"Hey… No," Joe sputtered.

"It must be somewhere very interesting," Mike teased Joe some more.

"It's a lollipop…in the peaches vicinity," Jillian whispered.

"Not just a lollipop…There's a butterfly, too," Bethany joined in the teasing.

"Alright. That's enough!" Joe exclaimed. "Honestly. I need a better class of friends."

"You started it by pointing out my…below the clavicles," Jillian pointed out.

"What are y'all talking about?" Jessup, Joe's son with Dex Lawson's late sister, asked, seemingly appearing out of nowhere.

"Tattoos," Jillian answered honestly and diplomatically all at once.

"Uncle Dex got a new one," he said proudly. "It's a caduceus because he's a nurse. On his forearm. Where is Uncle Dex?"

"He went outside to help Kenny," Joe answered.

"Kenny's in the kitchen playing jacks with Meghan, not outside," Jessup noted. "Oh, there he is swinging with Miss Johnson."

They all turned their heads to look out the front window.

"Well, I'll be…" Mike mused.

———

Aunt Bertie napped sitting in the chair. She was old enough that she called herself a spinster, born in 1932. Violet Gardner Pruce had been 7 years older than Bertie. After the end of World War II, and after Violet had given birth to Louis Pruce, she had hired Bertie as a young teen to help her with the baby and housework after school. Bertie had spent many, many days in this lovely home. Violet was a sweet young mother, and Bertie had loved working for her.

As she napped, she became aware of the soft, sweet smell of Violet's favorite perfume, Lily of the Valley. Violet, young with her hair coifed perfectly for church, dressed in a pretty navy-blue dress with little light blue flowers on it and a wide, white Peter Pan collar and little white gloves, stood over young Bertie, sitting in the chair old Bertie slept in. "It was a lovely wedding, wasn't it, Bertie, Dear?" she asked, excitedly.

"Yes. Quite nice," young Bertie answered.

"I like the young man," Violet whispered. "Is he one of my family?"

"No. He's my family. He's Frank's grandson."

"Oh, well, Frank has a lovely grandson. He's taking good care of my house," Violet noted.

"The bride is yours, Mrs. Pruce. She's young Gordon's daughter."

"My Gordy? Oh, that's nice."

"And the little blonde girl, Missy, is the bride and groom's child."

"So, she's both of ours! Wonderful!" Violet proclaimed. "I'll protect them all. I'm still here, you see."

Bertie snored loudly and startled herself awake. She was old spinster Bertie again, and Violet was long dead. Oddly, though, she still smelled the Lily of the Valley perfume.

"Pam, dear. I am ready to go home. I don't want to miss the evening meal," Bertie announced. She lived in an assisted living facility in Colonial Beach.

"Oh, of course, Aunt Bertie," Pam said, jumping up from where she sat on the sofa, looking through pictures on a tablet with Missy.

"Bye, Pam-ma," Missy giggled.

"Bye, Sweetheart," Pam giggled back, kissing the child

on the top of the head. "Come on, Kenny. Let's take Aunt Bertie home and get home ourselves."

Kenny obeyed happily. He was a good boy, Bertie noted. Too bad the war had scrambled his brain like that. But he walked and talked. The doctors had said he wouldn't ever do either again. He proved them wrong. He was the strongest of them all, Bertie thought, as he helped her to her feet.

"You should come live in the apartments I live in, Kenny, my boy. There's an empty unit now that old Al Harris is gone."

He smiled. "I'd like that, Aunt Bertie."

Pam frowned. She knew he was capable of surviving in assisted living, and his VA benefits would cover it. It was her holding him back. Bertie didn't understand why. But she'd hinted enough for today. Kenny was Pam's child after all. It was not her place to interfere.

CHAPTER 6

As dinnertime approached, the six of them decided to ask Ruth West, Bethany's mother, who lived in a small trailer next to Bethany and Joe's house, to watch the kids so they could go out to eat and go dancing. Joe and Dex walked Ryan, Jess, Missy, and Meghan back to Ravens' Roost, while the others made plans. By the time they returned to Mike's house, they had decided to go to Dockside in Colonial Beach. Jack Clark, another of their classmates from high school, had a band performing there tonight. The band, called The Watermen, played a mixture of country and rock and were pretty good for a local band.

As Jillian, Kristin, and Bethany disappeared into the bedroom to change, Mike looked at Joe. "This is going to take a while, right?"

"There are three of them. We should get a snack," Joe affirmed.

Dex laughed and slapped Joe on the back. "Hey, Kenny… he seems okay. You had me worried when you called."

"He handled it better than I expected," Mike said. "It's not like Jillie and I are brand new or anything. We've been on again/off again since high school. Maybe he just had time to process the inevitability of it."

"That's true," Joe said, nodding. "But he handled the news about…Kristin…well, too. I think he's…doing better."

Mike teared up. "He has good days and bad days, Joe. We got lucky, and he had a good day. But you know what…he can walk, and he can talk, and he's not in Arlington. So, I'll take all the bad days he can dish out."

"Amen to that," Dex toasted, holding up his beer. The other two clinked their cans against his. "Um…so that girl… Kristin…I get she's your stalker, Joe, and um…your sister? But she's kinda hot."

"Dex likes the uptight librarian type," Joe explained.

"Ahhh. She fits the bill," Mike said, stifling a laugh. "But seriously, Kristin's great. She's always helped me with Jillian… and Missy. She kinda went a little overboard with her crush on Joe, but I think she's just lonely. And under those cardigans…if memory serves from high school, she's not bad looking. If you're interested, Dex, you should definitely go for it."

"That's your sister," Joe snickered.

"For all of about five minutes… and she's 32 years old. It's not like I think she's a virgin."

"I don't know, Man. I wouldn't bet on that," Joe added.

"Trust me on this one," Mike replied.

"Ehhh. I wouldn't be surprised."

"Oh, come on. Don't say that. Now you got me nervous," Dex interjected, elbowing Joe.

The bedroom door screeched open, and footsteps sounded on the hallway floor. Then they crossed the foyer.

Kristin Johnson appeared in the living room through the open arch from the foyer. Her hair, which had been back in a tight ponytail all day, was down. It fell to her shoulders in long, dark, silky ringlets. Bethany and Jillian had done her makeup. They had given her smoky eyes, which enhanced their dark color. Her lips were a deep, glossy red. And there was a shimmer to her skin. She was dressed in Jillian's clothes, a short, black, flowy, skater dress with off-the-shoulder short sleeves and a sweetheart neckline, fishnet stockings, and knee-high, stiletto black patent leather boots.

"Wow," Joe said, staring.

"Um. Yeah. Uh. Wow," Mike added.

"You…look lovely," Dex said, smiling.

She smiled a big, toothy grin. "Thank you. All of you!" she exclaimed.

Jillian came in behind her, wearing an ivory-colored sleeveless A-line dress that fell to the knee with a jewel neckline, a rather conservative look for her, but the jeweled stiletto sandals gave the classic cut of the dress a sexy edge.

"I decided I still wanted to look like a bride," she announced. Mike stared with his mouth open. Joe reached over and shut it for him.

Bethany emerged dressed the same as she had been all day. She patted her tummy. "Melanie makes it so nothing Jillian has fits me. I could go home and change, but I'm afraid it's all more of the same."

"You look beautiful, Sweetheart," Joe said, smiling. Dex knew he meant it. And he had to admit, she did.

But Kristin. Kristin was drop-dead gorgeous.

———

They enjoyed their dinner and then paid their cover charges to get into the bar.

"Just ginger ale for Bethany…How about you, Kristin?" Dex asked, smiling at the transformed teacher.

"Amaretto Stone Sour," she replied, taking a seat next to Bethany.

"Jillian?" he asked, turning to the bride.

"That sounds good. I haven't had one of those in a while," she concurred.

"I'll come to the bar with you," Joe proclaimed, slapping Dex on the back. "Beer, Mike?"

"Yeah, whatever's on tap," Mike said, reaching for his wallet as he took a seat.

"Nah!" Dex waved him off. "We got this. Your money's no good tonight."

"Oh, well, thank you," Jillian yelled above the rising din of the band warming up. Kristin leaned toward her stepsister and motioned for her to lean toward her. Bethany, sitting between them, leaned back.

"Should I have offered to pay?" she shouted behind her hand.

"No!" both Jillian and Bethany shouted.

"I think I should offer to pay when he comes back with the drinks," Kristin insisted.

"It's a date, Kristin! Didn't you get that when Jillie and Bethy were giving you the makeover?" Mike shouted. "You're on a date."

The three women glared at him, and he laughed. He enjoyed teasing Jillian. He always had. Letting her know that they all knew what was going on was fun. She wasn't exactly being clandestine. She smiled back at him and blew him a kiss.

The band really was good. They danced a lot.

As the band took a break, they headed back to their table. Dex and Kristin had begun to hold hands to and from the dance floor. Halfway back to the table, someone stepped in front of them. "Is there any particular reason you're holding this boy's hand, Miss Johnson?" Big Billy Walsh hissed. There was a particular tone to the word "boy" that caused Dex's head to shoot up and his spine to stiffen.

"Crap!" Mike exclaimed, standing. "Get lost, Billy!" he said coldly, moving in next to Dex.

"He a friend of yours, Deputy?" Big Billy sneered.

"He is. Now, fuck off," Mike said.

Dex shook his head as Big Billy skulked off, waving for his group of friends to follow.

"I'm so sorry, Kristin," Dex offered.

"What on earth for? He's the ass. You're great," she replied, kissing his cheek.

Dex grinned. Mike chuckled and slapped him on the back.

Back at the table, they ordered another round of drinks and some appetizers. A shadow fell across the table as Mike reached for a nacho. He looked up, expecting one of Big Billy's cronies. Instead, he looked into the face of Jillian's first husband, Rich Lowe.

Mike sighed. "Hi, Rich. What can I do for you?" he asked, taking a bite.

"I guess she didn't even wait for the ink to dry on this divorce before she ran back to you," Rich sneered.

"You've been divorced for 8 years and married to uh… Sienna, Sierra?"

"Kierra," Rich's wife answered from behind him.

"My apologies. Kierra. You've been married to *Kierra* for 6 years. Why do you care?" Mike asked.

"I just hate for my daughter to have to keep suffering through break-up after break-up is all," Rich huffed.

"Ah, well, you don't have to worry about that. Missy's my daughter, not yours. I have a check for you to cover *all* the supposed child support you've paid over the last 8 years." He reached for his wallet in his back pocket, took it out, and unfolded it. He pulled the check he'd written out of the billfold and held it out to Rich.

"The hell you say," Rich shouted.

"Oh, please. Like you didn't already know. Your blood type. Hers. It's impossible. Mine…hers…possible. You might as well take the money. We've already sent in the DNA for testing… yesterday. Oh, and uh, my lawyer is Filmore Morgan. If you have any questions, talk to him," Mike said. He sounded calmer and cooler than he felt. He knew how to defuse tense situations. It was part of his job. But Rich had always been kind of a wildcard. Mike thought he was more possessive of Jillian than all her other exes combined.

He needn't have worried. Rich snatched the check and walked away, with Kierra running after him.

CHAPTER 7

The rest of the night passed uneventfully. They had a good time. Mike saw why Kenny held Dex in such high regard. He was a good guy. He was fun to be around. And he was a gentleman, unlike so many of the jackasses he had grown up with. The older he got, the more disdain he felt for people like Rich Lowe, Lyle Fox, and Big Billy. Big Billy at least had the excuse of being an uneducated jackass. But Rich had a good education, having been to one of the best private colleges in Virginia. Lyle also had a decent education, having received his associate's degree in computer science before transferring to Virginia Tech. He hadn't graduated, but he was only a few classes short of earning a bachelor's degree. He worked for a DOD contractor in Dahlgren and made a good living. And yet, they were both just terrible people.

Joe had joined the Marines out of high school, just like Kenny. That's where he met and befriended Dex. He had briefly dated Dex's sister, Jemma, though that was a rebound kind of thing. She had gotten pregnant, but they decided marriage would be a bad idea. They were planning to co-parent, but she sadly died after giving birth. It was a tragic situation. Joe took custody of his child and did his best to raise Jessup well. And somehow that tragedy had cemented Joe and Dex's friendship even more.

Kenny, as he had all his life, followed Joe. And Joe never minded. So, if Joe was friends with Dex, so was Kenny. Dex welcomed Kenny. And Mike was forever grateful for that. Kenny had been a surprisingly good Marine. Even so, his fellow Marines weren't always so kind. Kenny had been an honor student.

He had never been stupid. But he had never been…normal, whatever that meant. Mike had suspicions that Kenny may have been on the autism spectrum, though certainly high functioning. But there was no way to confirm that now. The traumatic brain injury was severe and permanent.

Joe had always felt guilty about that. He shouldn't. He did everything he could to protect Kenny before and after the injury. When Kenny was driving and hit an IED, Joe had been right there. He had suffered primary blast fractures in his right leg, but he'd still managed to pull Kenny, unconscious and severely wounded, from the overturned vehicle and to shelter in a rock crag, protecting him with his own body until they were rescued by their unit some 3 hours later. Mike had always considered Joe a good friend. After that, he considered him his brother.

He later learned that it had been Dex who had insisted on searching for the two of them, thus initiating their rescue. He was his brother, too. Mike was a decorated police officer. He was brave in his own right. But these two men were his heroes. And his odd brother…Kenny was the bravest man he knew. He'd seen him fight to learn to feed himself, talk, walk, and live again. It was the most painful process he'd ever witnessed. Ever. He defied anyone to speak ill of Kenny.

Thinking of Joe, Dex, and Kenny, he found himself openly crying as he drove home. Jillian reached over and touched his arm. "What's wrong, Sweetheart?" she asked.

"Sorry, Hon. It's nothing. I was just thinking about Kenny. And Joe and Dex. I was such a shit. I let him go to war. I broke up with you. I was as big an ass as Rich."

"What are you talking about? I hurt you. I was the one who dated Rich while we were still together," she replied sweetly, closing her eyes and laying her head back against the headrest on her seat.

He was quiet. She really blamed herself. He pulled over

and cut the engine. "Jill. Our breakup. The first one. That wasn't your fault. That one was on me," he said, taking her hands.

"You wouldn't have broken up with me if I hadn't cheated," she retorted.

"You didn't cheat. Even I know that. You went out on two dates with him...because your mother and Max asked you to. You hadn't even kissed him at that point. I...I was unreasonable. I wanted...I wanted to go to Ole Miss. And stupid me...I thought that meant we'd break up, anyway. I hurt you. I pushed you away, right into Rich's arms. And I've regretted it ever since. I'm so sorry. Even almost 14 years later. I'm still so sorry. I started this vicious cycle. And I hate that I did it." A tear rolled down his cheek.

He looked at her in the moonlight. A car drove past them. The harsh headlight flashed across her face. He furrowed his brow. God, he hoped she'd forgive him.

She spoke at long last. "I know. But I gave you the excuse. And I saw how it hurt you. So, let's leave it in the past. We've hurt each other enough for three lifetimes. We're both sorry. We've both matured. I love you. I always will. You love me. I know that with every fiber of my being. Let's just stop blaming each other and ourselves. It's pointless. Okay?" she pleaded.

He nodded. "Okay," he whispered. "And I do love you, Jillian. I'll never hurt you again. Not if I can help it."

"Me, too." She smiled and kissed him.

He restarted the engine and pulled the truck back onto the road. They were home within minutes. They had called Ruth before leaving the bar. Missy was asleep in bed with Meghan, so Joe and Bethany had offered to let her stay overnight. They had the house to themselves.

As they approached the front door, Mike swept Jillian up into his arms and kissed her as he carried her over the threshold. She laughed. It was such a beautiful sound.

Inside the door, he let her legs slide down so that she stood again, but he pulled her close and kissed her deeply. His hands slid up the back of the dress. His fingers fumbled briefly with the catch at the top of the zipper, but only briefly. He deftly unzipped the dress and led her to their bedroom.

———

Tom Palmer knocked on the door, feeling somewhat awkward. Aaron had told him that Jillian and Mike were together again, and Jillian's car was in the driveway. It was 5 am. He thought he was probably interrupting something, and that made him very uncomfortable.

The window to his left opened, and Mike's head appeared. "Tom?" he said sleepily.

"Oh, hello. Mike, sorry. Um…I…we found a body," Tom said cryptically.

"Okay. I'm not on duty until Sunday night," he replied.

Tom fidgeted with his hat. "No. Um. It's Billy Walsh…and he was murdered…and I understand you had an altercation last night and the night before."

"Ahhh. Gotcha. You aren't here to include me in the investigation, but to question me. Sure. Give me a second to put on something, and I'll let you in," Mike said calmly. Thank God, Mike was a professional and understood. He felt like a complete Judas being here and interrupting the deputy's reunion with his lady love.

A few seconds passed, then the light inside the front door switched on. Mike, somewhat disheveled, obviously just awakened, opened the door. Jillian stood in the hallway off to the left of the foyer.

"You should go on home, Jillian. This might take a while," Tom said, nodding at her.

"I am home," she said simply.

She held up her left hand, revealing a wedding ring.

Tom gaped at her. Then he turned to Mike, who held up his left hand, revealing a matching band.

"Oh. O…kay," he said.

"Plus, I was there during both 'altercations,'" she said. "Coffee?"

"Oh. Sure. Sounds good," Tom agreed and followed them both to the kitchen.

————

Jillian made the coffee as Mike and Tom sat at the kitchen table. As the coffee pot finished filling, she took three mugs from the cabinet and asked, "You like it black, right, Tom?" She grabbed the creamer from the fridge. The sugar dispenser was on the table, so she poured out the coffee, shoved a mug at Tom and a mug at Mike, before adding creamer and two spoons of sugar to her own.

Mike took a sip as she stirred hers. The clink, clink, clink of the spoon against the mug filled the silence.

"What do you need to know, Tom?" Mike asked, setting his mug down.

"Well, I heard you shot at him…"

"I shot at his truck. If I had shot at him, I wouldn't have hit the truck," Mike said, matter-of-factly.

"What happened?" Tom asked.

"He pulled into my driveway at 3 in the morning, yelling for me to come out, saying Jillian knew what would happen to me if she got back with me. I took it as a threat of physical violence. So, I shot out his flood lights and headlights with a BB gun and told him to get lost. I know I shouldn't have, but I've had enough of his threats."

"He threatened you often?" Tom asked.

"Sure. All the time."

"Was he ever involved with Ji…"

"God! No!" Jillian exclaimed, horrified. "Big Billy is

a disgusting human. I realize I'm not exactly a pillar of the community, but he's the dregs of society!"

"Was," Tom corrected her. "Then why the threats if you got back with Mike?"

"Because he's delusional! I don't know. He said something about 'the boss' ordering it…didn't he, Honey?" she asked, turning to Mike.

"Yeah, Big Billy Walsh liked to pretend he was a big boss, but he was just a low-level thug. Someone hired him to intimidate Jillian and me."

"Do you know who?" Tom continued.

"With certainty? No. I have a suspicion. My father," he answered.

"Um…Frank's been dead for a while now, Mike," Tom chuckled.

"Yes, he has been, and we all know he was my grandfather," Mike chided his superior officer.

"Yeah. I wasn't too certain…you…"

"I figured it out when I was 9, Tom," Mike chuckled.

"Oh. Who is your father?"

"Maxim Johnson. Pam confirmed it today," Mike replied.

"Maxim…Isn't he a lot older than…" Tom asked.

"Criminally so, yes. He was 34. She was 15," Mike retorted.

"But the statute of limitations is long up. If she was 15, it was a misdemeanor statutory rape. If she was 14, that would have been a felony statutory rape, and there would be no statute of limitation," Tom extolled.

"I know the law, Tom. But he's a doctor and a politician. He wouldn't go to jail if it came out, but he'd lose his medical license. She was a patient. He treated her for melanoma. And he'd probably lose his political career, too. Me? I look like Pam, but Kenny looks just like him. With Jillian and me together, it's bound to come out. It did come out," Mike explained.

"I see. And Maxim knows? About your being married?"

"Yep. Kristin and Mama were here for the wedding. He didn't come," Jillian interrupted.

"Can you account for your whereabouts at 2 am?" Tom asked.

"We were at Dockside. That was just after last call. Us, Joe and Bethany Gardner, and Kristin and Dex Lawson. We talked to Jack Clark as we were leaving at a quarter after 2. Um…Leslie Sisson was our waitress. She could probably place us there, too.

"You didn't leave Dockside until after 2…even after the altercation with Big Billy?"

"No. We stayed until closing. We had fun," Mike replied.

"Okay, Mike. I need to confirm your alibi, but it sounds solid."

"Sure. In the meantime. I'll see you tonight when I come into work…unless I hear otherwise."

Tom chuckled and drank down his coffee in one gulp. Holy cow, Jillian thought. How'd he do that without scalding the inside of his mouth?

———

Joe rolled over and climbed out of bed. He sleepily ran his fingers through his hair as he walked into the hallway from the bedroom and toward the front door. He yawned as he looked out the window to see Deputy Tom Palmer standing on the front porch. He yawned again before he moved to the front door and opened it.

"G'morning, Tom. What's up?" Joe asked.

"Where were you last night?" Tom asked abruptly.

Joe scratched his head. "Um…Bethany and I spent the day with Mike and Jillian. They got married. About 6, we decided to go out for dinner and dancing to celebrate. Um. We went to Dockside. We ate, and at about 8, we moved from the restaurant to the bar to listen to The Watermen play. Um…We left at closing time… around 2 am. Why?"

"Just confirming the events of last night. So, just you, Bethany, Mike, and Jillian?"

"No. My friend, Dex Lawson, and Kristin Johnson were with us, too." Joe responded.

"They left at the same time?"

"Yessir," Joe said.

"Where does this Dex Lawson live?" Tom asked.

"Um. He lives with his cousin in Stafford County. He's Jess's uncle. Why?"

"Oh. He's African American? Did Big Billy…"

"Yeah, Mike handled it. Dex ignored it," Joe answered.

"When did Dex leave?"

"Same time we did," Joe answered, starting to get annoyed.

"Did either he or Mike ever leave Dockside after y'all arrived?"

"No," Joe affirmed, shaking his head.

Tom nodded. "I know this is…frustrating, Joe. But trust me. I need your answers without your understanding why I am asking. You did great. Now I hate to ask, but…may I speak with Bethany? I promise, it's important."

Tom sat down on the sofa, and Joe walked back to their bedroom. He shook his sleeping wife's shoulder, leaning over her. "Babe, wake up. Deputy Tom Palmer has some questions for you."

"Who? What?" she asked, rousing and sitting up.

Moments later, she sat with Tom. Joe left them alone. When Tom got the answers he was looking for, he stood and shook Bethany's hand. He walked toward the door.

"Thank you both. You've been a great help." As he reached the door, he turned to look back at them. "You confirmed your friend's alibi. I can't say much. I still need to check the CCTV at Dockside and talk to a few more people, but it's good. You did just fine. Go back to bed." He smiled and was gone.

Joe looked at Bethany. "Yeah. Call her," he said.

Bethany ran and got her phone. She made a call.

"Jillian! What's going on?"

———————

Kristin heard the knocking on her door, but she pulled her pillow over her head and moaned. She had drunk a little too much the night before. Dex Lawson had driven her home. Her car was still at the Dockside…and Dex…

Dex was answering her door, having slept on her sofa.

She sat bolt upright. In a panic, she threw on a robe and ran downstairs. Dex, shirtless, sat where he had slept with Deputy Tom Palmer sitting in her armchair.

"Hey," she said in surprise.

Dex and the deputy looked up at her where she stood halfway down her staircase.

"Rough night, Miss Johnson?" Tom chuckled.

She sighed and smoothed her hair. "Yeah. I had a good time and drank a little too much. I must look a fright."

"You look beautiful," Dex said, blushing.

She smiled.

"Um, yes," Tom said, clearing his throat. "If you don't mind, Miss Johnson, would you please join us? I have some questions about last night."

Kristin continued down the steps and sat beside Dex, who quickly pulled on his T-shirt. "What is this about, Deputy?" Kristin asked.

"It's better if you answer without knowing why I'm asking. Please."

"Oh, of course," she said, furrowing her brow.

"First, is your father Mike and Kenny Poole's father?"

She was taken aback. That little nugget had spread fast. "I…That's what Pam Poole said. And…Kenny does resemble my father. I suppose it is possible. But that's a question you should ask Ms. Poole...or my father," she answered, blinking nervously.

The deputy nodded. "I understand. I assure you, I am not going around spreading a rumor. It's pertinent to my investigation. You were with your stepmother yesterday at Mike Poole and Jillian Fox's wedding?"

"Yes. Jenny left around lunchtime. Something about the Pruce property makes her very uncomfortable. I stayed," she answered.

Tom turned to Dex. "Um, yeah, I was there. Joe called me the night before last and asked me to come keep an eye on Kenny, help to keep his anxiety down. I got there early," Dex concurred.

"And the two of you went out with Mike and Jillian and Joe and Bethany?"

"Yes. At about 6, we all decided to go to dinner and dancing at Dockside. Jack Clark's band was playing. We probably got there around 7 and ate...and moved to the bar around 8," Kristin agreed.

"When did you leave?"

"We stayed all evening. It was fun. The band sounded great. We danced a lot," she chuckled.

"You and Mr. Lawson...exclusively...or did you dance with others?"

"I...danced a few with Mike and Joe..." She knew her answer sounded more like a question.

"But not anybody else?"

"No. I was there with a group."

"You didn't dance with Billy Walsh?"

"Eww...no..." she responded.

Dex chuckled. "Is that the redneck who..."

"Yeah, that's him," she answered.

"Who what?" Tom asked.

"It was nothing. He tried to make a fuss...because he's a

racist pig. Dex ignored him. Mike told him to get lost."

"Anybody else try to make a fuss?" Tom asked.

"Not about us. Rich Lowe was a jerk…as usual. Mike gave him a check to cover all the child support he's paid since the divorce and told him Missy is his…Mike's, that is."

"Really?"

Kristin nodded.

"He could afford to do that?"

Kristin laughed. "Sure. It's only like $6,500 in total. And Mike's been putting money away for years to cover it. He started saving as soon as he got home from college and saw Missy…all that blonde hair and those blue eyes…"

"So, Rich and Mike had an altercation?"

"I wouldn't call it that. They had an exchange of words, is all," Dex clarified. "That Rich guy took the check and left in a huff."

"Ah. Okay. And did Mike ever leave at any point?"

"Nope. We were all there until closing," Kristin answered. "In fact, my car is still there. Dex brought me home because I was in no shape to drive. He stayed on my couch because it was so late…and so he can take me to get my car this morning," she explained.

"Got it. Thank you both. And Mr. Lawson, I apologize. Billy is a punk," Tom added.

"Why would you apologize?" Dex laughed.

"Billy's his nephew," Kristin whispered.

"Oh. Well, still not your fault," Dex said.

————

Mike went back to bed after Tom left. Jillian had moved in the day before yesterday, but the house was still essentially Mike's, even with some of her stuff being used. She set about making the home feel a little more like hers before she had to leave for work. She started in the kitchen, cleaning and putting away her kitchen things. She went to the basement to retrieve her boxes marked as "kitchen."

The basement was semi-finished. The Pruces had installed a full bar and a half bath in the finished half of the basement at the bottom of the stairs back in the early 60s. The other half of the basement housed the washer and dryer, the furnace, the water heater, and general storage.

Elmer and Violet Pruce had used the finished portion of the basement for entertaining for decades. It was dry and clean but very dated. It had not been updated since it had been finished.

But Mike had had an inspection done, and the electricity and plumbing were all good. He had asked what she thought about updating it to a family room. She thought he meant a room to watch sports…which he probably did, by the size of the TV he was looking at. She didn't care. Let him have a mancave. But they had arranged some of their furniture in the room, and she had to admit it wasn't looking bad. As she flipped on the light, she smiled. Mike had hung a painting she had done of the Baptist Church years ago over his old sofa. She hadn't painted in a few years now, not since before she'd married Lyle. It wasn't bad, she noted. She should get back into it.

She walked on through to the storage room and dug through the stacked boxes until she found the three that she was looking for. She pulled them out and set them at the bottom of the stairs. She returned to the storage room to turn off the light and shut the door.

She screamed when she saw him…the child hiding behind the boxes at the back corner of the room. He was dripping wet, with dark saucer eyes and pallid skin.

The child screeched and lunged at her. The room filled with the scent of Lily of the Valley, and a sudden warmth pushed through her. A blur of light enveloped the frightening child, and then both he and the blur vanished. The scent, however, lingered.

Mike came running down the stairs. "What happened? Are you okay?" he yelled as he came.

"I just saw a ghost...no, two ghosts!" Jillian exclaimed, throwing herself into his arms and trembling.

"Honey, there are no ghosts," he said, holding her close. He flipped on the light again.

"Look. It's just boxes."

"I know what I saw, Mike!" she cried. "It was a little boy... and he was wet and...scary. But then there was a comforting presence. It smells of Lily of the Valley...and she got rid of that evil, wet...thing."

"She?" he asked.

"Yeah. She didn't have a form, but I'm pretty certain she was my great-grandmother, Violet."

CHAPTER 8

Mike walked into the sheriff's office and made his way to his desk. He sat and logged into the computer, checking his email.

"Hi, Mike," Aaron Muse greeted him.

"Hey," Mike replied without looking up.

"So…you and Jillian?"

"Married," Mike answered, holding up his left hand before returning to typing.

"Oh…wow. I wasn't expecting that," Aaron said, sitting at his desk across from Mike.

"Really? I've always expected it," Mike chuckled, looking up finally.

Tom Palmer and Jon Briars entered together. They had been on the day shift and were ready to go home.

"Did you clear me, Tom?" Mike asked as the superior officer heaved a sigh of relief, lowering himself into his own desk chair.

"Yeah, you're clear. Not only did everybody corroborate your alibi, but the band was also videoing their show, and you're on camera at the time of death…and so is your friend, Dex. Nice guy, by the way. But Kristin should be prepared. It's not easy… even now. There are always going to be dumbasses like Billy."

"Isn't Billy your sister's kid?" Mike chuckled.

"Yeah, unfortunately."

"So…do you want me to work the case, Tom…or would you prefer a different detective?" Mike asked.

"You are by far the best and most qualified, Mike. The sheriff wants you on it. Just tread lightly. You're cleared, but I still think it has to do with your altercation."

Mike nodded. "Well, I don't know enough to agree or disagree at this point."

Tom picked up a folder and tossed it onto Mike's desk. Mike opened it and viewed the crime scene photos. "Jesus!" he exclaimed.

Billy Walsh was a big man...hence the nickname "Big Billy." He weighed 320 pounds if he weighed an ounce. He was 5'10". He had been stabbed multiple times, then gutted. His watch was broken and stopped at 2:05. There was a link listed. Mike went to the site, which was shut down to the public. The murder and gutting had been livestreamed. The assailant was wearing the camera, and therefore, was never seen on camera. He...or she...wore long sleeves and black leather driving gloves. No skin was showing, so there was no way to identify skin color. Height was estimated to be 6'1" with the camera worn on the assailant's forehead. The crime scene was at Billy Walsh's trailer in a Westmoreland Shores Trailer Park. His body, at the end of the livestream, was shoved off the back of the deck, down the embankment, and into Monroe Bay. He did appear to recognize his killer, though, as he opened the door and asked, "What do you want?" before being attacked.

Mike shook his head. That was brutal. But he played it again...and again. He sat there for two hours. He concentrated on the opening door. There was something. He took a screenshot and zoomed in. On the floor...behind Billy...a purse sat on the floor...and beside it, two high-heeled shoes.

He jumped up. "Holy shit! There was a witness!" he exclaimed. Only Aaron had gone out on patrol. He was alone in the office.

He rushed out past the night desk clerk. "I'm going to the crime scene, Janine!" he hollered over his shoulder as he ran out the door.

It was only 6:00, and the days were getting longer, so the sun was still up when he got to the trailer. Crime scene processors were gone for the day, but Mike had a master's in forensic science. He slipped on latex gloves and crime scene shoe covers before slipping under the yellow tape and entering the trailer. The attack had occurred outside on the attached deck. The assailant never entered the trailer, and neither had CID. The purse and shoes lay on the floor right where he'd seen them on the livestream. He carefully opened the purse and pulled out the wallet. "Oh, no," he chuckled, seeing the driver's license. "Kierra Lowe."

He called Tom, who, though he was off duty, called the sheriff. The sheriff, Tom, and Aaron all arrived at the trailer within half an hour. Mike was waiting for them with the bagged purse, shoes, and wallet in his cruiser as they each pulled up. He showed them the purse and shoes on the livestream. He showed them his photographs of where he had found the items. Then he showed them the driver's license.

"How the hell did CID miss that?" the sheriff bellowed.

"Because Jameson is a moron," Tom complained. He had been complaining about Larry Jameson for decades. Jameson ran crime scene processing for the Crime Investigation Division that Tom headed. But the sheriff had been reticent to act on Tom's complaints, believing the rift to be personal and not professional. Even the sheriff had to admit the processing of this scene had been sloppy thus far.

"Glad you caught it, Poole. Of course, we have no idea how long the purse and shoes were there."

"Not more than 4 hours," Mike interjected. "She was carrying that purse and wearing those shoes at Dockside last night." He pulled up the video from Dockside on his tablet. He found Kierra and paused the screen. She was indeed carrying the purse and wearing those shoes.

The sheriff shook his head. "You and Muse get over to the

Lowes' place and find out if she saw anything," he grumbled.

————

Jillian finished her shift at the convenience store and nervously opened the front door to her new home. Missy stood behind her, looking at her like she was crazy. She'd spent the day at Bethany's house. After the experience this morning, Jillian was uncomfortable leaving her alone in the house. As the door swung open and she flicked on the light, she was greeted by the sweet smell of Lily of the Valley. "All good in here, Great Gran?" she asked the empty foyer. The perfume wafted, hitting her right in the face, and she felt a warm, welcoming sensation. "Oh, a hug," she exclaimed.

"Are you okay, Mama?" Missy asked, pushing past her.

"Um, yeah. How about we get a dog?" she responded. A customer had told her he had a one-year-old female St. Bernard he needed to rehome when she had mentioned wanting a dog. He was selling his farmland and moving to Baltimore, and the dog was just too big. She had taken down his information. She pulled out her phone and stepped back out onto the porch to make the call. "Mr. Turner? Hi, it's Jillian from the Stop In. You mentioned you have a young St. Bernard you need to rehome? Can you bring her over? Yes, I'll take her bed, cage, food…everything. Yes. I can Venmo you the money. $700? No problem. I'm home now. Great. See you in a few." Then she sat down on the swing.

Missy came back out and sat beside her. "Did you see the creepy boy, Mama?"

Jillian jumped. "Did you?" she exclaimed in horror.

"On my phone, yes. But you don't need to be scared. He's only scary because he's scared," Missy told her.

"Says who?"

"You won't believe me," Missy announced.

"I always believe you," Jillian said, putting her arm around Missy as they started to swing.

"Alec Gardner. He was the boy in the barn with me. And I see him…sort of…sometimes when I'm at the Gardners' house." Alec Gardner had died in Vietnam. He had lived at Ravens' Roost.

"Really? Well, I've seen a freakin' ghost myself, Baby. So, I guess I have to believe you."

"Will a dog make you feel better?" Missy asked her.

"I think so," Jillian affirmed.

"Okay. I like dogs," Missy said, laying her head on her mother's shoulder.

It was only 5 or 10 minutes before Mr. Turner pulled into the driveway with the large dog in the back of his truck. He climbed out of the truck and grabbed the dog's leash. "Hey, there, Jillian," he called. "I swear I didn't even know this house was here! Looks like your new husband has been clearing away lots of overgrowth." He smiled. "This here is Lily. She's a great dog. I'm gonna miss her, but there's just no room for her to run where we're moving. Looks like you got lots of room here, though. It's a nice piece of property."

The dog jumped out of the back of the truck and wagged her tail. She was a beautiful St. Bernard, with the classic white and brown markings on her coat.

Jillian stood and walked over. She held her hand out, palm up, for Lily to give it a sniff before petting her. "Hi, Lily," she cooed, "aren't you a beauty?" Lily wagged her tail and licked Jillian's hand. "Come on over, Missy, and let her smell your hand before you touch her," Jillian called.

Missy did as she was told. Then Lily sat, and Missy dropped to her knees and hugged the dog's neck, as Lily covered her face in dog kisses.

"Look at that," Mr. Turner winked. "She's already made herself at home."

Mr. Turner handed Jillian the leash. "I'll put her stuff on the porch for you," he offered. He unloaded Lily's stuff as Jillian and Missy played with the dog. He walked back to his truck, and Jillian transferred the money to him.

They led Lily inside the house. Jillian brought in her bed, cage, and supplies. "Lily," she announced. "What a great name! You match the smell of my great-gran. That's what we call a good omen."

Missy laughed. "You've lost it, Mama."

"Maybe, but I feel better," Jillian confided.

————

Mike pulled into the Lowes' driveway. They lived out on Route 205 by Potomac Beach, almost to the King George County line. It was a large red brick split-level home. Aaron pulled in behind him. His phone beeped. He looked at the text as Aaron walked up to his cruiser.

"The wife checking on you?" he teased, as Mike got out of the car.

"Nah. She just texted that she got a dog. Name is Lily," he replied.

"Aw. You got a cute little puppy named Lily, huh?" Aaron giggled.

Mike's phone beeped again, and it was a picture. "Oh, my God!" he gasped. He held it up for Aaron to see.

"Jesus! It's Kujo!" Aaron said, laughing loudly.

"She's definitely a big girl," Mike chuckled. "Jillian got spooked this morning. She swears she saw a ghost."

"Which one?"

"The kid who died in the gravel pit back in the '80s," Mike told him as they walked together toward the door.

"Isn't that just a local legend?"

"It's taken on the feel of a legend, that's for sure. But it really happened. I did a report on it for a history class back in the day."

"What does she think a dog can do against a ghost?"

Aaron snickered.

"No idea. But it's fine if it makes her feel better, and hey, at least it's a real dog." Mike rang the doorbell, and from inside, a little dog began yapping. Both he and Aaron burst out laughing.

Rich opened the door. "What the hell do you want?" he glowered.

"We have a few questions for Mrs. Lowe," Aaron said, standing straighter and trying to sound serious.

"About?" Rich asked.

"An ongoing investigation," Mike said curtly. Then he smiled.

"Fine. Wait here," Rich blustered. "Muffy, shut it," he yelled at the Shizu bouncing around his feet. "Kierra, two deputies would like to speak to you about an ongoing investigation."

Kierra Lowe came to the door. She looked furtively from Mike to Aaron to Rich. Mike reached out to shake her hand. Her hand shook as she took his. He knew that look in her eyes. Kierra Lowe was terrified. He also noticed a bruise peeking out from under the short sleeve of her T-shirt on the side of her bicep.

"Can you step out here to talk to me for a minute, Kierra?" Mike asked, giving Aaron a look. Aaron understood and blocked Rich from joining Mike and Kierra on the sidewalk.

"So, Rich? Mike paid back all the child support you ever paid to Jillian. Does that mean you aren't contesting his claim that he's Missy's father? I mean Missy kinda looks like him…a lot more than she does you, anyway," Aaron taunted. It would seem confrontational to those who didn't know what he was doing. He was making sure he had Rich's full attention, so that Mike could get more from Kierra. The art of distraction was a powerful tool.

Mike leaned in closely. In a low tone, he asked, "Were you with Big Billy last night, Kierra? Were you there when he was killed? We found your purse and shoes."

She took a jagged, fearful breath. "I didn't see anything.

I…I hid in the closet in the bedroom."

"You and Big Billy?" Mike asked. She nodded.

"He…he was nice to me. I know what he came off as…but he was nice to me. Way nicer than…Rich."

"How long?"

"Two years," she whispered.

"Did you hear anything? A voice? Did Billy indicate who was at the door before he opened it?"

She shook her head. Then she paused. "The truck. I heard the truck pull up. It was running rough…missing. It backfired," she said.

"You're sure it was a truck, not a car?"

"Um, yeah, pretty sure. He drew back the curtain when it pulled up. I saw it for a second. I mean, it was dark, but it was a truck. Orange…or red. A roll bar behind the cab. Chevy, I think," she recounted.

"How old?"

"Old. Late 90s, early 2000s."

"Good job, Kierra. Do you need help? Do you feel unsafe here?" he asked earnestly.

She swallowed hard. Her bottom lip quivered. "I don't have anywhere to go. And I can't leave Dahlia," she pleaded.

"We can get you and Dahlia out and into a shelter. But you have to make the call, Kierra. I'll get a social worker out here right now. But you can't go back later tonight. Do you understand?" He desperately wanted her to leave, especially for Dahlia's sake, but he had no recourse if she refused.

She nodded. "I…he won't hurt me. We've already fought about it. I'll be fine," she insisted.

He sighed and thanked her. "We're done here, Aaron," he called to the other deputy. They started to walk back to their squad cars. "I'm going to stop at home to meet that monster of a dog, so when I walk in at 5 in the morning, she doesn't take my head off," he announced. "Call in an order for pickup at Angelo's. I'll pick it up when I'm done."

———

It was dark by the time Mike pulled into the driveway. He opened the door to his house. "Hey, Honey," he called from inside the door. Lily, in the living room, at Jillian's feet, sat up and barked a deep warning at him.

"Lily. Down. That's Daddy," Jillian said to the dog.

"Hello, Lily," he said. "Come here."

The dog obeyed the command. He scratched behind the ears. "Oh, you're a good girl." Lily wagged her tail. "Get a good whiff, girl. Recognize me when I get home in the morning."

He walked into the living room. Lily followed at his heel. "She's well trained, anyway. Looks like she was well cared for. How much?" he winked.

"$700. Including all her stuff," Jillian answered.

"Do you feel safer, Baby?" he asked.

"I do. I know it's irrational. But I do."

"Then it's money well spent," he told her, smiling.

He reached down and petted the dog's head. "Listen, Jill...I think Rich is beating Kierra. I'm telling you this so you stay away from him. He's pissed at me. I don't want him taking it out on you. Let Mr. Morgan handle things with him. Don't put yourself in trouble's way. Got it?"

She stood and put her arms around his neck, taking a step closer. "I got it," she whispered. "But what about Kierra and Dahlia?"

"There's not a lot I can do if she won't report it, but I'm keeping an eye on her. Okay?"

Jillian nodded, laying her forehead against his.

He smiled, and they kissed. "I'll see you in the morning, Babe."

"Hmmm," she sighed. "I'll see you in the morning." She

let go and stepped back.

————

After he left, Missy emerged from the bathroom, having taken a bath. "Did I hear Mike?" she asked.

"Yeah, he stopped in to meet Lily, but he's working, so he couldn't stay," Jillian said, patting the sofa beside her. Missy sat. Jillian wrapped her daughter up in a hug. They watched TV for about half an hour. "You have school tomorrow, Babydoll. You should get to bed," she said to her daughter.

Missy rose and looked Jillian in the eyes. "Can Carly come home with me on Thursday and spend the night?"

Jillian nodded. "Yeah. I work an early shift on Thursday. That should be fine. But Jessup's birthday is on Saturday, and Easter is on Sunday, so she can't stay Friday night…Understand?"

"Yes, Mama. Thank you. Good night," Missy said happily before she skipped off to bed.

Jillian finished watching the show before she rose to go to bed herself. She straightened the blanket on the sofa and turned to walk to the bedroom. The scent of Lily of the Valley filled the room. Jillian looked around but saw nothing amiss.

"Alright then, Great-Gran. I'm going to trust you're watching out for us. I really like this house. Night," she said to the empty room.

CHAPTER 9

The week passed. Mike had suggested they canvass the neighborhood again to ask about the truck, but so far, no one had come forward.

Thursday would be his last shift overnight for a while. He would be off Friday, Saturday, and Sunday. Monday, he would return to the day shift. As he got ready for work on Thursday afternoon, he was grateful that he would have a few days with his family. His and Jillian's schedules had not meshed this week, and he had missed her.

Missy and her friend Carly burst into the house just as he kissed Jillian goodbye. He patted Lily on the head and told the girls to have fun before he walked out the door.

He was halfway to Montross when Janine called him on the radio. "Joe Gardner called from Mason's garage in Colonial Beach to tell you he has a truck in the garage that matches the description of the truck in the Walsh homicide," she told him.

"Okay. I'm turning around. I'll check in after I see what Joe's got," he replied. He headed back to Colonial Beach.

Joe came out to meet him as he pulled into the garage's parking lot. He wiped his hands on a rag as he approached. Mike got out of the cruiser and followed Joe around the back of the building. The truck was parked between a late-model Odyssey and a classic '68 Ford F-100. It was a bright orange 1998 Chevy 1500. A roll bar was installed on the bed behind the cab.

"Curtis Tilly brought it in," Joe said.

"Curtis...Curtis Tilly...Jacob Tilly's father?" Mike asked.

"I dunno. He's Ned Telly's father. Who's Jacob Tilly?"

"The kid who dove into the gravel pit and died back in…1989, I think it was," Mike answered. He walked around the vehicle. "Fresh mud," he said, pointing at the tires and running boards. "Ned…his daughter Chloe is Big Billy's baby mama?"

"Yeah, so says the grapevine," Joe answered. "Not my crowd."

"Yeah. Ned was probably around 16 years old when Jacob died…Curtis must be 80 or older. Is the truck registered to him?"

"Curtis? Yes. But he had Ned drive it in. He drove his Olds. Said the truck was too big for him to drive on the street. He said that it was fine last week, but now it's out of alignment, and the transmission is stripped. Like somebody drove it who didn't know how to drive a stick shift. But there's more wrong than that…and for longer than a week. Those spark plugs haven't been changed in years. It misfires."

"Does it backfire?" Mike asked.

"Yep," Joe replied. "What do you think?"

"I think it's worth checking into. Thanks, Joe," Mike replied.

————

Thirty minutes later, Mike was standing in Curtis Tilly's yard. The old man shuffled out the door and across the yard. "Good evening, Mr. Tilly," Mike greeted him.

"Deputy. You're the one who bought the Pruce land… right?"

"Yessir, I am," Mike replied. "I married Gordon Chisholm's daughter, Jillian, last week, too."

"Ah. I heard somethin' about that. Congratulations. It's been over 35 years. But I still can't stand to go out that way…to the Pruce property, that is. I drive all the way out the long way to avoid it. O' course, I don't hold it agin' the Pruces none. Jacob did it to hisself. But it's still painful."

"I imagine it is, Sir. And I'm sorry if my being here brings up painful memories…" Mike offered.

"Don't be silly, Son. I daresay, you weren't even born yet. I'm just in a melancholy mood. Pay me no mind. What can I do for you?"

"Your old Chevy 1500. Joe Gardner told me you thought someone might have taken it for a joyride and caused some damage. It matches the description of a vehicle used in a crime… and I was hoping you could tell me about what happened."

"Oh. Really? I'd 'a' called the cops if I thought that was the case. I just figured it was kids. Yeah, last Saturday, when I went to bed, it was parked out by the garage. I'll show you," the old man said, walking toward a detached garage behind his house. Mike followed. "See the way the grass is flattened? And when I woke up Sunday mornin', it was parked about a foot out and three feet forward." He pointed to another patch of tire tracks and flattened grass.

"Do you mind if I take some pictures and look around?" Mike asked.

"Help yourself. You need me to make a formal report?"

"Yessir, I'll take your statement in a minute. I want to get the pictures before it gets too dark."

Mike looked inside the open garage. The old man's Cadillac was parked inside. Bikes and fishing gear lined the walls. Back in the corner was an old 4-wheeler being used as a bench of sorts. Nothing appeared out of order. He snapped a quick photo, just in case.

As Mike finished snapping pictures, Ned Tilly drove up. "Hey, Daddy," Ned called. "What's up?"

"The deputy here says that my truck matches the description of one used in a crime."

"Really? Which crime?"

"Billy Walsh's murder," Mike answered, putting away the camera.

Ned huffed. "Good riddance," he mumbled. "I get you're just doin' your job, but my Chloe will be better off without that trash."

"I couldn't agree more, Ned," Mike smiled. "But it is my job. Besides…the person who did this…they need to go away. It was…beyond brutal."

"We'll cooperate fully, Deputy. Don't you worry. You need my permission to search the truck?" the old man offered.

"That'd be great, sir. Thank you."

————

Missy and Carly, with Lily, set off to explore the old gravel pit road. Joe had cleared it for Mike over the last few days, using an old bulldozer that belonged to his boss to level it. He stopped short of the gravel pit enclosure.

Missy reached the top of the hill. "It's all grown over," she said. "There's a hole in the ground, but it's all full of trees."

"Still dangerous, though," Carly observed.

"Yeah. Mike says to stay away from it. He says he hasn't figured out what to do to make it safe yet. He's still researching it," she agreed, stepping up to the rusty chain link gate that was locked with a heavy-duty rusty chain and padlock. I wish I could see it, though."

"Why?" Carly laughed.

"Just curious," she replied. "The ghost boy died in there."

"That's morbid," Carly sneered.

"Maybe. But I want to help him. Seeing where he died might make that easier," she pondered. "But I did promise Mike I wouldn't go in, so I guess I won't."

The girls stepped away from the fence and back onto the newly leveled old road. Beyond this point, it was rutted and overgrown. It might be passable on foot, but Jillian had warned them about copperheads, and Carly didn't want to risk stepping on one of the venomous snakes hiding in the high grass.

Missy stood looking wistfully past the gravel pit toward the marshy woods beyond. Carly put her hand above her eyes to block the sun. "Hey, is that a house?" she asked, pointing into the woods.

"Yeah. I think they call that the Pruce Homestead. Daddy says the Pruces, my Mama's people, owned this property back before the Revolutionary War. That house was built in the early 1800s or something. It was the original house," she explained.

"Wow, that's kinda cool," Carly said, sounding impressed.

"Yeah, and there was a Civil War battle here, too…across the street where the Event Center is. Burnt House or something like that. There are ghost stories about Civil War soldiers roaming around back in these woods. Muhaha," Missy teased.

"You're so mean," Carly giggled, giving Missy's shoulder a gentle push.

"I'm teasing, but there are stories. And that house is supposed to have a gray lady haunting it, a young bride waiting for her groom to come back from the battle, only he never did. Ewwwwahhhh," Missy said in a spooky voice.

"Stop it. I'll never sleep," Carly giggled. "How does Mike know so much?"

"He researches stuff that catches his interest. He's always been fascinated with this place," she explained, using her father's words.

"All my daddy knows is football and building stuff," Carly mused. Her father was an architect. Missy wasn't sure what an architect did, but it wasn't anywhere near as cool as a detective.

As they stood looking at the house, Missy could swear she saw something moving at the upstairs window. Lily barked. The two girls looked at each other, screamed, turned, and ran back toward Missy's new house.

Lily looked at the old house in the woods and at the retreating girls. She decided to follow them.

––––––––

Early Friday morning, Mike pushed open the front door and smelled Lily of the Valley.

"Wow. A little less perfume, Mrs. Pruce," he chuckled. Lily's bed was in the foyer, and she raised her head when he spoke and wagged her tail. "G'morning, Lily," he said. "I'm going to bed."

He was so tired; he didn't even have the energy for a shower. He went straight into the bedroom, removed his uniform, and collapsed onto the bed. Jillian awoke and sat up.

"Sorry," he moaned. "I'm exhausted. I didn't mean to wake you."

"That's okay," she replied. "Come under the covers with me."

"Mmmmm. Okay," he agreed, snuggling in the bed with her. Even as tempted as he was by her skin against his, he fell asleep immediately, but he did so clinging to her.

He didn't wake up until close to 1 pm. He could hear Jessup and Ryan in the living room with Missy and Carly. He remembered the kids were on Easter break. He moaned and struggled out of bed, put on a robe, and went to shower.

He stood in the shower, allowing himself to come fully awake under the hot cascade.

He'd searched the truck the night before and found blood transfer traces on the driver's seat. He was waiting for the lab to get back to him, but he was sure it would be Billy Walsh's blood. He had also finally gotten a statement from one of the neighbors who confirmed an orange truck had backfired at around 2 am. He was closing in, but he still didn't know who killed Billy or why. He'd also interviewed most of Billy's gang. They all pointed their fingers at Butch Kennedy, a rival thug, but Butch had an alibi…a good one. He had been arrested in Fredericksburg last Friday and was still in custody at the time of the murder.

Mike was looking forward to some time off, even if it meant Easter dinner at Jenny and Max's.

He turned off the shower, dried and wrapped the towel around his trim, muscular waist. Jillian's name was tattooed just above his hip, and the top of the J peeked out at the top of the towel. He didn't have nearly as many tattoos as Jillian, but he did have a cuff around his upper arm, and between his shoulder blades, he had the Marine Corps shield with "My brother, my hero" in script above it and "Kenneth Anthony Poole" in script below it.

He shaved and dried his hair before slipping back into his robe and removing the towel, which he hung neatly on the rack. He ran a comb through his hair and brushed his teeth.

Then he went back into his bedroom and got dressed… in jeans and a T-shirt, thankful it wasn't his uniform. And damn, Nikes felt so much more comfortable than tactical boots.

He emerged feeling refreshed and hungry.

The kids were playing on the PS5 in the living room. He found Jillian in the kitchen, making grilled cheese sandwiches and tomato soup. He wrapped his arms around her from behind. She leaned back against him. "Hey, Babe," she greeted him, "are you hungry?"

"Hmmm, starved," he told her. "You smell good."

"Ha," she scoffed.

"I'll settle for a sandwich and some of the soup," he chuckled. He released her and turned to open the fridge. "Oh… strawberry pie," he said.

"Don't you dare touch it. It's for Sunday."

"Not even one piece?"

"No," she commanded.

"Do you work tonight?" he asked, teasingly.

"No. I have off until Monday," she smirked.

The doorbell rang. "I'll get it," he offered with a smile,

leaving her to finish preparing lunch.

He opened the door to Gordon Chisholm.

He blinked. "Um... Hello," he stuttered. Gordon was a very fit 53 years old, with laugh lines around his eyes, a full head of prematurely gray hair, and broad shoulders on a 6-foot frame.

Gordon laughed. "Hey there, Son. I hear you married my daughter, finally."

"Y...yessir," Mike replied nervously. He stood there, staring for a long time. Then it occurred to him he should probably invite his father-in-law inside. He stepped aside and said, "Come on in. Jillie's making lunch, and Missy's in the living room playing on the PS5 with some friends. I just got up...I mean, I showered. But I worked last night. I'm rambling. Come in."

"Do I make you nervous?" Gordon asked, leaning towards him and winking.

"A little, yessir," Mike answered with a smile.

———

Gordon reached down and picked up his duffle, as Jillian came out of the kitchen, calling, "Kids, lunch." She stopped dead in her tracks at the kitchen door. "Daddy!" she exclaimed. She ran at her father and jumped into his arms.

She had reason to be excited to see him. He and her mother had gotten married after Jenny had graduated from high school. He had been a year ahead. He had joined the Navy. Jenny had tolerated the military life for a few years, but when he was transferred to Japan, she had come home. Jillian had been 3. They remained married for a few more years, but it was doomed. They had divorced when Jillian was 8. And Jenny had remarried when Jillian was 10. Gordon, saddened by his failed marriage, had finished his illustrious military career after 25 years in the service as a Master of Arms Chief Petty Officer and took a job in San Francisco. He rarely came home, mostly because Jenny preferred that he not. But he did his best to see Jillian on her birthdays and holidays.

Even so, it had been 5 or more years since Jillian had seen her father. He'd been unable to attend her wedding to Lyle, having tested positive for Covid the night before he was scheduled to arrive.

"What are you doing here?" she squealed, kissing his cheek.

"My company is transferring me to Dahlgren," he said, smiling. "I wanted to surprise you."

"You're kidding? You're here to stay?" she squealed again. "Missy! Granddaddy is here!"

Missy came running from the living room and jumped into his arms, too.

"Where are you going to live?" Jillian asked, and she noticed Mike blush.

Her father was as congenial as always and winked. "Wouldn't you know, as soon as I sell my house, they want me to move home? Nah. I'm kidding. I rented a townhouse in Dahlgren. But the thing is, it won't be ready for me to move in until May 1. I was hoping…I could use my old room."

"I haven't really been through the attic yet," Mike blanched. "But, of course, you're welcome to it. I might be able to get a friend or two to come help me shift stuff from the attic to the basement."

"Yeah, Grandma was a packrat. I didn't think about that. I can get a hotel room," he offered.

Jillian felt herself pout involuntarily. Mike looked at her and sighed. "Let me call Joe," he said, taking out his phone, "… and Aaron might be awake by now."

She grinned and kissed him. "I love you, Michael Gabriel."

"Yeah. I know," he smiled back. So much for his restful afternoon, she thought. He must really love her or something.

———

Mike wolfed down his sandwich and soup before Joe knocked on the door. Joe brought Dex with him. "Hey," Mike greeted them. "I didn't expect Dex to be here today. I thought he'd be here tomorrow."

"I will be. I'm staying at Joe's. Pops wasn't feeling well and sent his birthday gift for Jessup. I have a date with the lovely Miss Johnson tonight, so I thought I'd just make a weekend of it," Dex explained.

"That's great, Dex. Really. She couldn't find a better guy," Mike said. "Thank y'all for coming on such short notice."

"You helped me replace windows and paint my house in December," Joe guffawed. "Like I could say no."

They quickly got to work. They had tackled moving the vintage Christmas decorations in the corner closest to the stairs when Aaron Muse also arrived to help. They set up a system where 2 of them got the boxes upstairs and took them to the landing by the back door, and the other two picked them up from the landing and took them to the basement. Doing this, they had all the boxes cleared quickly.

The bigger pieces of furniture, other than the bedroom furniture, they moved together. It only took a couple of hours. Gordon and Jillian cleaned the room after they had cleared it. Mike thanked his friends before they left.

He went to the bedroom, peeled off his shirt, and collapsed face down on the bed. He must have fallen asleep because he opened his eyes to see that the light had shifted. Jillian had come into the room and was massaging his back.

"Hmmm," he moaned. "That's amazing."

She leaned down and kissed his shoulder. "Thank you," she whispered.

"What for?"

"For doing all that work so Daddy can stay," she replied.

"Of course, Darlin'. He's your father." Jillian rubbed

his neck muscles and then down his spine with her thumbs. "Hmmmm," he moaned again. "Speaking of your father…Did he get settled in?"

"Yeah. His old Pioneer stereo and cabinet were up there with a bunch of his albums from when he was in high school. He and the kids are having a blast listening to them."

She lay down beside him. He leaned up on his elbows and kissed her, pulling her under him.

The doorbell rang, and Lily started barking. "God damn it," he swore, rolling off her to his back.

"That'll be Carly's mom," she giggled.

He nodded.

Jillian got up and walked out of the room. "Lily! Quiet," she called. He heard the door open. He heard Carly's father's voice, muffled but angry. He said Mike's name. Mike sighed and got up. He found a clean shirt and pulled it on over his head as he emerged from the bedroom.

Doug March stood in the doorway, his wife, Carrie, behind him, looking rather sheepish, on the front porch. Mike walked up behind Jillian. "Hi, Doug. What's up?" he asked.

"Did you have a bunch of strange men here with my daughter?" Doug asked confrontationally.

Mike was taken aback. "Woah. They aren't strange men. My father-in-law surprised us by showing up today. I needed help moving stuff out of the attic bedroom to the basement to clean up the room for him. Joe Gardner, whom you know, came over. Our friend Dex Lawson came with him. Dex served with Joe and Kenny in the Marines. He's Jessup's uncle. And Deputy Aaron Muse came over to help as well. That's it. The kids were playing on the PS5. We didn't even see them the entire time," Mike explained.

Doug looked stunned. "But there was a black man…"

"Are you fucking kidding me?" Mike yelped. "Dex

Lawson is a Nurse Practitioner. He's a decorated Marine. And he's my good friend. So, watch what you say," Mike said, gritting his teeth.

Jillian put her hand up. "Please stop, Doug." She glanced nervously toward the living room.

Jessup stood there. He was breathing heavily. His lip quivered.

"Oh, son of a bitch," Mike swore and moved quickly, swooping the boy, thirteen tomorrow and 5 feet tall, up in his arms. "You listen to me, Jessup Gardner. Your skin color…is beautiful. Uncle Dex's skin color is beautiful. People who want to attach a lack of character to it are the ones who lack character," he whispered, cradling the child's head against his cheek. Jessup's cheek was wet. The back door slammed. "You need to get out of my house, Doug," he yelled over Jessup's shoulder, hugging him tighter as the boy started to cry harder.

"Look, I'm not sayin' all black men…"

"Shut up!" Mike bellowed. Gordon emerged from the kitchen and took Jessup from Mike.

"Come on, young man. You don't need to hear this trash," he said, walking away with him.

"I mean…if you know him well…"

A truck pulled into the drive, and Joe Gardner jumped out of the vehicle without shutting off the engine.

"Oh, crap," Carrie whispered.

Dex jumped out of the passenger side. "Joe!" he called. "That won't settle it."

"Don't care!" Joe bellowed as he stormed toward the porch and Doug March. As he reached him, he grabbed him by the shirt and pulled him out the door. "What did you say, you racist fuck?" he screamed.

Joe was 6'3" tall. Doug was 5'10" tall. Joe had a 6-inch reach on the smaller man. But he didn't punch him. He showed some restraint. He lifted Doug by the collar. "Apologize to my friend and to my son," he spat through his clenched jaw.

"I...I...I'm sorry. Okay, I'm sorry," Doug yelped.

Joe lowered him and yelled, "Jess, Honey, come out here."

Jessup reluctantly emerged from the house. He paused at the door before he flung himself at his father, wrapping his arms around Joe's waist and burying his face in Joe's shirt. Joe glared at Doug.

"Jessup, I'm sorry. I shouldn't have said...I shouldn't have judged... based on color," Doug stammered. "And that's the truth. It's also true I didn't even realize I was doing it." He turned to face Dex. "I... I don't know what to say."

"There's nothing you can say, Man. You have to recognize that you are racist before you can fix it. Do you recognize it?" Dex asked.

Doug nodded.

"Then change it."

CHAPTER 10

Kristin had a great time with Dex last week. It inspired her to come out of her shell a little. She wore her hair down to work for the first time ever…and she did it all week. She weeded the cardigans out of her wardrobe…except for one. That one had sentimental value and was so comfortable. She did some shopping and bought some jeans a size smaller and some dresses inches shorter. She left two buttons undone on her blouse instead of one. She wore more makeup…correction…she wore makeup.

She heard the comments from the female staff and faculty. She felt the approving looks from the male staff and faculty. She felt transformed.

And she was excited to see Dex again, one-on-one, without her stepsister and Mike and their friends acting as a buffer. She was nervous, too, because it meant he didn't have them as a buffer, either. He'd see her…just her.

Friday evening, she sat on her sofa, ready and waiting. She wore the new jeans, a red blouse with the top 3 buttons undone, and a pair of vintage Candies shoes. She sat bouncing her leg and biting her thumbnail, staring at the clock on the wall. He was late. Just 5 minutes. But she was on the verge of tears when the doorbell rang.

"Oh, thank God," she murmured as she stood and walked to the front door. She opened it to Mike Poole. "Mike," she said, her heart falling to the pit of her stomach.

"Hey, Kristin," he said. "I know you weren't expecting me."

"He isn't coming. He hated me," she said, pouting and

turning away.

"No, Honey. He likes you…a lot. He was ready to come pick you up an hour ago…Then Joe's truck slipped into gear and…ran over his foot…" Mike grimaced.

"What?" Kristin asked, whirling back to face him.

Mike sighed. "Listen. Gordon showed up today. And his new house won't be ready until May. He asked to stay with us. I needed to clean out the attic room quickly. So, I asked Joe and Aaron to come help. Dex was with Joe. And we got everything cleaned out quickly. Then, later, Doug March showed up and yelled at me for having a strange black man in my house with his daughter…in front of Jessup. Ryan ran out the back door and went home to get Joe, who naturally jumped into his truck to come confront Doug. Dex came with him again to try and keep him from ripping Doug's head off. Anyway, when they pulled in, Joe just slammed the truck into park and got out. So did Dex. Duke…on the other hand…Joe and Doug didn't actually fight, and when Dex turned to get back in the truck, Duke got excited and knocked the truck into gear," he gushed.

"Duke…the…dog…ran over my date's foot?" she echoed.

"Um. Yes," Mike replied, grimacing again.

"Where is he now?"

"The dog? At home," he answered.

"No, you dork. Where is Dex?" She shoved his shoulder. He chuckled.

"Mary Washington ER," he replied, laughing.

"So, he's not coming?"

"Oh. No, Kristin," he said, grabbing her arm, "that's not what I'm saying. He's just going to be late."

"Why didn't he just call me?" she sniffed.

"He did, Honey. Your phone is off," Mike pointed out.

She stared at him and took her phone out of her back pocket. He tried to keep a straight face. She closed her eyes and pursed her lips. "I'm a moron," she whispered.

Mike grinned and hugged her. "His foot is broken, just a minor fracture. He's getting a boot and will be here in about an hour."

Dex sat in the passenger seat behind a big bouquet of roses. "Do you think she still wants to see me?"

"She said she did when she spoke to you...and again in the text. She understood, Man. Just go knock on the door," Joe huffed, rolling his eyes.

"I swear I saw Confederate soldiers in the field across the street before the truck rolled over my foot."

"Uh-huh," Joe snickered. "Worry about modern-day racists, Dex, not the dead ones."

Dex opened the door and staggered out, limping with one crutch to Kristin's door. He rang the doorbell. And stared at the roses.

Kristin opened the door. "Hi," she said, smiling. "Are those for me?"

He looked up. She was breathtaking. He nodded and held them out to her. Then he waved for Joe to leave.

She took the flowers.

"Well, we could go to Monroe Brewery. They have a live band tonight, but you're kind of out of commission," she said, smelling the roses.

"Yeah, I'm so sorry about that. I was looking forward to tonight," he smiled.

"I made spaghetti. We could eat here and watch a movie..." Kristin suggested.

"That sounds nice. And...I really need to put my foot up," Dex said with a laugh.

Kristin moved aside and let him in. He took a seat on the sofa while she went to put the roses into a vase. Kristin's sofa was one of those with a chaise lounge on one side. He grimaced as he lifted his leg and sighed in relief.

Kristin returned quickly. She placed the vase on the buffet table in her dining area of the great room. "I'll bring you a plate. We can eat in the living room, since the sofa is the best place to put your foot up. One meatball or two?" she said, turning to face him and smiling nervously.

"Two," he replied, hoping she could cook meatballs.

She disappeared again. She returned with a bottle of wine, a corkscrew, and two wine glasses. "Would you open the wine?" she asked, as she walked away again after placing them on the coffee table.

He reached over and opened the bottle, pouring wine into both glasses. She returned with two plates full of spaghetti and two forks. She set one plate down on the coffee table in front of him and another plate next to it. She handed him a fork before she sat.

They ate, talked, and laughed. They finished the bottle of wine. Kristin excused herself again to take their plates to the kitchen. "The remote is in the basket on the end table by you," she called to him as she loaded the dishes into her dishwasher. "Pick a movie."

He found the remote and scrolled through the choices, laughing when he saw *My Cousin Vinny* on the guide. He selected it and waited for her to return.

"Oh! I love this movie!" she exclaimed, sitting beside him again.

"Me, too," he replied.

Halfway through the movie, they paused, and Kristin got a second bottle of wine.

By the time Vinny stood in court in the velvet tux, they were snuggling up close, Dex with his arm around her shoulders. As the end credits ran, she leaned forward and picked up the remote. "Another movie or…" she stammered. He took the remote and turned off the TV.

He returned the remote to the basket. He turned back to her and reached out, caressing her cheek. She closed her eyes, her shoulders relaxed, and her lips parted. He leaned in and kissed her softly.

Kristin laid her hand gently on his shoulder. As the kiss deepened, she moved in closer, moving her hand up and around his neck. She swallowed hard as the kiss ended.

"I like you, Kristin. I really do," he assured her, pulling back. "I think I should go home…or back to Joe's…now. I don't want to rush it…or you."

She took a deep breath and nodded. "I'll take you, if you want to go." She paused, not moving. "I was in love once, I thought…He used me. He pretended to love me to make his ex jealous. He broke my heart. And I…I threw myself at Joe… because I knew he wasn't interested. It was a great way to prove I was…over it…and still not have to actually…date anyone."

"Oh. I see. We can take it as slow as you want, Kristin. I'm in no hurry."

"No…that's not what I mean. I mean…I haven't…I haven't put myself out there in a long time…and I wasn't all that experienced as it was. I…I don't…know if I'll be any good…at any of the physical…emotional. I want…with every part of my body…I just don't know how to convey that…" she stammered.

"You don't want me to go?" he asked.

She shook her head.

"Are you sure?"

"I'm sure," she said determinedly.

He smiled. "How about we…watch another movie, cuddled up here together under a blanket and just…" She shook her head.

He smiled again and traced her lips with his thumb.

"Music?"

―――――――

Jillian opened her eyes in response to the sound of the doorbell and Lily's barking. Mike's arm was around her, holding her close. His breath, warm and steady, tickled the back of her neck. She moved his arm and sat up. She slipped on her slippers and grabbed her robe off the hook on the back of the door.

She pulled on the robe as she walked toward the front door. "Good girl, Lily," she praised the dog, who wagged her tail. She looked out the window. Kristin was pacing in front of the door. Jillian opened the door and greeted her, "Hi, Honey. What on earth are you doing here at this hour? It's not even six, yet."

"I…I just brought Dex back to Joe and Bethany's," Kristin stammered.

"Oh…I see. And?"

"Jesus, Jillian. I'm…I don't know what I am," Kristin pleaded.

Jillian laughed. "Human. You're human. Did you have fun?"

"Oh, God," Kristin said, blushing and covering her eyes with her hand.

"Come on in, Miss Johnson. I'll make some coffee, and I can explain why you have nothing to feel ashamed about," Jillian snorted, winking.

She moved aside, and Kristin moved past her to enter, stopping short when she saw Lily. "Jesus, that's a big dog."

"That's Lily. She's a good girl," Jillian cooed at the animal. She closed the door and took Kristin by the arm, leading her to the kitchen. Jillian started the coffee. "Want some cereal?" she asked.

"Cereal?" Kristin echoed.

"Yeah. Breakfast?"

"Oh, that's right, you can't make breakfast," Kristin giggled.

"I am a great cook...as long as eggs aren't involved," Jillian agreed.

"How about an omelet?" Kristin asked, looking in the fridge.

"Sounds wonderful." Jillian laughed, handing Kristin an apron.

"Fine. I'll make the eggs. Can you make toast?" Kristin offered.

Soon, the two of them had breakfast well underway.

Missy was the first to succumb to her curiosity and hunger. She stood in the kitchen doorway watching her mother and aunt for a moment. "Hi, Aunt Kristin," she said, taking a seat at the table.

"Hey, Bugaboo," Kristin greeted her, kissing her cheek and setting a plate with an omelet, bacon, and toast in front of her.

Gordon came down the steps and entered the back of the kitchen. "Kristin? Wow. You look amazing. Good morning, Jillie, Missy, Lily," he said, peering beyond the kitchen to the dog sitting in the foyer watching the activity in the kitchen.

"Thank you, Mr. Chisholm. You look pretty good yourself," Kristin smiled.

"Gordon, please," he said, sitting.

Jillian placed a plate in front of him and kissed his cheek.

"I didn't realize you and Kristin were so close," he whispered.

"It's a relatively new occurrence," she whispered back. "She's...Mike's sister."

Her father's mouth dropped. "Max is..."

"Yes."

Then Mike came in, shirtless, and wiping his eyes. "What's

going on?" he asked.

"Go put on a shirt," Jillian commanded her husband.

"What? Why?"

Kristin called, "Hi."

"Oh, who cares? It's just Kristin," he retorted, sitting down.

Kristin rolled her eyes and shook her head.

"The date went well?" he asked.

Kristin blushed. "Um. Yes. Thank you."

He looked at her for a beat. "Oh. It went really well."

"Shut up, Mike," she said, blushing deeper.

He laughed.

They ate. Jillian stood, grabbed Kristin's arm, and said, "Mike and Missy will do the dishes. Come on, Kristin." She pulled her stepsister into her bedroom.

"Well?" she asked, closing the door.

Kristin sank down, sitting on the side of the bed. "Oh, my God. I'm such a slut. I can't believe I did that."

Jillian chuckled and sat beside her, laying her hand on Kristin's knee. "Kristin, you are not a slut. He's what? The second guy you've ever slept with? That is not a slut. I'm a slut."

They both laughed.

"Do you like him?"

"Gee, I hope so," she replied sarcastically.

"That's great, Honey. Really. He's a good-lookin' guy," Jillian said.

"I do like him…a lot. And he is really good-looking. And I think about him constantly. We like the same movies and books. And we laugh so much. And I haven't talked this much in years… And I swear Jillian…I look in the mirror…and I'm suddenly pretty."

"You were always pretty," Jillian laughed.

"No. I had the potential to be pretty. But I was a sour puss," Kristin said. "Do you know I haven't put my hair up in a ponytail in a week? And I threw out all my cardigans…except for Quinton's…which I couldn't bring myself to do."

"That is the one you need to throw out. Quinton Tilly is a piece of crap. Forget him."

"I…I don't have feelings for him anymore. I know he used me. He was ten years older and exciting…and I was naïve. He was never going to leave Arleen. I was just a means to an end. But I did love him, Jill…enough to…" She looked down. "I want to… open my heart up to Dex. I want to take a chance. And I haven't wanted to do that since I gave away my baby. I'm afraid to tell him, though."

"So…you chased Joe because…?"

"Because he wasn't interested, and I wasn't risking anything…" Kristin blurted.

"Oh. Jesus, Kristin. That's one of the saddest things I've ever heard." Jillian meant it. Her heart broke for Kristin. Mike had been right about her. She wasn't an uptight, skanky bitch. She was a hurt, sweet…sister.

Noises from outside drowned out their conversation. They both turned to see a truck full of sod in the circular drive. "Oh, the guys are here to lay the sod," Jillian noted, stating the obvious.

There was a knock on the bedroom door. "I need a shirt," Mike's muffled voice called.

"What'd I tell ya?" Jillian yelled.

"Jill," he pleaded.

"Yeah, yeah, yeah. Come in," she laughed.

He opened the door, walked over to the chest of drawers, and opened the third drawer, pulling out a red T-shirt. He pulled it on, turned, walked over to Jillian, and kissed her on the mouth. "You're mean, Jillian Poole."

"Say it again," she giggled.

"You're mean," he repeated.

"Not that part," she whispered.

He smiled, wrapped his arms around her, and kissed her deeply. Then he pulled away and said, "Jillian Poole."

CHAPTER 11

Jillian and Kristin went shopping. Kristin needed a gift for Jessup and clothes, having been invited to the birthday party by Dex and later to a drag race at the Colonial Beach Dragway, which was closer to Oak Grove than Colonial Beach, but that was irrelevant. What mattered was that Kristin had nothing to wear to the Dragway. She was a closet motorhead. She knew how to dress, but not for a date. No one had ever asked her to go to the drag strip on a date. She needed her stepsister's opinion.

Mike watched them drive away as he supervised the installation of the new front yard. He'd decided to seed the back but sod the front. He looked up and waved as they left. The men leveled the yard first with a small bulldozer, depositing a pile of dirt out back by the garage. Then they laid the sod, cutting the edges to fit the circular driveway and around the porch. Mike was not the kind to just watch and worked as hard as the men he'd hired. Gordon and Missy, however, watched contentedly from the porch swing with Lily lying on the floor at their feet.

They had nearly finished laying the sod when Pam pulled into the driveway, with Kenny in the passenger seat. Lily let out a low growl, then a bark. Gordon tightened his grip on her leash. Mike nodded in satisfaction.

Mike heard Missy's squeal of delight. "Pam-ma!" she called, jumping up.

"Pam-ma. I served there," Gordon retorted.

"Huh?" Missy asked.

"Nothing. Never mind. It's just a granddad joke, Baby," Gordon laughed.

Kenny, excited, clapped as he exited the car. "Oh, you got a dog! I love dogs!"

"Be gentle, Kenny. She has to get to know you before you roughhouse, okay?" Mike called to his brother as his sister/mother approached him.

"He wants to move into the assisted living apartments," she sniffed as she came within earshot.

"Yeah. That would be good for him, Pam...for you, too," Mike said, giving her a hug.

"Mike, I can barely keep him safe when he's with me. How can I do it if he lives in an apartment?"

"What do you mean?" Mike asked, noticing Kenny was limping as he walked up the porch steps.

"He got jumped by some teenagers yesterday on his walk on the boardwalk," she whispered. "He fought 'em off...cuz he's strong as an ox, but he took a few good punches to the head and got stabbed in the leg."

"Jesus! Pam, why didn't you call me?" Mike bellowed, dropping the sod he was holding and running over to the porch and up the stairs. "Kenny, take off your hat!" he demanded, grabbing his brother's arm. Kenny did as he was told. "Jesus!" Mike swore again. Kenny's jaw was purple and swollen. He had a black eye, and his nose had a bandage across the bridge and was twice its normal size.

"I'm okay," Kenny assured him.

"And you were stabbed?"

"I'm okay," Kenny repeated in a sterner voice.

Mike choked back the tears. "Okay. Okay. But why didn't anybody call me? I want to know these things, Ken..."

"What were you going to do? Pam took care of it. I got a tetanus shot and stitches. I don't have a concussion. It was your first day off since you got married."

"Who did this?"

"You can't fix it."

"I can sure the hell try. Who?" Mike demanded.

Kenny clamped his mouth shut.

"The O'Malley boys, Steve and Caleb. And that Green kid…Ray. Colonial Beach Police picked them up. They're in custody at the Colonial Beach jail," Pam said from behind him.

Mike pulled his checkbook out of his back pocket, signed a check, and thrust it at Pam. "Pay them when they're done," he said, bounding down the steps and getting into his truck. He didn't head out toward the Beach, though. He turned the other way and drove toward Ravens' Roost.

Joe and Dex came out of the house when he pulled into the driveway. They were all smiles as he rolled down the window. He quickly told them what happened to Kenny. They both frowned. Joe turned and yelled toward the house, "Bethy, Dex and I are goin' out with Mike for a bit. Something happened to Kenny."

Bethany appeared on the porch. "Is he alright?" she asked, genuine concern etched on her pretty face.

"He's okay, but he's pretty beat up. He and Pam are at my house now if you want to talk to him, Bethany," Mike called. She nodded. Joe and Dex ran around to the passenger side. Joe got into the front seat, Dex in the back of the king cab. Mike backed out at full speed and spun his tires as he pulled away, this time heading toward Colonial Beach.

They didn't speak as Mike drove. When they arrived at the small police department, located in the BB&T Insurance Services Building on Colonial Avenue, they all three got out of the truck without speaking.

Jon Briars, a deputy in Mike's unit, was inside talking to officers Hopkins and Foster. "Oh, crap," he said as the three entered.

"It's alright, Jon," Mike glowered. "We just want to know what happened."

"Their parents bailed them out after they went before Judge Sanders this morning. I don't know what to tell you, Mike. I don't know what got into them boys," Officer Foster explained. "They know Kenny walks there, and they admitted he wasn't botherin' them."

"Can I see the police report?" Mike asked.

"Sure. But you gotta let the court handle it."

"Hank, I'm a veteran officer. I know what to do and not to do," Mike replied.

"Sure…but your friends?"

"They do, too," he retorted.

"I'll get it for you," Foster answered, and he walked into a back room.

"Like I could get in a fight with my foot in a boot and walking with a crutch," Dex chuckled.

"What exactly happened?" Jon laughed.

"Joe's dog drove a truck over it," Dex teased.

"Say what?" guffawed Officer Hopkins.

"I got out of my truck and left it runnin', and Duke knocked it into gear," Joe blushed.

"At the time, it wasn't funny. But this morning…I admit I laughed. Dex was rollin' around in…basically dirt, because we tilled my yard, but there's no grass yet, and Duke was barkin'. And our dog, Lily, was barkin'. Joe was chasin' the truck. And the rest of us were standin' there wonderin' what the hell just happened," Mike chuckled.

"Yeah, funny," Dex grumbled.

"Don't tell me you didn't milk that injury for all it was worth last night. I know exactly what time you got back to Joe's this mornin' after your date last night," Mike pointed out, laughing.

"You spyin'?"

"No. She rang our doorbell and made me breakfast," Mike

laughed heartily.

"His date made you breakfast?" Jon asked.

"Sure. Why not? She's family," Mike snickered.

"Who is?" Hopkins asked.

"Um...Jillian's stepsister...my half-sister...Kristin," Mike replied nonchalantly.

Hopkins had taken a swig from his water and choked. "Kristin Johnson? Delegate Johnson's daughter...that means he's...your..."

"Biological father, yes."

Foster returned from the back and handed Mike a file. Mike opened it. Joe and Dex moved to look over his shoulder. The three teens, ages 16, 17, and 15, had been skateboarding on the boardwalk around 8 am. Kenny had been on foot. He walked on days with good weather on the boardwalk in the morning, when there weren't many people around and the temperature was temperate. He had in his earbuds and ignored the boys' catcalls and teasing hurled at him as he walked. This angered Ray Green, who chased him down and sucker punched him. The other two boys jumped in. At first Kenny had just balled up, but when Steve O'Malley stabbed him in the leg, he had turned Hulkish and beat all three of them severely before Janelle Young had pulled him off. He cried when she called his name, and she held him until the police arrived. She had been opening the *Everything's Beachy* Store when she'd witnessed the boys attack Kenny.

Mike handed the file back to Officer Foster. "Thanks," he said. The three of them walked back out, Dex hobbling on his crutch. Mike drove to the boardwalk. They made their way to the gift shop. He walked up to the counter.

"Janelle Young?" he asked.

The clerk pointed to a young woman in her early twenties.

Mike approached her alone, so that they wouldn't scare the poor girl. "Janelle?" he said, walking up behind her. She turned.

"Yes sir?"

The "sir" stung, he had to admit.

"Hi, I'm Mike Poole. My brother is Kenny Poole," he started.

"Oh, yes. Kenny. Is he alright?"

"Yeah. He seems to be. Thank you for your help yesterday."

"Oh, no problem. He handled those punks like a pro, though," she smiled.

"Yeah, I imagine he did…literally. He was a Marine. He suffered a traumatic brain injury," Mike explained. "Those two guys there served with him and are like family." He pointed at Joe and Dex, who waved awkwardly. "We just…want to know what happened exactly. Full disclosure, I'm a deputy with the Westmoreland County Sheriff's Department, but I'm off duty, and this isn't my case. I'm a brother right now."

"Sure. I understand that. Um…I told the police. Kenny was just walkin' along, mindin' his own business. Those punks were skateboarding out front of the store. I heard the tall skinny one say, 'Hey, that's the guy we're supposed to jump,' and he took off runnin' after Kenny and jumped him. The other two jumped on him, too. The short, fat one stabbed him in the leg, and then Kenny just went off on them. He threw them off him and beat the crap out of them. I know Kenny from his walk. I called his name, and he stopped, started crying, and hugged me. So, I just hugged him until the police came," she told them.

"Wait…He said, 'That's the guy we're supposed to jump?' What does that mean?" Joe asked.

"That means someone put them up to it," Mike explained. "Thanks, Janelle. You've been a big help."

They walked back to the truck. "That isn't what the police report said," Dex pointed out.

"Nope. It sure wasn't," Mike said.

At the Beach Gate, the crossroad of Route 205 and Colonial Ave, the only way onto the peninsula that was the town of Colonial Beach by land. Mike turned right instead of left.

"Where are we goin'?" Joe asked.

"Ray Green is Toby and Ella Green's kid. They live next door to Rich Lowe," Mike said through gritted teeth. He looked up to see that Jon Briars was behind him and remained so until he pulled into the Lowes' driveway. Jon pulled in right behind him.

Dex and Joe got out of the truck but stayed beside it. Mike walked determinedly up to the door and rang the bell.

Muffy started yapping inside. Rich swung open the door. "You're not in uniform. Does that mean this is not an official visit?"

"No. Uh. I'm not here on official business," Mike said. He thought he was showing great restraint.

"I got the notification of the DNA results. Missy is your daughter. I cashed the check. We're even. I'm not suing," Rich grumbled.

"Oh, well, that's good, but it's not that. Kenny was jumped by your neighbors' son and two friends."

Rich looked genuinely surprised. He unfolded his arms and stood straighter. "Is he okay?"

"Yes. Thank you. The thing is...according to a witness, Ray indicated they were instructed to attack Kenny."

"I'd never do that!" Rich protested. "Kenny has nothing to do with our issues. He's an American hero."

"Sure. I...I believe you...but have you seen the kid talking to anyone? Did he come into money? Anything?"

"No. Nobody. I think Max said hi to him when he was here the other day, but they were literally in different yards, and it was one word," Rich replied, sincerely.

Mike nodded. "Mmkay. Thank you. Let me know if you

think of anything…I'd…really appreciate it." Then he turned and walked back to the truck. The three of them climbed back in, and Mike started the ignition.

"Is he telling the truth?" Joe asked, scowling at the man, as he went back into his house and closed the door.

"I honestly don't know. I'm suspicious of him. But he did seem sincere. I don't know," Mike replied.

Jon backed out of the driveway and drove away. Mike decided it was time to give it up for right now. But he wasn't giving up entirely. Someone put those kids up to hurting his brother, and he was going to find out who.

———

Pam turned and looked at Gordon as Mike drove away.

"Howdy, Stranger," she said with a sweet smile.

"Hello Pamela Jean," Gordon replied.

She laughed. It sounded like music. She was as pretty as ever.

"God, you're gray," she teased.

He brushed his hand through his hair. "Yeah. I got old. You didn't. You look exactly the same," he said, blushing. He felt like a school kid. What the hell was happening?

"Liar," she chuckled.

Kenny looked at them both. He kind of stood there with his mouth open for a second. "Can I take the dog for a walk?" he asked awkwardly.

Gordon handed him the leash. Kenny turned stiffly and walked off with Lily. As he reached the end of the drive, Gordon heard him say to the dog, "That was weird."

It was kind of weird.

Pamela Jean Poole. She was 5 years younger than he was. When he'd left home at 18, he'd seen her as a little sister. He'd always pictured her that way…the little girl of friends of his family. He'd seen her a few times when he'd visited Jillian over the years. He'd known, like everybody did, that she had gotten pregnant and had the twins at 15. He'd never judged her for that. Shit happened. But Mike had said Max Johnson was his father. Max was…nearly 20 years older than Pam. He'd been her doctor. Gordon suddenly felt incredibly angry at his ex-wife's current husband. And it wasn't just normal outrage. That bastard had dared to lay his hands on Pamela Jean, *his* Pamela Jean.

Why was he feeling so possessive of Pam all of a sudden? He hadn't seen her in years. He'd never dated the woman. He'd never wanted to date her as a girl. Had he?

He'd thought she was pretty…that was all.

"It's alright, Pamela Jean," he remembered himself saying as he wrapped her in a towel and hugged her to his chest after she'd looked down in the gravel pit and seen…Jacob. She had only been 12. But she'd had a better figure than Jenny.

He could still smell her hair…pure summertime: strawberry scented shampoo, cocoa butter, suntan lotion, baby powder. What the actual hell?

He shook away the memory and looked at her now. She was 5'7" tall, curvy in all the right places, and fit. She obviously worked out. She looked 10 years younger than her 48 years. She climbed the steps to the porch. He watched her go up. Her hips swayed and by God, she had the best ass he'd ever laid eyes on.

The yoga pants showed it off beautifully. The Ole Miss T-shirt's hem fell around her hips and moved maddeningly with them. Her waist looked like it was missing something. His arms around it.

"Damn, Pamela Jean," he teased.

———

Gordon Chisholm. He was still so damned appealing. He'd gone gray, but it looked good on him. Pam knew her ass was one of her best features. She made sure to walk up the steps before he did. She felt his eyes on her and smiled.

"Damn, Pamela Jean," he said, his Northern Neck drawl drawing out each syllable.

She turned and looked over her shoulder. "Eat your heart out, Gordy," she said, batting her eyes.

He grasped his chest with both hands and stumbled backwards, laughing. "When did that sweet little girl turn into a stone-cold femme fatale?" he asked.

Her stomach did a flip-flop. Gordon had always been so damned handsome. Even now, his body was muscular. Other than a few laugh lines, his face was youthful. She'd always had a thing for him, and here he was flirting with her. She was relishing every second.

She sat on the swing and patted the seat beside her.

"I don't bite…hard," she said.

He grinned, looking so self-assured, and her heart was in her throat. She was faking it, and she could only hope he couldn't tell. The truth was she was nervous as hell.

"Too bad," he countered, climbing the steps and sitting beside her. His hip brushed against her, and she felt a rush of electric energy surge through her. "Seriously, though. Pam…you look really good to me. I suddenly feel like I'm home."

———

Kristin got out of her '64 ½ Mustang. It was her pride and joy with a metallic fleck candy apple red paint job. She grabbed the present from the back seat and closed the door with her hip. She was wearing off-white leggings and a soft pink cashmere sweater with off-the-shoulder short sleeves. She chose canvas Keds because she wanted comfortable shoes to wear to the Dragway. She wore sunglasses, and her hair was down. She had liked the way she looked when she left home, but as she looked up, she realized that everybody was looking at her…and that they had stopped talking. Jillian jumped out of the truck behind her Mustang and ran to her side, taking her arm.

"Do I look alright?" Kristin whispered to her. "Do I have spinach in my teeth, or a booger in my nose...or, God forbid, toilet paper hanging off my shoe...or worse yet..." Kristin quickly looked down at her shoes and around at her back end.

"No, you look great," Jillian assured her.

"Then why is everybody staring at me?" Kristin asked.

"Because...you're hot," Jillian laughed.

Jessup's birthday party was being held in the new barn, which had just been built in March. So, they made their way to the back yard. Kristin laughed, realizing that Mike was shooting the evil eye at several of the dads present. Kenny followed along beside Mike, apparently oblivious.

Wayne Beck, a volunteer firefighter, approached Mike as they entered the barn. "Who's the stone-cold fox with Jillian?" she heard him ask. Wayne had known her all her life.

"What do you mean?" Mike chided. "That's Kristin."

"That's...Kris...tin?" Wayne stammered. "What happened to her?"

She didn't hear Mike's answer because she'd found Dex. She smiled, and he smiled back. She walked up to him. "Hi," she said.

"Hi," he said back.

Jillian took the gift from her, but she barely noticed, except that, almost involuntarily, she moved closer and hugged the man in front of her. He hugged her.

"I'm glad you're here," he whispered in her ear.

"Me too," she whispered back before she kissed him.

"Woah, Man...your uncle is Miss Johnson's boyfriend?" she heard one boy say to Jessup Gardner.

"Um...I...guess," Jessup replied.

She laughed. Dex laughed. Then he screwed on a fake disapproving expression. "Hey, you got a problem with that?" he barked.

"Uh, no. No sir," the boy replied nervously before he ran off. Dex laughed again.

"Ah, intimidating children...my favorite part about teaching," she teased.

"You should try it being a nurse practitioner. I get to do it while holding a big needle," he grinned, flexing his eyebrows like Groucho Marx. He even tapped the ashes off the end of an imaginary cigar next to his cheek.

They found a seat at a picnic table near the refreshments table. Soon, Mike, Kenny, and Jillian joined them. Kenny was passionately making a case for something.

"I know I can do it," Kenny said vehemently.

"I know you can, too, Kenny. That's not the problem," Mike retorted.

"Yes, it is!" Kenny yelled, slamming his fist down on the table.

"Kenny," Kristin interjected calmly. "Breathe with me." He looked at her, and she breathed in deeply through her nose and out through her mouth. Kenny, held by her gaze, did as she did. She kept it up until he unclenched his fist and laid his hand flat. She covered his hand with hers and smiled. "Okay?"

He nodded.

"Now, tell me what's going on...calmly," she said in her most soothing voice.

Pam had started over when Kenny had punched the table, and she stood back a few feet, watching this interaction.

"I want to move into the assisted living apartments. I want to have my own place. And I know I need...more than a regular apartment...because of the seizures...I need someone there. I know that. There is an apartment open, and my VA benefits will cover it. But Pam doesn't think I'm capable of even that. Neither does Mike," he said tearfully.

"Oh," Kristin said, glancing at Pam's worried expression.

"I don't think they have doubts you can do it, Kenny. They, of all people, know how much you went through and how strong you are. Mike has told me that *you* are the strongest person he knows. And he has a tattoo the size of a billboard on his back proclaiming you as his hero." A collective chuckle arose from everyone, even Pam. "I think that they're worried about Pam," she whispered. "She's scared, but I think she will come around, Kenny. It's just because she loves you. And she nearly lost you. So, she's holding on really tightly. I know that you can do it. And she does, too. She just needs some reassurance. I know Olivia Pope over at the Assisted Living Apartments. She's the administrator. She's about to retire, but she may still be able to help. I know they offer short-term trial periods of a month to see if assisted living is the right choice for their tenants. I'd be happy to ask her to offer you that option."

"But I want to stay…" he started.

"I know, and if you still feel that way at the end of the trial period, you can stay…and if you don't…then you don't have to. You can take that month to prove to Pam that you both can handle it," she explained.

Dex nodded. "It's true. The facility where I work is more of a nursing home, but a lot of assisted living facilities offer that. Heritage Gardens, in Colonial Beach, is one of them," he agreed.

"I…might be able to convince her of a trial," Mike agreed.

"I'd agree to that," Pam said, stepping forward.

Kristin smiled and patted Kenny's hand that was still under her own. "See, there's a way."

Kenny nodded.

Mike mouthed, "Thank you."

As Kenny began to feel overwhelmed by the noise of the party, Pam agreed to take him home. As he walked away, Kristin heard him say, "I like Kristin a lot. She's nice."

Pam agreed.

"I wish she had been my sister when I was myself."

Pam rubbed his back as they walked away. "She was. Don't you remember? She always was."

Dex leaned over and kissed her cheek. "You really are beautiful…inside and out," he said tearfully.

"Who beat him up?" she asked quietly, sadly.

"Ray Green and Steve and Caleb O'Mally," Mike replied.

"Why?"

"Just because. I think someone asked them to do it."

"Caleb O'Mally?" she asked. "The kid Dad hired to help take care of the lawn? Excuse me." She stood and strode toward her car.

"Oh…shit," Mike gasped before jumping up to follow her.

CHAPTER 12

Mike sat in the passenger seat of the old Mustang. It was meticulously restored and ridiculously spotless. He had always thought the Mustang was an odd car for Kristin...at least the Kristin she had become after the baby. It didn't seem to fit with her personality anymore, though once upon a time, it would have been exactly the kind of car she would have driven. Maybe it was a sign that the old Kristin had always been there.

He looked over at her now. In a week, she had transformed back into the kind of girl he expected to drive a classic muscle car...and he didn't just mean her new look. True, her look was part of it, but there was more. She was still a little...unsure of herself, self-conscious, and a little timid, but she knew she looked good. She had no problem flaunting her figure as she had previously. She was unafraid, despite her self-doubts. She was a butterfly emerging from a chrysalis.

"What?" she asked, wiping her cheek. "Do I have cake on my face?"

"No," he laughed. "I was just thinking about how you are more..."

"More?"

"More...you...like you used to be, back in high school," he replied.

"I did used to be bodacious, didn't I? I missed that." She smiled and made the turn off Route 205 heading back toward Westmoreland Shores. "My father shaped me into a schoolmarm and tried to shape Jillian into a housewife. And he...just tried to ruin you and Kenny at every turn. He's not a very good father in the end."

"Nope. He's not," Mike agreed.

Minutes later, they pulled into the driveway of the Johnsons' mid-century ranch.

Mike followed Kristin as she walked in without knocking.

"Dad," she called.

Max Johnson was sitting in the formal living room off to their right as they entered with a man neither Mike nor Kristin recognized, clearly mid-interview as a cameraman with a TV6 News placard was between them.

"Cut!" called the man, clearly frustrated.

"Kristin," Jenny said, rushing forward. "Your father is being interviewed about the effect of the changes to the Chesapeake Bay Act. I sent you a text. Why is Mike here? Where's Jillian?"

"Jillian's fine. She's with Gordon at Joe and Bethany's," Mike said, dismissing her.

"Kristin, why are you dressed like a…" Max started, standing.

"A what, Daddy? Woman on a date? Because I have a date tonight," she retorted.

"You look very nice," Jenny soothed.

"Why did you instigate Caleb O'Mally and his brother to beat up Kenny?" she demanded.

"Never mind, keep rolling," the man whispered to the cameraman.

"What are you talking about?' Max Johnson blustered.

"You know exactly what she's talking about," Mike interrupted.

"Stay out of this, Mike," Delegate Johnson said, shaking his finger.

"No can do, Daddy," Mike said sardonically.

"What?" asked the man, shoving a microphone at Mike's

face.

"My mother was 15 years old, you sick fuck," Mike said, stepping forward. "You actually got a kid to stab my brother in the leg to warn me off? What's wrong with you?"

"What?" Jenny asked.

"Daddy is Mike and Kenny's biological father," Kristin said, crossing her arms.

"You can't prove that!" Max shouted.

"Of course we can prove it, Daddy. I gave him a DNA sample. We have a paternal DNA match," Kristin said, shaking her head. "So, Pam Poole was almost 16…and a patient you were treating for melanoma, while you were 34 and married…and expecting a baby… they're three weeks younger than me. Dad. How gross are you? And then you do everything you can to keep Jillian and Mike apart. Me I could understand. We're siblings, after all. But Jillian? She's not related to him, though you did your damnedest to convince Jenny they were. You meddled with their relationship time after time after time…because you didn't want anyone to see you next to Kenny? He looks just like you."

"Kenny is not of sound mind," Max insisted.

"There's nothing wrong with Kenny's mind. He's doing great. And he's recovered as much as he has because of the strength of his mind. You think he's disposable?" Mike interjected.

"No. That's not what I mean…I…" Max sat hard. "You really gave him a DNA sample, Krissie?"

"Yeah," she replied. Mike was so proud of her. It was the truth, but he hadn't expected her to reveal it on camera so callously.

"I never told anybody to hurt Kenny…he's my son. I wouldn't do that," he said sadly. Mike took out his handcuffs and stepped toward Max, reading him his rights as he cuffed him.

"Have a seat, Dad," he sneered. "Aaron Muse will be here momentarily."

They sat for a moment in silence. Then Mike added, "Did you hire Big Billy Walsh to intimidate and threaten me?"

"I'm not answering any questions without my lawyer," Max said.

"Okay," Mike replied. "You wanna take that camera out of my face?" he said to the cameraman.

———

Mike and Kristin returned to the party, appearing an odd mix of dejected and triumphant. Dex hobbled over to his girl, and he had decided she was his girl now. "What happened? Are you alright, Baby?" he asked.

"Yeah, I'm fine. He wouldn't admit it. But he asked those kids to jump Kenny. I know it," she sniffed, wrapping her arms around his waist and leaning against him. He staggered for balance with his broken foot but quickly regained his footing and wrapped his arms around her.

It didn't take long. Dex's phone notifications buzzed. He took his phone out. The Richmond Times-Dispatch was reporting that Delegate Maxim Johnson was arrested by his biological son, conceived by a 16-year-old patient with whom he'd had an affair when he was 34, for hiring three teens to attack the officer's fraternal twin brother, who was a decorated, wounded Marine. He had been confronted by his daughter, with whom his wife had been pregnant at the time of the affair, and her half-brother, while he was being interviewed by Brian Scott, a reporter with NBC News 6. He was in custody for the attack in Westmoreland County. Phones buzzed around the barn.

The looks of the adults started to fall on Mike and Kristin. Dex shielded her face with his hand from the barrage of flashes as several people started snapping photos.

"Come on. Let's go," he directed, trying to shield her and hobble on the crutch at the same time. Joe came to her rescue, draping a tablecloth from one of the tables over her head.

"Mike," Joe called, nodding for his friend to come with them. Jillian grabbed Missy. Mike swooped his daughter up and they made a run for their vehicles.

———

Mike opened his door to find Pam and Kenny on his front porch. They'd been inundated by reporters at Pam's townhouse in Colonial Beach. Kenny's anxiety was through the roof. He was hyperventilating.

"Come in," Mike said calmly, taking his brother's hand. "You're alright. Breathe. Like Kristin showed you. That's right." As Kenny practiced breathing the way Kristin had taught him, Mike led him gently into the living room.

"Why are those people screaming at me and shoving things in my face, Mike?" Kenny asked, near tears.

"I'm sorry, Kenny. That's my fault. I found out what happened. Caleb O'Malley is willing to testify. Max paid those boys $200 each to jump you. I arrested him…while he was being interviewed by News 6. He's been charged with solicitation to commit assault and battery with a weapon and three counts of contributing to the delinquency of a minor and child endangerment. I created a huge controversy."

"Why would you do that?" Pam cried. "You know that's exactly why I never…"

"Because I am sick of it!" Mike cut her off. "I've had enough. That's all there is to it. He…hired…people…to…hurt…Kenny. He needed to be taken down. Next time, it might not be kids."

Pam sat down hard on the sofa. "You're right. Of course you're right. What do we do now?"

"The state will pursue the criminal charges. Kenny needs to bring a civil suit against him," Mike suggested.

"Can't you?" Kenny pleaded. "He's hurt you lots."

Mike sat beside him. "Yes, he has hurt me, but not

physically. It's not actionable. This…what he did to you…it's actionable, Kenny. And I know it makes you anxious. And I won't make you do it. But you can make him pay, Kenny."

Kenny sat there for a minute. He almost appeared to be listening to something with his head cocked to one side. Mike wondered if he was about to have a seizure. He often had auditory auras. But Kenny swallowed and nodded without seizing. "The boy says to make him pay."

"What boy?" Mike asked, concerned.

"The wet one," Kenny answered, pointing to an empty corner of the room.

"There's no boy there, Buddy," Mike said.

"Oh, God," Pam said, shivering. "Jacob. Jacob would want to make him pay."

"Jacob? Tilly?" Mike asked, remembering his report on the accident that had occurred on his property back in 1989, when Pam was just 12.

"That's true enough," Gordon agreed, coming into the room. "That was a terrible day. I'll never forget the look on your face, even from a distance, when you saw the body."

Pam nodded. "It was awful. You and Jenny were running up the hill at us. I was going to jump in, but I looked down, and there he was, floating, face down in the mucky water, naked. I'll never forget it. It haunts my nightmares to this day."

"What's any of that got to do with Max?" Mike asked, hearing for the first time that his sister/mother had been at the gravel pit that day.

"Oh, nothing," Gordon said, shaking his head. "Jacob just really hated Max for some reason. Max lived in a small house on Buzzard Point…in Placid Bay…back then, across the street from the Tillys and Jenny's family."

Later, after Pam and Kenny went home, Mike sat staring at the wall. Jillian sat beside him.

"Did I make a mistake? Should I not have done that?" he asked, without looking away from the wall.

"Kenny will be fine," she assured him.

"I know. He's stronger than he knows. I just…I wanted to make Max pay. I think my motives…were all wrong," he admitted. She put her arm around his sagging shoulders and pulled him close.

'Baby, you're the best man I know. You love Kenny. You considered the fallout. I know you did," she said, hugging him tightly.

"I think I may have underestimated it," he sniffed.

"Max is a narcissistic megalomaniac. He used three teenage boys to do his bidding and tried to eliminate an obstacle to what he wanted…and that obstacle was his own son. I've never liked him. I've never…been comfortable around him. I'm not comfortable with Missy around him," she mumbled.

He turned and looked at her. "Wh…what? Jillian… what?" She didn't answer. "Jillian?" Panic was rising in his voice. "When?"

"When I was 16. That's why I…married Rich…to get away."

"Why the hell didn't you tell me?"

"Because…you would have given up your scholarship. It was the same reason that I didn't tell you I was pregnant," she confessed.

"Was it possible that he…"

"No. I avoided being alone with him after…" She started to cry.

"Has he…Missy?" he asked.

"No. She's too young. She's still a felony. Once she's 15… though," she theorized.

"Kristin?"

"I…I shouldn't say. Probably," Jillian replied.

"Does your mother know?" he asked, still dumbfounded.

"No. I'm sure she doesn't want to know. She believes everything he says, anyway."

Mike wrapped his arms around her waist and squeezed. "God, Baby. I...I'm such a dick. I didn't have a clue."

"I know you didn't. None of that was your fault. I wanted you to go, Mike. I wanted your dreams to come true. More than anything." Tears ran down her cheeks. She pursed her lips. "I was very good at hiding it. I didn't want you to know."

He wiped away a tear with his thumb.

"I...Jillie...he's a serial statutory rapist. I...need to talk to Kristin. I need to find other victims."

She nodded. "I know."

"Do you know of anybody else?"

She shook her head. They sat there for a minute more.

"Want to have sex?" she asked.

He chuckled. "God, yes."

––––––––

Dex limped toward Joe, who was bent over in the engine bay. "Try it now!" Joe yelled above the din of the race taking place behind him. His boss, Norm Mason, turned the key, and the engine whined and then growled, flames bursting from the racecar's dual tailpipes. Joe grinned and slammed the hood shut. He gave a thumbs-up to Norm and stepped back.

Dex placed a hand on Joe's shoulder. "Hey!" Joe yelled at him.

"I can't hear you!" Dex yelled back, laughing.

"Where's Kristin?" Joe yelled.

"What?"

"Where's Kristin?"

"Oh. She's over there, on the bleachers," Dex yelled again, pointing to his new girlfriend. She waved frantically. Joe waved to her.

"Ryan, Jessup! Go sit with Uncle Dex and Miss Johnson," he told his sons as the noise lowered between races.

"Bethany and Meghan didn't come?" Dex asked.

"No, the fumes make her sick…and Meggy doesn't like the noise. Plus, I'm busy working…but the boys love it."

"Gotcha," Dex laughed, nodding for the boys to come with him. They made their way to Kristin, who had decided she didn't care if she had to battle the press.

She had been promised a date at the Dragway, and she was going to have her date. Dex's instinct was to protect her, but she was fearless. He thought he might love her for that. Or maybe he just loved her. He hadn't decided yet. But either way, he was definitely at least halfway to being fully in love. He'd never fallen this quickly or hard before.

"Hi, Miss Johnson," Jessup yelled, sitting in front of her. "Thank you for the Legos." Dex sat beside her.

She grinned. "You're welcome, Jessup. Happy Birthday. Popcorn?" she offered, holding the box out to each boy. She smiled so sweetly and popped a kernel into her mouth. Dex had never wished to be a popcorn kernel before. This was a new experience for him.

"That Honda Civic that Burt Fredericks is racing will be tough to beat, but for me, nothing beats American Muscle. Norm Mason's Camaro is by far the sexier car," she yelled into Dex's ear over the din.

"Ummmm," he brilliantly replied.

She smiled coyly. "I really love the old ones…nothing like the '68 Camaro Z/28. 302 cubic inch small block V-8 with 290 horsepower, 4-speed manual. Just…pure…sex appeal. Norm's 2023 has a 632 cubic inch V-8 engine. Obviously, a much bigger engine and wow, the horsepower…650 I think…but I don't know…it's like…Chris Hemsworth vs. Steve McQueen. They're both sexy as hell…"

"Holy…" Dex breathed.

"What?" she asked.

"I think I love you."

Suddenly, Mike Poole was there, motioning for Kristin. She leaned over and kissed Dex's cheek before standing, climbing past the Gardner boys, and making her way to her brother. Jess and Ryan giggled and nudged each other with their elbows.

"Shut up," Dex said, marveling at the woman walking away. Sure, he realized she drove a vintage Mustang, and she'd admired his Galaxie, but that woman just spoke…motorhead.

As she conversed with Mike, Dex watched with deep concern. Her demeanor changed. Her smile disappeared. And Mike looked…gutted. Now she was fighting tears, and Mike grabbed her and hugged her. She shook her head. Her brother nodded. And then they parted. She gave a shiver, put a smile back on her face, and made her way back to Dex. But the spell was broken. She was miserable. And no matter how she tried to hide it, Dex could see it.

They stayed to see Joe's boss race his car. He won.

Then Dex took the boys back to Joe, yelling that they were leaving. Joe looked confused but nodded, understanding.

As they made their way back to the car, they passed Mike, sitting sullenly in his truck.

Dex walked over and knocked on the window. Mike looked at him and rolled down the window.

"Is Kenny alright?" Dex asked.

Mike looked past Dex at Kristin. "He's fine. It's not him I'm worried about. Dex…Jillian…my mother wasn't the only one," he said, looking forward at the windshield.

"Your father?"

Mike nodded.

"He did something to Jillian?" Dex asked.

Mike nodded and glanced again at Kristin.

Dex felt an uncontrollable rage rush through him. "And Kristin? That's what you and she were talking about? He...his own daughter?"

Mike nodded. "I want to kill him," he said quietly. "I won't...but God, I want to."

————

Gordon lay back on his old bed in his old bedroom and stared up at the ceiling. "Pamela Jean?" he asked the room.

He could almost hear his grandmother laugh good-naturedly and say, "That Pamela Jean Poole is such a nice girl." She'd often followed it with, "Way prettier than Jenny Wade."

He laughed. That had always been true. Pam was always the prettiest. The prettiest baby. The prettiest child. The prettiest girl. The prettiest woman. Pretty hadn't been why he hadn't ever...thought of her that way. Because he had. Of course, he had. Who was he kidding?

He put on his headphones and let the records on the turntable play. *REM* played. *The B-52s* followed. *George Michaels... Tone Loc.*

Junior/Senior prom. He'd gone with Jenny, of course. He'd thought she was on the verge of breaking up with him, and, stupid him, he'd thought proposing to her would be the way to fix it. He was still on crutches from his Achilles tendon surgery. His scholarship had been revoked, and he had just signed his enlistment papers for the Navy. They'd had an argument about that early in the evening. It was all kinds of wrong. Jenny had been in a bad mood all night.

Jason Thorn, the prick, had brought Pam, who was 13 and way too young to be at prom, as far as Gordon was concerned. He'd flipped his lid when Pamela Jean walked into the cafeteria in that dress. When he'd learn it was a bet...to get her to put out, he'd thrown away his crutch and chased after them as they left the dance to go out to Jason's car. He'd caught up to them just outside the main doors on the circle. He'd shoved Jason. Pam had screamed at him then. "Why do you think you have a say? Don't you have a diamond ring for *Jenny*? Who I date is none of your business, Gordon Dylan Chisholm!"

"You're too young to date, Little Girl!" he'd screamed back. "What the hell's with that dress? Playing dress up don't make you grown!"

"I'll have you know that everything in this dress is *real!*" she'd retorted, adjusting her very real cleavage and stamping her feet.

"Just cuz they're real ain't no God damned reason to show 'em off! Put on a fuckin' sweater!"

"Go to hell, Gordon! Get married. See if I care!" Then she had stormed off. She got a ride home with Helen White, now Madison, thank God.

Jason cussed him out and spent the rest of the prom with Kayla Jenkins, his real date. Gordon had never spoken to him again. Not ever. He wouldn't speak to him if he saw him now. And suddenly Jenny's mood had changed. The fight was like it had never happened.

Funny. He could remember the argument with Pam down to every last detail. All he remembered about the fight with Jenny was that it had been because he'd joined the Navy, but he couldn't recall what words they'd used or even where they'd been. Was it at her house? No…maybe in the car? Or in the cafeteria? What color was her dress? Pam's had been a bright teal with spaghetti straps and matching high heels that she kicked off after asking who cared if he got married.

Holy shit! Had Pamela Jean cared?

The headphones' jack came loose, and *If Wishes Came True* by *Sweet Sensation* played on the turntable. The volume increased. The song filled the room. The overhead light blew out.

———

After Dex and Kristin left him, Mike sat there feeling guilty. Not only had he made his family the center of a controversy, but now he had gone and ruined Kristin's date. She was just emerging from her chrysalis. He hoped he didn't send her retreating inside it.

That's when he noticed Ray Green. Ray was the oldest and tallest of the 3 boys who had attacked Kenny. He was 17 and close to 6 feet tall. He was also incredibly skinny. Lanky was the word, Mike thought. Ray Green was lanky...all arms and legs. He couldn't weigh more than 150 pounds. He had shaggy, greasy hair that fell halfway down his neck, probably dark brown in color...the grease made it appear darker than it was, though. He dressed like any skateboarder. Lots of black, an anarchy symbol emblazoned on his T-shirt, and holes in the knees of his jeans.

Mike jumped out of the truck and made a beeline for the boy.

"Ray Green!" he bellowed, pointing at the teen.

Ray looked around like a trapped animal, as Mike closed in. Trapped animals were dangerous, Mike reminded himself.

"I just want to talk," he said calmly, imploring the kid to stay.

Ray looked around and nodded.

"Why? Why would you do that...for Max?"

"Money," Ray scoffed.

"No. I don't buy that. I've checked your record, Ray. You're not a delinquent. You're basically a good kid. So are Steve and Caleb. I don't understand," Mike implored. "Make me understand."

"Max is just a cool dude. I don't know what to tell you. He gets it. He gets us," Ray replied, shrugging.

"And for that...you're willing to hurt another human being?"

The boy shrugged again.

Mike nodded and turned away. Those kids were willing to do that for Max. They wouldn't have done it for just anybody… but for Max. Max was scum. He couldn't understand. Of course, he had always been popular. He'd never been lanky or awkward. He was a football star who earned a scholarship to Ole Miss. Ray was a skinny anarchist who hung around with a short, fat kid and his younger brother…the outsiders…

Max picked kids he knew he could manipulate. He only went after girls once they were old enough not to be a felony, but young enough that he could intimidate them. He married Jenny, who believed his every word. Max was smart. He pitted those he could control against those he couldn't. Those he couldn't control, he attempted to keep away or destroy. None of this was new behavior. He'd been doing this for a long time.

He quickly got back into his truck and headed home at a breakneck speed.

CHAPTER 13

Kristin unlocked her front door. Dex was standing so close. He hadn't said anything, but it was clear Mike had told him. She wanted to disappear.

He put his hands on her shoulders and turned her to face him.

"Dex...I," she started.

He kissed her, pulling her against him. She hadn't expected the kiss. She surprised herself. She didn't push him away. Instead, she surrendered to the kiss, melting into his embrace, responding to his want with her own. She pulled him inside and slammed the door behind them. She tugged at his buttons on his shirt, desperate to undo them, as his mouth explored her neck.

Lter, as he lay sleeping beside her, she watched him breathe. His face was so serene, so handsome. She was going to fall in love with him. She knew it. She was already well on her way.

His long, dark lashes fluttered, and his eyes opened. An enigmatic smile graced his lips. "Hey, Baby," he whispered huskily.

"Hey," she replied, snuggling her head down into the pillow.

He took her hand into his, interlocking their fingers. "Are you okay?" he asked for the first time since he'd spoken to Mike.

She nodded. "It's not the same for me as it was for Jillian. He didn't...take it as far. Maybe even he couldn't...cross that line...or maybe I just wasn't his type. I dunno. But...it was enough, Dex. It...he...screwed me up. You should run."

"Never," he confessed. "We're all screwed up, Kristie...in one way or another. That's...the human condition."

"You seem pretty perfect," she objected.

He burst out laughing. "I'm far from perfect. I had bad anger issues as a younger man. I got into lots of fights. Joining the Marines saved me and taught me to channel that anger. I beat a guy near to death, Kristie. In a bar fight. He held up his hand with the scarred knuckles. He called me...'Boy'...and I exploded."

"I'm sorry. It's awful that people still...think that way," she responded.

"That's not the point. Yeah, he was a racist prick. But my response...was not productive. I just reinforced his beliefs."

"So, what, you're just supposed to take it?"

"No. God, no. But I am smarter than that. And I didn't act it."

Kristin nuzzled under his ear. "I like it when you call me 'Baby'," she whispered.

"Hmmm. I think I might love you, Baby," he admitted.

She smiled. "I think I might love you, too."

————

Mike dug through the boxes they moved to the basement. He knew approximately where the box was located. He remembered seeing it when they'd moved the stuff from the attic to the basement. It should be in this corner with Gordon's stuff from high school.

He opened a large box in the corner. On the top were the football trophies...and at the bottom, three yearbooks. He didn't see the fourth. He opened one and discovered that 9th grade was not included, so there would be only three.

He made his way to a sofa and sat, flipping through the yearbooks, starting with 1987-88. Gordon had been in 10th grade. He was on the football team, as expected, and his picture appeared throughout the book. This was before he'd started dating Jenny

Wade. The autograph of Valerie Dixon indicated, and several pictures confirmed, that she had been his girlfriend for most of that school year.

He laid it aside and picked up the next: 1988-89. Jenny was a cheerleader. Gordon was the quarterback. They were the "it" couple. But that wasn't what he was looking for. He flipped through to the class of 1991, then sophomores. He found Edward Tilly. Ned was an awkward teen. One picture of him appeared... his school picture. He wasn't in any clubs or sports or on any committees.

Mike picked up the last yearbook: 1989-1990. Gordon was still the quarterback. He and Jenny were still going strong. Unfortunately, though, he tore his Achilles in the Homecoming game against King George High School. In a moment, his free ride was gone. He ended up joining the Navy. He earned his degree, but it took longer, and his football career was over. Not that it affected his outlook. Gordon Chisholm was a lot like himself, Mike realized.

He looked for Ned. It was the same as the year before. Ned Tilly had not stood out in high school.

Mike sighed and shut the yearbook. He tossed it onto the floor and leaned back, closing his eyes. If Max was a serial statutory rapist, could he have been a serial...what would you call it? Master manipulator? User and abuser of fringe kids? Complete psychopath?

"Yeeeeesssss," came a soft hissing whisper.

Mike opened his eyes dubiously to look at Jacob Tilly, wet, pallid, and horrible, in the deep, dark saucer-like eyes.

"Well, you are creepy. She's right about that," he said nonchalantly.

"Aren't you scared?" the phantom asked.

"Of you? No. You're dead and buried. And I'm clearly dreaming."

"The pitcher of tea flew across the kitchen," the ghost reminded him.

"Sure. Still didn't hurt me. There's nothing to be scared of."

Slowly, the child morphed from a terrifying shade into an image of a clean-cut child, dry, normal coloring, with blue eyes, like his brother Ned's.

"There you are. Feel more like yourself?" Mike asked.

"Yeah, I do."

"You were saying something about Max?"

"Yeah, he did things to Jenny, you know. Bad things. But Jenny isn't what she seems, either. He convinced her she was the one who...um...what do you call it when you come onto someone and make them all horny?" Jacob asked, sounding very much like a 12-year-old boy and less like a haunting apparition.

"Seduce," Mike said.

"Yeah, Max convinced her she seduced him. And she still believes it. I saw it when she was here the other day. He convinced Ned that I was bad, too. Ned used to love me, but lately...well I guess not lately...but before I died...he started framing me for stealing stuff...making me look like a liar...It was weird."

Vaguely, Mike became aware of Lily barking fiercely, followed by Jillian's scream. He opened his eyes and sat bolt upright. He'd fallen asleep looking through the yearbooks. The dream still vivid in his mind, he blinked and looked around, assuring himself he was indeed alone in the basement.

Jillian screamed again. Lily's barking became more insistent. He jumped up and ran up the stairs, yelling, "What? What happened?"

Jillian came running into the kitchen in her nightie, screaming and panicking. She flung herself into his arms. "Man! There's a man!" she screamed in terror.

Lily was going crazy now, jumping at the closed door with

her whole body, growling and barking.

"What man? Where?" Mike asked sternly, pushing Jillian behind him and moving quickly toward his gun safe in the cabinet in the foyer. He grabbed a rifle and cocked it.

"Looking in the bedroom window on the front porch!" Jillian screamed.

Mike grabbed Lily's collar and opened the door before releasing her. She took off like a shot, running for the old gravel pit road. He grabbed a flashlight and followed.

Lily chased the man halfway up the hill. She pounced, and the man fell forward. She landed, straddling him with her two front paws on his shoulders and her two rear legs on the ground by his legs, her mouth on his neck.

Mike ran up and commanded her to heel, raising the rifle, taking aim at the man. "Stand up...slowly!" he yelled.

The man obeyed, peeing his pants as he did.

"Turn around," Mike commanded.

The man slowly turned. Mike lowered the rifle. "Ray?" The man was just a lanky teenage boy. "Where are Tweedle Dee and Tweedle Dum?"

"Who?"

"Steve and Caleb," Mike answered, irritated and not hiding it.

"Oh, they took off when Kujo started barking, and Mrs. Fox started to scream," the boy answered, shaking.

"Poole. Mrs. Poole," Mike corrected him. He searched the teen, finding a bowie knife and a handgun. "Move." He motioned with the rifle for the boy to walk back toward the house.

Ray started to cry.

"It's too late now, Ray. You crossed the line. And you'll be going away. Congratulations. You're a criminal," Mike said coldly, zip-tying the kid's hands behind his back and forcing him to march forward in front of him.

Back at the house, Mike walked over to his cruiser. "Sit," he commanded.

"Where?" Ray protested.

"On the ground," Mike replied through gritted teeth, shoving him down. He opened the cruiser door and turned on his radio, calling dispatch.

———

Jillian started to run to Mike the second he came back into view, but she stopped short when he shoved the man down to call in the disturbance.

He finally looked at her and smiled. She ran to his open arms and hugged his neck as he wrapped her up in his loving embrace. "It's okay, Baby. We're okay," he reassured her.

"He's just a kid," she said, glancing at Ray.

"No. Not anymore. He came here to hurt us. He's no longer a kid," Mike advised her. Lily sat beside him and pawed at his leg. "Good girl," he said, rubbing her head. "You made a good decision with this little lady, Jill. She's a good dog. Good dog." He smiled at Jillian, and she hugged him tighter. The fear was subsiding, but her heart ached. She loved Mike more than words could say, but her stepfather…his father…was so evil…to go to this extent. Would there ever be any peace for them?

He read her thoughts. He knew her so well. "We'll be fine, Jillian. I promise. I'll make it so he can't hurt us anymore. But it's gonna hurt…and not just us. I don't see a way around that. Kenny…Pam…Kristin…your mama…we're all gonna pay a price. Can you endure it? For me? For our family…our future?" he whispered.

She nodded against his shoulder, and he held her closer. In his arms, she knew. He loved her. He loved Missy. He even loved that silly dog…that amazing, silly dog she bought out of fear. She'd never find happiness like this with any other man… and despite the threats against them from outside forces, she was happy.

Five months ago, her daughter had been trapped in a collapsed barn. Her husband, Lyle, chose that moment to leave her. Mike, who had been on duty and assigned to a case at the other end of the county, had monitored the situation from his cruiser. He'd left as soon as he could and raced toward the scene, only to hear Missy had been rescued halfway there. He'd signed off and gone straight to the hospital. He beat the ambulance there. Jillian had ridden in the ambulance with her traumatized baby. Her mother had followed in her car. But when the ambulance doors opened, and the EMTs offloaded Missy, there he was, standing there, anxious, scared, crying. She had thrown herself into his waiting arms and collapsed into tears, much to Jenny's chagrin.

A year before that, he'd taken her home...to the home she shared with Lyle...after she'd been held up at gunpoint at work. It had taken every ounce of restraint she had to not give in to the temptation to kiss him. She had nervously spilled her coffee on him in the car. He had quickly pulled off his shirt and put on a clean one behind his cruiser after she'd gone into her house. She'd seen her name on his waist and known he'd always love her...no matter what.

Every breakup, every time they reunited, their bond became stronger. She'd been right. She couldn't be happy without Mike. Max wouldn't win. There was no way around it.

"I'll go anywhere with you," she said. "I'll follow you wherever you lead. I love you."

He kissed her, and she felt it in her knees.

———

Missy looked up at her grandfather as his hand fell gently on her shoulder. "Granddaddy, what's going on?" she asked, hugging her doll. She was 13 now and looked older most of the time, just like Pam had, but at that moment, she seemed so much younger.

Gordon pulled her into his arms and hugged her. "Your dad and Lily caught an intruder, Babydoll. Let me tell you. Your dad, he's a bit of alright."

Missy, still mostly asleep, asked anxiously, "Did someone get into the house?"

"No. Are you kidding? They came up on the porch, and Lily nearly went through the door to tear 'em apart. And your dad…he's a police officer. He didn't even hesitate. You, Princess, are safe," he assured her with a wink. "Why don't you go on back to bed, Sweetpea?"

She shook her head. "I…don't want to…not by myself. Can you…read to me? I know that's stupid. I can read my own self, but I just like the sound of your voice," she tried to explain. He understood. She was unsettled. His heart swelled that she found his presence a comfort. He'd missed so much. Coming early for his new job had been the best thing he'd done in a long time.

"Sure, Missy. What do you want me to read?" he asked, leading her to her room. She climbed back into her bed and pointed to her backpack. "My tablet's in there. We're reading *The Outsiders.*"

He chuckled. "Hold on. I'll be right back," he told her. He ran up to his room, his old room, and retrieved a box from under his bed. He dug through it until he found Jenny's old copy of the book. Real pages. He grabbed his reading glasses and headed back to Missy's room.

She was sitting up in her canopy bed, hugging her knees.

Gordon smiled and held up the book. "This was your granny's copy of that book. She left it here a long time ago. You can have it," he said, winking again. He sat in her desk chair and leaned back, crossing his long legs at the ankles. "Where do you want me to start?"

"At the beginning. I've already finished it. I want to start over," she answered.

"Alright then, lie down. I take it you're big enough, you don't need a tuck," he teased.

"No," she giggled, lying down and pulling the covers up to her chin. She stared at him with those sleepy, big blue eyes while he read. He'd only made it to the drive-in when he noticed that she was sound asleep. He pulled Jenny's bookmark out of the pages of the old book and marked his place with it, laying it on Missy's desk. He pulled off his reading glasses, rose from his seat, kissed her cheek, and left her room.

————

Missy awoke just before dawn as an old woman rifled through her desk.

"Who are you?" Missy yelped, frightened by the strange person in her room.

The woman turned. She was pleasantly plump. Her flowered dress hung just below her knees. Her "stockings" curled down on her legs to her black orthopedic shoes. Her hair was white. Her eyes were a steely blue, almost gray. She held up the book Granddaddy had been reading to Missy the night before. She tossed the book into the trash bin and then vanished.

Missy screamed.

Mike was there in seconds. He burst into the room; Lily was right behind him.

"What? What is it?" he asked, sounding scared.

"There was a woman by my desk. She threw my book in the trash and…disappeared," Missy cried. She pulled the blankets up tighter around herself.

Mike looked confused at first, but then he looked relieved. He sighed and reached into the trash, picking up the book. "I think you were dreaming, Honey," he said, calmly, placing the book back on her desk. He smiled and took a step closer. "I think the events of tonight have you spooked, and I don't blame you.

I…I wanted to talk to you about it, but your grandfather got you back to sleep. I thought it could wait until morning…but…maybe not," he offered.

Missy sniffed and pulled her knees to her chest under the covers.

"Was…the man…dangerous?" she asked, meekly.

Mike sat on the side of her bed and opened his arms to her. She quickly wrapped her arms around his waist. He hugged her to his chest and gently stroked her golden hair.

"Yes. He was dangerous…mainly because he was stupid, Missy. He didn't know how to use those weapons. He was a clear danger to everyone, including himself."

"Would you have…shot him?" she asked.

Mike thought for a moment. He pursed his lips. Then he nodded. "I would have if I needed to, but I didn't need to."

"Have you ever…needed to shoot somebody?" she persisted, hugging him tighter.

He took a deep breath. "No…not a person. Only about a quarter of all police officers ever discharge their weapon while in the line of duty, Missy. We are trained to apprehend people… without shooting them."

She leaned back. "Have you ever…discharged your weapon in the line of duty?"

"Yes. I've had to shoot a deer that was hit by a car," he said softly, smiling.

"That's it?"

"That's it," he replied.

"So, you've never been hurt by someone you were trying to arrest?"

"I didn't say that, Missy. I said I've never discharged my weapon at them. I've been hit, bitten, kicked, and stomped. Heck, you may remember that Bethany's father punched me in December before I cuffed him. And Lyle sucker punched me when I came to ask your mother to come identify the suspect in the Stop In armed robbery the Christmas before last."

Missy sniffed again. "But you're safe?"

"I do everything I can to ensure my safety, Sweetheart," he replied, kissing the top of her head.

CHAPTER 14

Kristin, in her big, fluffy terry cloth robe, with her still-wet hair wrapped in a towel turban on top of her head, opened the door to the insistent knocks of her stepmother, dressed like Carmen Sandiego. "Are you supposed to be incognito?" Kristin asked, amused by Jenny's attention-drawing attempt at disguising herself.

"Ha, ha," Jenny said, pushing her way inside. "We've got to stand behind your father. I can't believe what Mike Poole is saying. You don't believe it, do you?" She pulled off her ridiculously large hat and Ray Ban Aviators.

"Every word, Jenny. Every last word," she reiterated. "I know exactly who and what my father is. You, of all people, should as well."

"You have to believe him, Krissie. I know I was young... but I swear I was the one who..."

"Yeah, well, I wasn't the one who...Jillian wasn't the one who...And I guarantee Missy won't be the one who..." Kristin blurted out. "And to be honest, I don't believe you were the one who seduced him. I don't think Pam was, either. I don't think a 15-year-old can seduce a good man."

Jenny looked at her in such dismay, and all she felt was disgust for her narcissistic father and her deluded stepmother. Jenny was a good person. But she had a major blind spot when it came to Maxim Johnson. It was as if she couldn't accept the evil he'd done to her, so she internalized it all on herself. She was the one who had done wrong, not him. He was beyond reproach. Kristin had thought that way once upon a time.

Kristin had, until recently, allowed that kind of thinking to shape her life. She wasn't quite sure what had changed in her to wake her up to the truth. But it started with Mike and Kenny. It always had.

She didn't know the exact moment she'd realized they were her brothers. It might have been at her 10th birthday party. She'd certainly felt a connection to them that was stronger than with her other classmates. Drew Boyd had made fun of her. And Kenny had stood up to the much bigger Drew. When Drew made a move to hit Kenny, Mike had jumped in between and took the punch. And then Mike had beaten Drew up.

Or it might have been when she was 16 and her friends abandoned her at Central Park in Fredericksburg. She sat down in the restaurant area of Target and cried, knowing she was going to have to call her dad, and not wanting to sit alone with him that long. Mike and Kenny were just suddenly there. And even though they ran with a different group, the popular group, Mike took her home.

But whenever it was, hearing it from Pam's mouth last week hadn't been it. It was no surprise. Not to her. Not to Mike. Honestly, not even to Kenny.

It had certainly been prior to 9 years ago, when she had delivered her daughter. Kenny was in Afghanistan at the time. Jillian was still married to Rich Lowe. She had fallen in love with Quinton Tilly, only to have him rip her heart out of her and stomp all over it. When she told him she was pregnant, he told her to get rid of it. He had reconciled with Arleen, and that was all he had ever wanted from his relationship with Kristin…to make Arleen realize what she was giving up. She had *not* gotten rid of it. Instead, she opted to pursue her master's degree in English at St. Francis University in Pennsylvania and to give her child up for a closed adoption. She told no one.

As she labored, Mike had come into her room, telling the

nurse he was her brother and birth coach. She had burst into tears when she saw him. She'd asked how he had known. He had told her that he hadn't. He'd been in Philadelphia for a forensic science symposium and had stopped by her apartment to say hi, even though it was out of his way. Her neighbor had told him that she had gone into labor. He had figured she probably needed a friendly face, and he hadn't wanted her to go through it alone.

It was that way with them. They were always there when they needed each other. It was uncanny, like the universe was telling them that they were connected.

A year later, when Mike had received the telegram about Kenny having been severely wounded and being transferred to Walter Reed, she had been coincidentally standing right beside him. Jillian had left Rich but hadn't run back to Mike yet, but she had been struggling, and Kristin had a list of things Missy needed that Jillian couldn't afford. Mike had been living in a townhouse in Colonial Beach, where Pam and Kenny lived now. He rented it to his mother below market value. Anyway, Kristin had sneaked away to deliver the list of things Jillian needed and was there when the telegram was delivered.

Then last week, when Dex had called her "pretty lady," something just clicked. She was a pretty lady. And her father, who had always told her she wasn't, who had always made her feel less than, was just a piece of crap.

There was no turning back now.

"He never crossed that line with me, Jenny. He just couldn't bring himself to go that far. But he was extremely inappropriate. He kissed…with tongue," she said with emphasis. "He touched where he shouldn't. And then he'd go to Jillian's room to finish what he couldn't bring himself to do with me. We figured it out. I would text her to warn her if he got handsy. She'd sneak out of her room. If she saw him leering at me, she'd let me know, and I'd sneak out. We started avoiding being alone with him. We helped each other as much as we could."

Jenny grasped at her chest and sat hard on a barstool at the kitchen counter. "Why? Why didn't you tell me?"

"We did. You didn't believe us," she replied coolly. It was true. They had tried. Jenny had shut them down.

"No. I can't believe it. It can't be true. He…he loves you both. He has invited a very nice man over to meet you. Howie Moore. He's a clerk in the Delegate's office. He wants the best for you both."

"Yeah, right. That was supposed to be Jillian's date, I assume. Dad was trying to get a new dud, or beast, in there before she went back to Mike, only she went back first, and this time she married him. My guess is that he'll try to weasel this Howie guy in there to split them up, but dating me is the excuse to get him at family functions. I already have a boyfriend, though, so that's not going to work," Kristin retorted.

"You have a boyfriend?" Jenny asked.

As if summoned, Dex hopped down the stairs on his one good foot, fresh from the shower, "Hey, Babe, have you seen my phone?" he called as he came.

"I think it's on the end table by the sofa, Honey," she called back, smiling coyly.

Jenny looked dumbstruck.

"Ah. Got it. Thanks," he said, finding the phone and walking over to the kitchen. The downstairs of the A-frame was an open concept with walls separating only the bathroom and a study under the loft, where the bedrooms and second bath were located. He leaned over the counter to kiss Kristin. "Hi. Happy Easter," he said.

"Jenny, this is my boyfriend, Dex Lawson. Dex, this is my stepmother, Jenny Johnson."

———

Jillian woke up and stretched. The sound of humming filled

the air along with the scent of Lily of the Valley. The humming was…*The Old Rugged Cross,* she was almost certain, but it was hard to be positive because it came from the other room.

Mike was still sleeping soundly, despite the sunshine spilling through the curtains. She delicately removed his arm from around her and got out of bed. She followed the sound, but it moved as she did, always moving. When she went into the kitchen, it came from the living room. When she went into the living room, it came from the foyer. When she went into the foyer, it came from the hallway. When she went into the hallway, it came from the kitchen.

"Okay, I'm just going crazy," she bemoaned to Lily, who barked and wagged her tail. "Yeah, I know. Breakfast. You deserve a feast, but all I have is kibble. That Farmer's Dog stuff I ordered hasn't come yet."

Her father came down the steps and stood on the landing by the back door. "Are you humming *The Old Rugged Cross?*" he asked, running his hand through his gray hair.

"You hear it, too?" she exclaimed. "I thought I was losing my mind."

"Grandma used to hum that old hymn," he said. He smiled. "It's kind of…comforting. Happy Easter, Sweetheart." He entered the kitchen and kissed her cheek. "What are the plans for today?"

"Church...then Pam and Kenny are coming over. Probably Kristin and Dex. Joe and Bethany are going to Waldorf to spend Easter with her grandparents and family," she replied. "We were supposed to go to Mama's, but none of us wants to be around Max. He was released on bail last night."

Mike walked into the kitchen, rubbing his hands through his hair and yawning. He looked good in his PJ bottoms and T-shirt. "Good mornin'," he said, wrapping his arms around Jillian's waist from behind and kissing her neck.

"Good morning," her father replied with a chuckle. "What time is the church service?"

"10 am," Jillian said, leaning back contentedly against Mike.

He was her person. In all her relationships, except for with Mike, she was cold. Lyle called her a "frigid bitch." Rich called her "a cock tease." Bruce called her a "lesbo cunt." Adam was less interested in a sexual relationship than she had been. But with Mike, she could barely keep her hands off him. That should have been a clue, Jill, she thought as she made the coffee.

———

Kenny straightened his tie and shifted in the old wooden pew. The church was old with white tin plate walls and ceilings, red carpeting, and those old wooden pews. Kenny liked the church, but the pews were very uncomfortable. They made his back ache. That gave him a headache. Headaches made him anxious.

Pam, ever vigilant, pulled a travel pillow out of her big purse and shoved it behind his back. He forced a strained smile. She meant well. But it honestly made him feel ridiculous that he needed his mother to take care of him at 32 years of age, 33 in a month. He loved Pam, and he knew she loved him, but she had devoted the last 8 years of her life to him. He wondered if she would be like Aunt Bertie, always single. He needed to let her have a life. He needed to get into the assisted living apartments.

Mike tapped him on the shoulder as he sat in the pew behind him and Pam. "You okay?" he whispered.

"I'm okay," Kenny answered.

Jillian looked pretty in her purple floral dress. She was Jillian, so she wasn't dressed like all the other women. The dress was form-fitting, not flowing. Her angel wing tattoos were on display as the dress's collar line was cut wide and low. The dress was a solid purple satin. The floral pattern was a black velvet.

She wore black stockings and black pumps. She smiled at Kenny and sat beside Mike. They looked good together. They looked happy.

When Gordon sat beside Missy, he felt Pam stiffen beside him and heard her catch her breath. Huh, he thought. He should make sure she sat beside him at supper today. Gordon was still a good-looking guy, still fit, still trim. He was only five years older than Pam. He could save her from the Aunt Bertie fate.

Roy Kelly and Charlie Porter were staring at him. He could feel it. It shouldn't bother him. He knew that. But it always did. They were just good ole boys. They didn't mean harm. They never had. Even now, as grown men with kids, they were the bane of his existence. In high school, they had been his tormentors. And today, they stared at him like he was some kind of alien.

He heard Roy whisper to Charlie in front of him, "What kind of life is that? His *sister*, wink wink, has to carry a pillow around for him."

"Ignore them," Pam whispered.

Charlie's kid whispered, "Look, Daddy, my teacher is here with a black man." And Kenny gripped the armrest hard.

Roy chuckled. "Miss Johnson, right? Lori is in her class, too. Nice body, but she…HOLY SHIT." The entire congregation gasped, and Roy's wife smacked him on the back of the head. "Dang, she's like a different woman," he continued, rubbing his head where his wife had hit him.

"Wow," Charlie agreed.

Kristin and Dex made their way to him and Pam. He scooted to let them sit in the aisle, Kristin next to him. She grabbed his arm and kissed his cheek. "Hiya, Handsome," she teased. "Let me see that eye, Bud. Oh, that's not too bad. You'll be fine in a few days."

"I'm fine now," he insisted.

"Semper fi," Dex whispered.

"Simper fi," Kenny whispered back.

Take that, Roy and Charlie.

————

Mike followed Jillian out of the church after the service ended. God, she looked sleek in that dress...and her ass was spectacular. He put his hand on the small of her back and moved up beside her. He leaned to whisper in her ear, "I love this dress, Jill. You look beautiful."

She smiled coyly. She knew perfectly well how she looked. The dress was chosen for its shock value. Between her brazenness, Kristin's transformation, and the rumors circulating about Maxim, they were a spectacle. He knew her. He knew that's exactly why she'd chosen it. Jillian's philosophy was to lean into controversy and let them stare.

Kristin had never subscribed to it before. But today...Her long, dark hair was down, showing off those soft, natural curls, instead of pulled back or up so tightly that it pinched her face. It was as if she discovered she had good legs and her pencil skirt, a raw silk in ivory, fell mid-thigh, inches above her knees. The hot pink blouse was tucked neatly in at the waist. A gold swagged belt hung like jewelry just above her hips, accentuating her flat stomach and elegantly curved hips. She had only buttoned the bottom two buttons and wore a silky camisole in the same ivory color as the skirt under the blouse, exposed to below her breasts at the top of her ribcage. A touch of lace traced along the top of the camisole at the top of her ample cleavage. Her legs were bare. She wore ivory high heels with peek-a-boo toes. Hot pink toenails peeked through the ends. They matched her manicure and lipstick. She held her head up high.

Even Pam, usually so conservative, seemed to have dressed to show off her attributes. At 48, she still had a good figure, though she rarely showed it. Today, however, she had also chosen a dress that showed her cleavage and hung on her trim frame to show off her shape instead of hiding it. She'd gotten a haircut. The new style, much shorter than she had ever worn previously, was more daring. She had dyed it too, going back to her natural honey blonde, and eliminating the grays that had started to appear around her temples. And Mike was not the only one to notice. Gordon took her by the arm and walked down the large front staircase with her upon exiting the church. "You look lovely today, Pamela Jean," he said with a smile, his tone like he owned the name. Mike's mouth dropped open as he reached out for his mother.

It was Kenny who prevented his interference. "Don't you dare," his brother demanded, grabbing him. "She deserves to be admired."

"How'd I miss that?" Mike whispered to his wife.

"Miss what?" she asked.

"That…" he said, pointing at his mother and her father, walking arm in arm down the stairs in front of them.

"Oh…oh," she said. Then she giggled and kissed his cheek.

———

As Gordon stepped off the stairway with Pam Poole on his arm, Beau Madison tapped him on the shoulder. Beau had been the kicker back in the day. After high school, he'd joined the Air Force and had served in Desert Storm as an airplane mechanic in Kuwait. Now he was married to Helen White…well…Madison… and owned and operated his family's dairy farm. Gordon didn't see Helen.

"Hey, Man," he said, greeting his old friend. The two shook hands. "How are you?"

"Good. Good to see you, Buddy. What are you doing back here?"

"Oh, I'm moving back. My company named me Director of Operations at our Dahlgren branch. I've rented a townhouse in Dahlgren, but it's not ready for me until the first of May, so I'm stayin' with my daughter and her family…back at Grandma's and Gramp's old house," he replied good-naturedly. Beau's eyes drifted to Pam. "Oh, you remember Pam Poole. Of course, she's more than a few years younger than us," Gordon laughed. "She's my son-in-law's…"

"Mother," she interrupted. Her voice cracked, but she said it loudly and proudly. Gordon winked at her. She was pretty darned cute.

"Oh, yes…I heard about that…I…" Beau stammered.

"Oh, don't worry about it, Beau. It's not like everybody didn't know already," she said, bursting into nervous laughter.

"Yes, well…I…" Beau stammered again.

"Hi, Pam. Love that dress," Helen Madison said, moving up beside her husband, a small child clinging to her hand. Helen Madison was bodacious. She always had been. Her Easter outfit, at age 52, was a leopard skin babydoll top over black leather pants with black leather boots. Her hoop earrings reached to her shoulders. Her platinum blonde hair was cut in a wedge, and she had on a black lace headband with a large rhinestone at the base of a huge black fluffy feather that rose 8 inches above her head.

Pam's eyes grew large. "Oh, thank you, Helen…you look…like a party."

"That's what I was going for!" Helen beamed, puffing her hair.

"Same ole Helen," Gordon chuckled.

"Yep, God love her. She does stand out," Beau said, adoringly.

Kenny reached the bottom of the stairs and stood quietly behind his mother. Beau nodded. "How you doin', Kenny?"

"I'm fine," Kenny answered again. "Joe's not home today, but Mike and Dex are here…and Kristin can help me breathe. Pam needs time off."

"I do not," Pam protested.

"She should go to a movie with Gordon Chisholm," he added.

"Oh, dear God," Pam exclaimed, blushing.

"Sounds like fun. Good idea, Ken. But not today. Today is Easter. Tomorrow, Pam?"

"We haven't been out for dinner and a movie in forever," Helen suggested. "Maybe Kelly can spend the night with Meghan tomorrow night."

"That would depend upon Joe and Bethany, I imagine, but we can always find a babysitter," Beau chuckled. "What do you think, Gordy? A double date...like back in the day?"

"Perfect," Gordon agreed.

———

Mike just stood there with his mouth open. "Seriously, how'd I miss this?"

"You weren't looking," Dex said, coming up beside him.

Mike was befuddled. Jillian lay a reassuring hand on his elbow. He felt a little foolish in fact. He was supposed to be a detective. And he'd missed all the signs. He could see them clearly now, in retrospect. But he'd completely missed...

He'd missed it. He'd missed who killed Big Billy. It had slipped right by him.

"Oh... crap...I have to go to work. Dex, can you please make sure Jillian and Missy get home?" he stammered. With that, he quickly kissed his wife on the mouth and his daughter on the cheek before running to his truck in the parking lot.

———

"What was that about?" Helen asked.

"He solved his case," Kenny replied quietly. "Or at least he knows who did it. He has to go to work to prove it."

Jillian sighed. "Yeah, Kenny's right. He's very dedicated." She smiled. He was amazing. Watching him made her heart flutter. And she watched him all the way to the truck, and as he drove away.

The conversation between her father and his old friends faded into background noise. Michael Gabriel Poole, she thought. His name was a mantra to her. Michael Gabriel Poole. She closed her eyes and let his name fill her.

She thought back to the robbery a year and a half ago at Christmas and the aftermath. Lyle, of course, had been furious that Mike had brought her home, even though he never came into the house and had only been doing his job. She and Lyle had fought well into March over it.

When Mike had pulled into the driveway near the end of March and walked toward the front door, Lyle had been drinking. He opened the door and sucker punched Mike, who was bigger and stronger than Lyle. He'd responded to the punch by shoving Lyle up against the wall and cuffing him in one swift movement. In much the same way that he'd dominated that kid last night, he dominated Lyle, forcing him to sit on the floor. When Jillian had come running into the living room from her kitchen, Mike had calmly stated that he had a suspect in custody and needed Jillian to come in for a lineup. Then he'd rolled Lyle like a sack of potatoes and removed the cuffs before leaving.

She'd already gotten the angel wings tattoos. He had seen them. She knew he had, but he'd never make a move to get her back until after she left Lyle. And she wasn't ready to do that yet. Big Billy had stopped into the convenience store where she worked just hours before, reminding her that Mike's life depended on her staying with Lyle Fox. At the time, she had believed it. Even seeing Mike handle Lyle like a rag doll hadn't persuaded her that he was safe. So much time wasted.

It turned out Mike had found the guy. According to Aaron Muse, he'd been relentless in his investigation.

"Mama," Missy said, interrupting her daydreams.

"Hmmm?" she responded dreamily.

"Granny wants to know when we'll be over," Missy said, holding up her phone.

"We won't be," Jillian replied haughtily. Dex winked at her in encouragement. Jillian noted he was holding Kristin's hand, and Kristin looked amazing.

Last week, some people might have found Kristin and Dex to be an odd pairing. But it made perfect sense to Jillian. Kristin had a wild streak she kept well hidden. Dex worked hard to tame his. She'd known it when Joe had introduced him at his and Bethany's wedding. He had scars from fights. And he had that 1966 Ford Galaxie 500…painted midnight blue with silver metallic flecks and a white convertible top and white leather interior. He was a man who joined the Marines to harness a demon or two. Kristin hadn't needed the Marines. But she definitely harnessed more than one demon. All it took was interest from the handsome ex-Marine to release at least one. Kristin wasn't going to take crap from anyone anymore; of that, Jillian was certain.

There was more than one of her students in the congregation, and oddly, it was the dads who were pushing the children to greet their teacher. The moms were not nearly as enthusiastic. Kristin was obviously aware. But she held onto Dex's hand even tighter and stood even straighter. Dex knew what was going on, too. He gave more than one dad a warning look.

"Are y'all ready?" Jillian asked, amused.

"You betcha," Dex answered good-naturedly.

"Can you ride with Pam and Kenny, Daddy?" Jillian asked her father. He nodded, still conversing with his friends. "Let's go, then. I have a ham to cook."

CHAPTER 15

Mike had rushed home and changed into his uniform before calling in to advise he was on duty. Within an hour, he had obtained the search warrant. Now he stood on the stoop in front of the door with a bevy of deputies behind him to execute the search.

He rang the doorbell, and Muffy started her incessant yapping. Rich Lowe opened the door. "What now?" he asked incredulously.

"I have a warrant to search the premises, Rich," Mike replied.

"For what? I haven't done anything," Rich grumbled.

"Nobody said you did," Mike retorted with a coy smile.

He handed Rich the warrant. "What are you looking for?" Rich demanded, letting the deputies inside.

"The murder weapon, and a skater or biking helmet with a GoPro arm mount," Mike answered.

"If you don't think I killed Billy, why are you searching my house?" Rich persisted.

"You're not the only one who lives here," Mike replied, laying a hand on his shoulder.

"Are you kidding?"

"No," Mike said.

"Got the murder weapon, Detective," a deputy called from the kitchen. He emerged with a butcher knife, bagged and tagged. "It matches the description you gave, right down to the nick on the blade from the livestream. It's also positive for blood."

"It's a butcher knife! Of course, it's positive for blood,"

Kierra interjected.

"A lot of blood…way more than all the others on the butcher block," the deputy added.

Thirty minutes later, another deputy emerged from Dahlia's bedroom with the adult-sized bike helmet with the GoPro mount. "This it, Detective?" he asked, holding it up.

"That's it," Mike confirmed. "Bag it. Kierra…you're under arrest for the murder of William Walsh." He cuffed her and read her rights before leading her out to his squad car.

Mike looked up as the prosecuting attorney sat across from him at his desk. "Good job," he said to Mike.

"Yeah. The evidence was there. I…just missed it. The witness said only the truck was in front of the trailer at the time of the murder…her car wasn't there. If she was in the closet, like she said, where was her car…the car she left in after Billy was murdered? She had been there. She left her purse and shoes on purpose. She drove to the Tillys', 'borrowed' the old truck, put on that bike helmet with the arm mount, which brought the height of the attacker up to 6'1" on camera, knocked on his door, and attacked him. She stabbed him multiple times, gutted him, and shoved him over the railing into the bay. He had started seeing Chloe Tilly again. And she wasn't going to have that. She took the Tillys' truck, thinking that would lead us to Chloe. But she used her own butcher knife, not realizing the fact that the sheer amount of blood would make it stand out under Luminol. She figured all the knives in her block would show blood…and they did…just not…all over. Plus, she missed the nick. She got rid of her bloody clothes…probably burned them, but she hadn't figured out how to dispose of the helmet and GoPro camera yet. She confessed right away. I think her conscience was eating at her," Mike reiterated.

"Well, whatever, you got there; you closed the case. That's

all we can ask for...a detective who does his job," the prosecutor winked. "And on your day off at that."

The Sheriff came out of his office to congratulate Mike as well. Mike stood as he approached. They shook hands. "You can finish up that paperwork tomorrow when you are scheduled to work," the Sheriff teased, with a hearty laugh.

"Thank you. Hopefully, I can make it home in time for supper," Mike said, grinning. He paused. "I was wondering if I might be permitted to look into the Jacob Tilly case."

"As a reward for a job well done, you want to look into a thirty-five-year-old cold case? Help yourself. I don't expect you'll find much," the Sheriff chuckled.

"I know. But his body was found on my property...and apparently, my mother was there. I never knew that. I...I owe it to Pam to at least look."

———

Pamela Jean Poole, you're too old to have a schoolgirl crush, Pam thought to herself, staring at herself in the bathroom mirror. But it was Gordon Chisholm, by God. And he was flirting with *her*. He was the hometown hero, the quarterback, the Navy man, the sophisticated executive who lived and worked in San Francisco. He was as handsome at 53 as he had been at 18, though he had gone gray prematurely. So had his grandmother. His face was young-looking. And, by God, his body was incredible. He clearly took very good care of himself.

She didn't look too bad herself, she decided. She was still in good shape. She wasn't overweight. Her boobs were pretty good. It was true that gravity had taken a toll, but not too badly. She bought good bras that fit properly. Her stomach wasn't completely flat, but she had given birth to twin boys after all. A small pooch was expected. Her butt was good. She didn't look like a 22-year-old. But she was 48. With the right makeup, she could pass for 40. That wasn't too bad. Now that she'd gotten rid of the grays in her honey blonde hair, she looked alright. Why wouldn't a man like Gordon Chisholm flirt with her?

"Because you have no higher education, and you've devoted your entire life to your kids. You're just a tad bit dull, Pamela," she said to the mirror.

"Nonsense," a voice said. She looked around. She even checked behind the shower curtain and in the medicine cabinet for good measure. She was in the bathroom alone. She shook her head.

She straightened her dress and smoothed her hair before exiting the bathroom. She had retrieved Aunt Bertie from the apartments. Kenny was pouting about moving into them again. The two of them were sitting on the couch conspiring against her. Gordon, who was conversing with Dex Lawson at the other end of the room, by the piano, smiled and waved.

She made her way toward the two men. "Can I get you a drink, Pam?" Gordon asked politely.

"I'd love a glass of wine," she replied. "My boy is trying to get rid of me, and my aunt is helping him…and I'm hearing things. The bathroom argued with me about my being dull," she sighed.

He laughed. "Grandma," he said. "She's been very vocal today. Jill and I heard her humming this morning. Here, hold my beer. I'll get you some wine." He handed her the bottle and walked away.

"What do you think, Dex?" she asked earnestly once Gordon had left the room.

"I think you should relax and enjoy the attention," Dex said, taking a sip of his own beer.

"I'm not a prude…I know what he finds attractive. I know what I find attractive. I just don't want Kenny getting his hopes up, set on some kind of relationship, when it's really just a physical thing…"

"Pam…Kenny's an adult. And he has trouble formulating his sentences…not his thoughts. He may be confused and unable to comprehend things in moments of stress, but he absolutely comprehends. You know that better than anyone. Don't use him as an excuse. If it's only physical, you wouldn't be talking about Kenny's feelings. You and I both know that. You like Gordon. He likes you. And…yeah…there's definitely a physical attraction between you two. You're either willing to pursue it…or you're not. It has nothing to do with Kenny," Dex answered her honestly. She sighed. Damn, that was annoying. She nodded and followed Gordon into the kitchen.

He smiled and held out the glass of wine he'd just poured her. She took it, downed it with one swallow, put the glass down on the counter, set his beer beside the empty glass, and took his hand. She led him to the back stoop and upstairs.

"Oh," he said halfway up the steps. "Okay, then…"

————

Jillian changed out of her dress and into jeans and a T-shirt. Kristin knocked on her bedroom door as she pulled the T-shirt on over her bra. She knew it was her because she called out Jillian's name as she knocked. "Yeah, come in, Kristin," she said, adjusting her shirt.

Kristin had brought clothes herself and had changed into jeans as well. Still…everything fit her differently than the clothes she'd worn just last week. Her wardrobe more resembled Jillian's than Jenny's now. What a difference.

Jillian chuckled.

"What?" Kristin asked, checking herself in the mirror.

"That," Jillian laughed. "The school marm is all gone. Hello, sex kitten."

Kristin grinned. "I look hot. And I like the sex."

They both burst out laughing.

"Is he as good as he looks?" Jillian teased.

"Better," Kristin groaned, sitting on the bed. "Honestly… he's awesome…and I'm going to marry that man. He just doesn't know it yet."

"Okay…Don't get your heart broken again, Kristie. He's a good guy, but you're moving fast."

"I know. I know. I think it's too late, Jill. But thanks for worrying," Kristin told her.

Jillian sat beside her and hugged her. "Well, there's something to be said for taking a leap, Honey. I wasted half my life not taking it," she said, smiling.

"Did you see his car?" Kristin asked.

"Yeah. Normally, I'd say that a car doesn't mean anything… but in this case…that car screams Kristin Johnson."

"It has a 427 cubic-inch V-8 engine with a 4-speed manual transmission. It's 345 horsepower of pure muscle car. And, yeah, it gets my motor running," Kristin sighed.

"I don't get the car thing, but it's obvious the two of you do, and that's good."

Missy came to the door. "Hey, Mama, Aunt Kristin. Where are Granddaddy and Pam-ma?"

"Living room," Jillian answered.

"No. I was just in there. Just Uncle Kenny and Mr. Lawson," Missy said.

Jillian leaned back on her hands and looked up at the ceiling. "Oh dear, God," she said, stifling a laugh.

Kristin tried, but the laugh escaped.

"What? Where are they?" Missy persisted.

"Never mind. They'll be back soon," Jillian told her, rubbing her forehead.

As Missy turned to leave, still unsure as to what was going on, thank God, Kristin looked at Jillian. "It's springtime," she guffawed.

"Hmmmm. That it is," Jillian responded, shaking with

laughter. "Let's go…cook."

The two women rose and went to the kitchen arm in arm.

———————

As Jillian started to put the honey-glazed ham into the oven, the doorbell rang.

"I'll get it," Kristin offered, walking through the kitchen doorway into the foyer. Lily sat at attention, waiting for a sign as to whether the guest was welcome or not. Kristin scratched her ears on her way past. She opened the door to Jenny, Howie Moore, and her father. "Oh…great," she groaned. Lily let out a low growl. "Easy, girl. They're just annoying, not dangerous," she told the dog.

"Howie, this is my daughter, Kristin Johnson," her father said in his smarmiest voice. "Krissie, this is Howie Moore. I thought the two of you might get along. He's a Penn State grad."

"Is he?" she asked, eyeing the skinny, nerdy man with spectacles and no muscle tone. "Dex is an ex-marine and a nurse practitioner with his degree from William and Mary."

"Who's Dex?" Howie asked, his hand still untouched and outstretched to shake hers.

"My boyfriend," she said, pointing into the living room. "Come in."

Lily barked. Jenny jumped. "I hate this house," she complained, stepping over the threshold.

"Granny! Granddaddy Max! Hi!" Missy exclaimed from the living room. She came running to greet them. At least someone was happy to see them, Kristin thought, rolling her eyes. A pan crashed to the floor in the kitchen.

"Ow. Shit," Jillian could be heard cursing.

"Go on into the living room. Dex or Kenny will get you drinks," Kristin said, pointing. Then she walked away, returning to the kitchen. "You okay? Did you burn yourself?" she asked her stepsister as she sashayed through the doorway. She could feel her father's shock. It felt more like Christmas morning than Easter.

"Hello, Mrs. Johnson. We meet again," Dex bellowed from the living room. Kristin smiled. Jillian, picking up the empty pan she'd dropped, looked up at Kristin, shook her head, and chuckled.

Kristin made her way to the back entrance, leaned into the stoop, and yelled, "Gordon, Pam…Jenny and my father are here…when you're done."

Jillian burst into raucous laughter. "Oh my God, where has this Kristin been hiding? She's freakin' hilarious."

"And evil! She's slightly evil!" Gordon yelled from upstairs. Pam's laughter filled the house.

———

Mike pulled into his driveway, and his heart dropped. They were here. You'd think they would have had the good sense to stay away, but nope, he thought, as he saw the "good" doctor's Mercedes. Jenny never drove it. Max wouldn't come alone. Therefore, they were both here. He wished he'd stayed at work momentarily, but then he thought of Jillian and Missy, and there was nowhere else he'd rather be than where they were. He cut the ignition and pocketed his keys before exiting the vehicle and climbing the front steps of his home.

As he opened the door and stepped inside, he heard Missy ask, "Why are Granddaddy and Pam-ma upstairs…and what are they doing that they should finish before they come downstairs?"

"Jesus!" he yelped, turning around and sitting on the swing instead.

Jenny came storming out in a flustered state. She looked at him with her mouth wide open. Then she started to pace the porch. "I can't believe Pam," she proclaimed.

"Pam is a grown woman, Jenny. She can do whatever with whomever she pleases," he responded.

"Then what are you doing out here?" she snapped at him.

"Mentally preparing myself," he replied, swallowing hard.

"I hate this house," she said, near tears.

"Why?" he asked. She had just spoken the truth about why she was on the porch.

She had divorced Gordon decades ago. Whatever love she had for him had dwindled long ago. She didn't care if he screwed Pam Poole one iota. She hated this house.

"You'll just think it's...stupid," she confessed.

He chuckled. "Jenny, you were here when they pulled a dead child out of the gravel pit. A child you knew well. That's a pretty big trauma. I might argue it's not the house, but...I'd never think it's stupid," he assured her, kindly.

"I think he's still here, Mike. Wet, alone, scared...scary. His presence permeates everything. And he hates me," she said tearfully.

"I don't believe that last part," he said, nodding for her to sit beside him. "I don't even hate you."

She laughed at his teasing and sat beside him. "You're good. I'll give you that. You're personable. People respond to you. You get that from..."

"From Max," he finished.

"Yeah," she agreed, looking at her hands.

"Let's pretend for a moment I'm not one of the dreaded bastard children...Tell me about Jacob Tilly. I'm...I'm looking into it, Jenny. Your perspective would be a big help," he told her.

"You are? Do you think that will help him...rest?"

"I think it will help you rest...give you closure. And that...that might dispel any ghost you feel is hanging around." He smiled again.

"I was 16, and Gordon had just turned 17. He had a 1981 Pontiac Trans Am...A *Smokey and the Bandit* model. He was...so cool. And I was cool because I was his girlfriend… Kind of like you…and Jillian," she started, smiling.

"I remember," he confessed. "I know what you mean."

"Anyway, Jacob was just a kid. He lived next door to me. He got it in his head that Max and I…the summer before."

"When you turned 15?" Mike asked.

"Yes, but it wasn't like that, Mike. It wasn't. I liked Gordon. Jacob just…got it wrong."

"Did he? Okay," he noted, smiling again.

"He started acting out. Getting in trouble at home… stealing, lying."

Mike felt like she'd slapped him. That's what the… dream…had said…well, sort of. In the dream, Jacob had said that Ned framed him for those things.

"Do you think he really did those things?" Mike asked.

Jenny huffed. "Good question. No. It wasn't like him. It was more like Ned."

Mike nodded. "And what about that day?"

She sighed. "I was here. I had ridden my bike over. Gordon was changing the oil in the Trans Am." She laughed at the memory of him covered in oil. "He pulled the plug before he had the oil pan in place and was still under the car. The oil gushed out all over his face."

She laughed hard. Then she stopped. "He chased me for laughing, and I ran toward the gravel pit. Your mother was about to jump in. He yelled for her to stop. She looked down…and screamed bloody murder. Not that I blame her. He was naked. Not even floating, just lying face down on the bottom of the pit in like two inches of water. It was really dry that summer. They said he snuck over alone and dove in to skinny dip, but there wasn't enough water. He broke his neck on the exposed bedrock."

"Is that what happened?"

"I don't know. It wasn't like him. He wasn't the skinny

dippin' type. He wasn't the swimming type. He didn't really like water much," she recalled. "He was a nice kid, Mike. It shouldn't have happened," she said, wiping away a tear.

"You're right. Things like that shouldn't happen. Not to people we know and like. I'm sorry."

"For what?"

"For what you endured. For the grief. If you let that go, I think your angry ghost will disappear. Instead, you'll remember a living child, not a dead one," Mike advised.

"And what will that do?" she scoffed.

"It will make it so you aren't scared of this house," he said, smiling again. He stood. "I think I'm ready to face Pam. Stay out here as long as you like." He left her sitting on the porch swing. "Hello, Lily," he said to the dog who greeted him with a wag of her tail.

Now he just had to have an uncomfortable talk with Kristin. God, holidays suck, he thought.

———

Kristin was perched happily on Dex's lap, much to her father's chagrin. He had been counting on her to help separate Mike and Jillian. Instead, she'd started dating this…ex-Marine. He didn't care about the color of his skin. He didn't object to his profession as a nurse practitioner. It was a noble profession. He didn't even mind his past as a juvenile delinquent. He'd paid his dues and changed his life. What he minded was that he was Kenny's guard dog. Kenny was the problem.

It was uncanny. Mike looked exactly like Pam. His hair was perhaps more of a sandy blond compared to her honey blonde, but they had the same blue eyes, the same mouth. And Kenny…Kenny had dark brown hair, just like he had, just like Kristin. Mike's hair was straight. Kenny's curly. Mike was trim, but muscular. Kenny had a thinner frame. While they were about the same height, Kenny looked taller at a glance because of his smaller frame. Kenny was the spitting image of Maxim as a younger man. And that was a huge problem.

When Jillian brought Mike Poole home in high school, he realized immediately that Mike could be his undoing. Mike was smart. Really smart. Kenny had not had the issues he had now, but he'd been a little oblivious. Mike was the curious one, the one who asked questions and found answers. Max was almost proud of that. Almost. But mostly, he was terrified of it. Mike could easily destroy his medical career if he asked the right questions. And then he could also destroy Max's political career. Mike and Kenny were a huge controversy waiting to explode. And so, he had begun his decade and a half long campaign to keep Mike and Jillian apart. It was all falling apart now.

Even after his arrest for what had happened to Kenny, Max had held onto the hope that he could spin things his way. If he could get Kristin to date Howie, then he could find a way to push a wedge between Mike and Jillian, and he could salvage things. But Kristin had given her DNA, proving Mike and Kenny were her half-brothers. And now she was refusing to date Howie.

Max scowled at his daughter.

Mike Poole strode in like he owned the place, which he technically did, Max reminded himself. He'd been unable to get Jenny to persuade the girls to bring this confrontation to his home turf.

Howie Moore cleared his throat to break the tension in the room.

"Hi, I'm Howie. I work as a clerk in the Delegate's office," he announced, holding out his hand to Mike.

Mike, self-assured as ever, shook it. "Mike Poole, one of the Delegate's bastard sons," he replied coolly. Kenny, sitting quietly beside Dex and Kristin, laughed. "That's my fraternal twin and the other bastard son, Kenny," Mike added. God, he was brash.

Gordon and Pam made an entrance. She was still straightening her dress, for Pete's sake. She was still a pretty woman, he had to admit, though he still liked them young. His wife, Jenny, was pretty enough, too. Just not young anymore. But she was a great shield. Pam was a liability.

"Mike," Pam admonished. "Stop."

"No. Sorry, Mama. That isn't happening."

"Mama is right. I'm your Mama. And I'm asking you to stop. Not in front of your daughter," she demanded, looking at poor little Missy. Now, Missy was turning into a beautiful young woman. She was a little too young yet, but soon...

Mike sighed and nodded. "Alright then." He turned and walked away. Max didn't know where he went, but he left the room. Still, he knew he'd lose this time. Jillian and Mike were not going to separate. Kristin was not going to help. Howie was useless.

Max breathed a little sigh of relief when Jenny returned. She actually seemed less jumpy. That's before Mike reappeared, no longer in his uniform with a serious expression on his face.

"Kristin," he said from the foyer. "We need to talk...about her."

Mike knew. Max was certain of it. And he was about to tell Kristin. "No," Max yelled, standing from his seat in the floral armchair by the piano. "You've poisoned my stepdaughter against me. You won't do it to my daughter."

Everybody stared...at him. He truly despised this son of his.

"She already knows what you did, Daddy Dearest," Mike sneered. "So do I. This...this is about how bad it turned out."

"What? What do you mean?" Kristin asked, jumping off the ex-Marine. "Mike...What?" She was panicked. And by God, Max realized, Mike was right. She did know. How long had she known? All along? Oh God...it was all along.

"In private," he said calmly.

Then Kristin did the unthinkable. She undid everything he'd done to hide it.

"No. No secrets. What's wrong with my baby? What's wrong with Dahlia?" she demanded, standing straighter.

"N…nothing. Dahlia's okay…But…I arrested Kierra…for murder. She brutally murdered Billy Walsh. She confessed," Mike said calmly. How was he so calm?

Kristin turned like a wild animal. She flung herself, all teeth and nails, at her father. "You gave my baby to a murderer! You son of a bitch!" she screamed like a banshee.

Dex had great reaction time. He grabbed her before she reached Max and flung her over his shoulder. He carried her out of the room, kicking and screaming.

Max sat there, stunned. "Well…she wasn't a murderer when I arranged for the adoption," he justified to the room.

———

Dex carried Kristin out the front door. She screamed the entire way. She kicked. She clawed. And worst of all, she cried. By the time he set her feet on the ground in front of him, her rear against his car door, she was sobbing. He wrapped her up in his arms and held on until the sobs slowed to gasps. Then he pulled back enough to take her face into both of his hands. He gently kissed her lips and wiped her hair back out of her face. "Calm down," he whispered softly. "It's okay. It's goin' to be okay. We'll fix it. Calm down."

"How? How do we fix it? Dex, I had a baby. And I gave her up for adoption. Only Mike knew, and only because he showed up unexpectedly. I didn't tell anyone. But…my dad…he's…omnipotent, I swear."

"I know you had a baby. It's okay," he said, kissing her again.

"How do you know?" she asked. She was so naïve. He

loved that about her.

"I've seen you naked, Honey. You've got a great body. You look...amazing..."

"But I have stretch marks. Of course..." she sniffed.

"Tiger stripes, Baby. You earned 'em," he chuckled, turning her head to make her look him in the eyes when she tried to look away.

"How do we fix it?" she repeated, crying.

"Well, first, how do you know Dahlia is your baby?" he asked.

"Mike. I...I wavered. I asked him to find out who the adoptive parents were. He found out Dad had intervened and that Naomi...that's what I called her...was adopted by a single mother...Kierra Folsom. She named her Dahlia. Then, when Jillian and Rich broke up a year later, she moved here from Maryland...and started dating Rich."

"So, did Rich ever adopt her?" he asked.

"Um...no," she answered.

"And you and Mike are sure?"

"Yes, I've seen her birth certificate." She breathed out a jagged breath.

Kenny stood beside her suddenly. He took her hand. "Breathe," he said. "In through the nose. Out through the mouth." She looked at him and followed his lead this time.

That's when Rich pulled into the driveway, with 9-year-old Dahlia in the passenger seat, and Kristin burst into tears again. "Good try, man," Dex said to his friend.

Mike emerged from the house and stood on the porch as Rich popped the trunk and got out of the car.

"What are you doing, Rich?" Mike implored.

"You gotta help, Mike. You know as well as I do, I'm...not a good father. And Kierra called CPS...from jail," Rich laughed. "They're going to take her, Mike. You know it. I know it. Kierra knows it. But I'm also pretty sure you know who her biological parents are. I'm willing to bet it wasn't a legal adoption. You can prove it. And if they want her…"

"You wavered? Did you sign the consent?" Dex asked.

"They said I did before she was born," Kristin sniffed.

"What state?"

"Pennsylvania," she answered.

"Oh, Jesus. Kristin? You never signed after she was born? In Pennsylvania, a birth mother cannot sign away rights until 72 hours after birth," Mike exclaimed. "I…I told you that!"

"Well, excuse me for being confused. I asked the lawyer after you told me that. He said I had already signed…and I couldn't back out."

"Of course you could back out!" Mike screamed in exasperation. "You have thirty days after you sign…and Quinton had thirty days after birth! And there should have been a consent hearing."

"Mike. Calm down," Kenny said, strangely, the cool one. Dex understood. Whoever this lawyer had been had done a number on Kristin.

"A hearing? The lawyer said I didn't need to do that because it was a private…" Kristin stammered.

"Who the hell was this lawyer?" Dex asked.

"The adoption was handled through Morris, Blackstone, and Granger. I didn't check deeper than that because they're a solid firm…and she told me she signed. I was just looking for who adopted Naomi. It never occurred to me to check if they stole the baby! Jesus, Maxim!" Mike said, sitting hard on his step and holding his head.

"You…You're Dahlia's mother?" Rich asked, looking at Kristin. "And you wanted to back out at birth?"

Kristin nodded.

"Dahlia, Honey, get out of the car. Your birth mother

wants you. She always did," Rich said, moving to the back of the car and removing two suitcases from the trunk.

"What do I do?" Kristin whispered to Dex.

"Call a lawyer," he advised.

Mike had beat him to the punch, though. He'd already taken out his phone and was saying, "Hi, Mr. Morgan. It's Mike Poole. My sister, Kristin, needs a lawyer immediately. Ham, I think. Yes, Jillian made strawberry pie. Of course, there's enough for you to join us. See you in a few. Thanks." He disconnected, stood, and walked to Rich. "You got the adoption paperwork, Rich?"

"Yeah. It's all in the box in the back seat. Mike…I'm not… I'm not intentionally a shit. I'm just…not equipped to be a father. That was always my problem. I want the best for Missy…and for Dahlia. It was just never me. And…do you want the dog? It's Dahlia's."

Mike looked in the car and nodded. He opened the back driver's door and took out the box. "Kenny, can you come get Muffy?"

CHAPTER 16

"Is this everything?" Dex asked a shellshocked Kristin.

"Um…Yeah," she said nervously. "Oh God, Dex. He was my lawyer. I trusted him. I feel so stupid."

Dex shifted the box under his arm and kissed her forehead. "I told you we'd fix it. And we'll fix it," he said encouragingly.

He'd brought her back to her house to get all her records for Mr. Morgan. She was grateful they'd taken his car to church and Mike's. She was in no condition to drive. He managed despite his broken foot without complaint.

"She hates me. Did you see the way she looked at me?" she gasped, fighting tears again.

"She doesn't hate you. She's a little girl who is being used as a pawn in grown-up games. She feels unwanted and unloved. We just have to make her feel wanted and loved. It will be fine."

"We?"

"Yes. We. I'm not goin' anywhere. I can barely walk on this broken foot," he teased.

It made her smile. She thanked God for him today…in so many ways.

"You have to go home," she whispered.

"Why?"

"What?"

"Why do I have to go home?" he asked.

She just looked at him.

"Your friend at Heritage Gardens is retiring. I was offered the job a month ago…before we met. I came last week looking for a place to live. I bought the lot across the street from Mike's on Monday morning. I start next Monday. Do you want to marry me, Miss Johnson?"

She just nodded in complete shock.

He kissed her.

"You should probably meet my pops. How about tomorrow?" he asked, smiling.

She nodded again, still shocked.

He reached into his pocket and pulled out a ring box. "I…I've been carrying this around ever since we met. Silly, I know. But…I seriously started thinking about it right away. This was my grandmother's." He opened it and took the half-carat diamond solitaire out. Kristin held out her left hand, and he slipped the ring onto her finger.

She smiled. "I told Jillian I was going to marry you," she said with a laugh.

"Really?" he laughed. "That's…good."

"You gonna kiss me?" she asked.

"Oh, yeah." He leaned in and kissed her softly on the lips.

Missy sat across the kitchen table from Dahlia. Neither girl spoke. Missy, 4 years older, looked at her nails. Dahlia brushed her dog, Muffy. Missy always ignored her, so she was used to it. Missy had been her stepsister ever since she could remember. Now it turned out, she wasn't. Nobody told her, but she'd overheard her mother and Rich talking about it. Missy wasn't his daughter. And her real father had returned all the money Rich had paid for child support. Now, it seemed Missy was her cousin…for real. Her mother wasn't her mother. Her mother was Miss Johnson, Missy's real father's half-sister. Dahlia had a basic idea of what was going on. She wasn't stupid. But it was all very confusing.

Her mother, who wasn't her mother, killed her boyfriend, the scary man she'd been seeing behind Dahlia's stepfather's back for the last two years. Then she called CPS because if she was miserable, everybody had to be. Maybe it was for the best. Rich wasn't exactly the best dad. He forgot she was home and left her there all day. When he returned, he'd only brought dinner for himself. He ordered delivery for her once he realized his mistake, but then there were the drugs. He had a problem. When CPS showed up, he panicked. At least he knew he couldn't take care of Dahlia. She was glad of that. While the CPS lady talked to Dahlia, he had packed up her stuff and dog. While the lady looked around the house, he rushed Dahlia out the door and into the car. The next thing she knew, she was sitting across from Missy, being ignored, holding Muffy.

Muffy was a white Shizu. She had yipped and yapped for a few minutes at Lily upon entering the house, until Lily returned the greeting by barking. The much larger dog's friendly response was louder and deeper than anything Muffy could produce and sent her scrambling to hide under the sofa.

Uncle Kenny had retrieved her and handed her to Dahlia. He told Dahlia to call him Uncle Kenny, so she did. Uncle Mike… Uncle Kenny told her to call Deputy Poole that, so she did…Uncle Mike was on the phone, apparently with the CPS lady.

"Yeah, she's here. Her birth mother is Kristin Johnson. Yes, she's willing to take her. Yes, Filmore Morgan is representing Kristin. It was an illegal adoption. Sure. Kristin and her boyfriend went to her house to get the paperwork for Mr. Morgan. They're there now. No. Dahlia's here. We thought it was best she stay with me as an officer of the law until Social Services were up to speed. Kristin says you can come examine the home," he said into his phone as he walked through the kitchen toward the back door. He gave the address to Miss Johnson's house as he walked outside.

"It's weird that we're really related," Dahlia said nervously.

Missy looked up. "Oh…yeah. Everything's weird, Dahl.

Our family is really messed up." But she smiled as she said it. Maybe she didn't hate Dahlia. Maybe she was just as confused as Dahlia felt.

Dahlia sighed heavily and fought back the tears. "Nobody really wants me."

"That isn't true!" Uncle Kenny insisted, sitting beside her. He wasn't like the other adults. He was almost like a kid, but not really. He rubbed his head. "Kristin wants you. I know she does. I promise."

"Then why did she leave?" Dahlia asked.

"Because Mr. Morgan asked her to get some things from her home, and you were left in my custody. She'll be back soon. Here," Uncle Mike said, coming back inside and setting an old camera down in front of her on the table. "That was out in my squad car." He reached into his pocket and pulled out a memory card. "These are pictures from when you were born." He winked and mussed her hair.

She picked up the camera and inserted the memory card. She scrolled through them. In every single picture, Miss Johnson looked at her with so much love. Even Uncle Mike held her and looked adoringly at her. Compared to the pictures from her mother's posts, where she was more of a prop than anything else, these photos were full of true emotions, including an overwhelming sadness.

"She wanted you, but she didn't know what else to do. She was supposed to be the perfect one. He wouldn't allow her to be like me," Missy's mama said. Dahlia hadn't even noticed her standing behind her, looking at the pictures over her shoulder.

"What's wrong with being like you, Mama?" Missy asked.

"Nothing," she said, smiling. "I'm just the wild one."

———

Kristin opened the door to Lois Dodge, the social worker who had called Mike after Rich had disappeared with Dahlia.

Fortunately, he'd left a note that he was going to the deputy's house with the child.

"Hi," Kristin said nervously. "Come on in. Can I get you something to drink? Coffee? Tea?"

"No. Thank you," Lois replied. "My understanding is that you'll be petitioning the court to negate the illegal adoption of your biological child, Dahlia Naomi Folsom. Is that correct?" she asked curtly, entering the house.

"Yes, Ma'am," Kristin replied, ringing her hands.

"You're engaged?" the social worker asked, pointing at the ring on her finger.

"Yes Ma'am," she answered.

"Will your fiancé be residing in the home?"

"Yes, Ma'am," she repeated.

"I'll need to interview him," Lois noted.

"He's sitting right there," Kristin pointed out. Dex was indeed sitting on the sofa, not 10 feet from the women. He smiled and waved.

"Oh. Sorry. I didn't see you." Turning back to Kristin, she continued, "You're an interracial couple?"

"No. He's white. He just stayed out in the sun too long," Kristin sputtered, sardonically. "Of course we're an interracial couple. What difference does that make?"

Dex snorted. He actually snorted. Lois just looked up from her notepad. "Oh, it doesn't make a difference. Just an observation."

Kristin was dumbfounded. This woman lacked all social graces and had zero humor. "Okay," she said in resignation.

"You're a teacher at Washington District Elementary School?" Lois continued.

"Yes, Ma'am. Fourth Grade," Kristin confirmed.

"Yes, my Harry is in your class."

"Oh, Harry Dodge. Of course. He's a good kid."

"He's a monster, but thanks for trying," Lois said, cracking a smile for the first time.

"He's…rambunctious," Kristin corrected, smiling herself.

"Your background check is on file with the school?"

"Yes."

"And what is your name, sir?" Lois asked, addressing Dex. "Full name, please."

"Dexter Jermain Lawson," he answered.

"And what do you do for a living?"

"I'm starting next Monday as the Administrator at Heritage Gardens Assisted Living and Nursing Facilities in Colonial Beach."

"Oh…you're the new Administrator. It's nice to meet you. I have some clients there. You're an ex-Marine, right?"

"Yes Ma'am. I served for 10 years. I was honorably discharged 4 years ago with the rank of Master Sergeant," he told her.

"And you're a nurse practitioner?"

He nodded.

"And your background check is on file with the state?"

"Yes," he said.

"God, you two are a social worker's dream. Show me the child's room."

———

Jenny felt like crying. But she'd been a delegate's wife for 15 years now, and a doctor's wife 6 years before that. She'd been married to the man for 21 years. 21 years of smiling in public. 21 years of never showing a crack or a flaw. He was 14 years older than she was, with a daughter just 1 year older than her own. He was respected. And he had money. He had provided well for her and Jillian.

She looked at Jillian, laughing, even amid all this mess, her arms around Mike Poole's neck. He looked at Jillian like she was a goddess, a queen. It was obvious that he loved her. It was obvious he was good for her. She glowed. She had never glowed before. She'd always seemed…angry. But she was laughing. Jenny had no idea what Mike had whispered to Jillian to make her laugh like that and wrap her arms around him, but that didn't really matter. It was like there was no one else in the room anyway. It wasn't intended for the rest of them.

When Jillian kissed him, she meant it.

Jillian was in love with that man. And he was in love with her. And Max had always endeavored to destroy that…just because it was inconvenient to him…just because he'd have to explain his penchant for sleeping with young girls. She'd been one, too, she told herself now, even though she'd denied it for more than 35 years. Was he looking at Missy? By God, he was!

As his gaze drifted lasciviously toward her granddaughter, Jenny let go of all that reserve. "You motherfucking son of bitch!" she screamed, grabbing the vase full of fresh flowers off the piano and hurling it at him. He ducked, and the vase crashed against the wall behind him.

"What the hell, Jen?" her husband sputtered.

She grabbed Missy's Easter basket up off the floor and began hurling colored eggs at him, one at a time. "You stay away from my granddaughter! You sick fuck! Don't even think about doing to her what you did to Jillian!" Pam quietly started handing them to her so that she didn't have to keep reaching for them.

"He did what?" Gordon gasped.

He looked at Jillian and then at Mike before he lunged, jumping over the coffee table. He punched Max repeatedly. Lily growled and lowered herself on her haunches to pounce. Mike flung Jillian off him to grab Lily's collar. Jillian stumbled and dropped to her knees in front of Aunt Bertie, who never even stopped knitting. Kenny didn't even pause. He pulled Gordon off Max, both of them falling backwards into Howie Moore. Poor

Howie was knocked over in the fray, his glasses flying off and sliding across the hardwood floor, his drink splashing up in his face.

The doorbell rang, and Missy calmly reached down, picked up Howie's glasses, handed them to him, and made her way to the door. Jenny heard her say, "Hello, Mr. Morgan," and lowered the egg she held.

"I want a divorce," she announced. "I suggest you move into your apartment in Richmond. Tonight. Now." She was breathing heavily, but she felt oddly composed. She handed the egg back to Pam and smoothed her hair back into place. She pointed her chin in the air and tugged her sweater down.

Howie put back on his glasses. "I'd very much like to go home," he said.

Jenny picked up her purse. "Max will take you back to *my house* to get your car, Mr. Moore. I'll ride with the police, who will make sure he gets his stuff. Mike, you'll call for someone?" she announced.

Mike, with his mouth wide open, nodded.

Jenny felt vindicated.

"You should have let me beat the crap out of him," Gordon said, lying back on the floor.

"It won't change anything," Kenny replied, lying back beside him.

Jenny stomped out of the room. But she didn't know where to go. She found herself standing on the back stoop, looking out the back door.

"You should leave," the angry voice of the dead child hissed in her ear. "You should leave before I kill you."

———

Mike looked at the mess. Eggs, everywhere. Broken glass. Water. Soda. Flowers. Furniture out of place. "My house," he whispered in despair.

"No worries, Dear. Gordon will clean it up," he could swear a female voice said.

Then Gordon stood, grabbing at his ear. "Ow ow ow ow," he said as he stood. As he got to his feet, the coat closet door opened, and the broom inside fell at his feet.

Gordon stared at it. Mike shook his head. "I think that's meant for you."

"I think so. And I think I'd better do what she wants," Gordon agreed, stooping and picking it up.

Mr. Morgan entered the room and took a look around. "Good Lord, what happened?" he asked.

"Jenny lost her ever-lovin' mind!" Max shouted. Gordon drew back his hand as if to strike him again. Max pulled back. "I'm going." He maneuvered around Gordon and ran out the door. Howie jumped up and ran after him.

Within minutes, Aaron pulled into the driveway. Jenny walked out and got into his squad car. And then they were gone.

As Mike stood, still in a state of shock, his mother walked over to Gordon, kissed him quickly on the mouth, and started to help with the clean-up. He let out a heavy sigh. "Excuse me, Mr. Morgan," he said as he turned and walked slowly to his bedroom. He slammed the door shut behind him, flung himself face down onto the bed, and screamed into the pillow before punching it five times.

The door opened and closed. He didn't look up. Jillian sat on the bed beside him. She ran her fingers through his flaxen hair. "What did that pillow ever do to you?" she asked, teasingly.

"Oh God, Jill. I opened a can of worms. Did you see the chaos I unleashed?" he moaned.

"Darling, you didn't do that. That was all Max's doing. I liked that vase, but it sure looked good hurling toward him," she chuckled. "Mama finally made a stand. It's all I ever wanted. Besides you, that is."

"You've got me. Now, and always," he said, leaning up on his elbows. He smiled. He rolled to his side. "Jill...does Kenny seem...like himself...I mean...like he used to be...today?"

"He's having a good day. Why?"

"It's nothing. It's just...sometimes he seems...less flustered and then..."

Pam's scream interrupted.

"Shit," Mike grumbled, jumping up and running out of the room.

"Is Uncle Kenny alright?" Dahlia cried, hugging her dog in the foyer.

"Uncle Kenny!" Missy cried from the living room. Mike burst into the living room to find Kenny in full convulsion. Pam was kneeling beside him, trying to roll him to his side. Gordon had grabbed a pillow off the sofa and placed it under Kenny's head. Mr. Morgan had the good sense to stand out of the way. He held Missy by the shoulders.

Dex and Kristin walked through the front door. Dex rushed forward on his crutch, pushing past Mike. "How long?" he asked, kneeling beside Pam, placing the crutch on the floor, and rolling Kenny to his side. He wrapped his hand in his shirt and swept his fingers through Kenny's mouth. "How long?" he repeated.

"Um...a minute," Pam answered, nervously. She was shaking. Gordon helped her to her feet and moved her back out of the way. She was crying. He pulled her close.

"Okay, it's slowing," Dex said. "Kenny? Ken? Buddy? Are you coming back?"

Mike watched, finding he was shaking. It didn't seem to matter how many times it happened. He was never prepared. He always felt helpless. He always was helpless. There was nothing he could do.

Kenny's convulsions slowed and stopped. Mike realized

he'd been holding his breath as he finally breathed in relief. He'd frozen. He never froze. Of course, Pam and Gordon had it covered, but he should have done what Dex did. Instead, he stood there watching, like someone who'd never seen a seizure before.

He felt the sob escape his chest. Kristin reached out and took his hand. Then she reached behind him, taking Jillian's hand. Quietly, with more understanding than any other person he knew, she placed Jillian's hand in his and released them both before stepping back.

Jillian opened her arms to him, and he embraced her. "God," he wept into her shoulder, "I...I hate this day."

————

Kristin gently maneuvered Dahlia out of the foyer and toward the kitchen. "He's okay," she whispered calmly. "Dex will take care of him."

The child looked up at her. Dahlia's eyes were huge. "Dex is your boyfriend?" she asked. Kristin smiled and pulled a chair out for Dahlia to sit. She reached out and scratched Muffy behind the ears.

"He's my fiancé," she told the little girl. "He's going to live with us. Does Muffy need some water?"

"She might," Dahlia answered, looking at her pet, who licked the end of her nose.

Kristin took a saucer from the cabinet and filled it from the tap. She placed it on the floor and gently took the small white ball of fur from Dahlia. "You can have her back when she's done," she promised.

"What do I call you?" Dahlia asked with an accusatory tone.

"What do you want to call me?" Kristin responded, setting the dog on the floor by the saucer.

"I don't know. 'Mama' isn't right. My mama is kind of

nutty. You don't act like her. I'm too old for Mommy. And you gave me away. Can I just call you Kristin for now?"

Kristin stood and smiled again. She felt the sting of tears in her eyes but held them at bay. Dahlia had every right to be wary. "That's fine." She took a seat across from her beautiful daughter, with dark curly hair just like her own. "Now, as for what's happening with Kenny..."

"Uncle Kenny," Dahlia corrected her. And she felt the tears well again.

"Um, yes, Uncle Kenny. He had a seizure...a tonic clonic seizure. Uncle Kenny has epilepsy. Do you know what that is?"

Dahlia shook her head.

"It just means he's had more than one seizure, and that he will probably have more."

"But why?"

Kristin thought for a second before answering. "Uncle Kenny was wounded in Afghanistan. He was a Marine fighting in a war, and his vehicle struck a bomb. His head was hurt. They thought he might never walk or talk again. But he is a very brave man, and he worked very hard to learn to do things that we do easily every day...like feed ourselves, brush our hair, brush our teeth, walk, talk, use the bathroom...He has epilepsy because of the injury to his brain. He takes medicine, but he still has seizures sometimes."

"Why did your...fiancé...stick his finger in his mouth with the shirt wrapped around it?"

"Well, he wanted to make sure Uncle Kenny didn't have anything in his mouth that he could choke on, but...you saw how he was moving? That was his muscles spasming and releasing. Your jaw has a muscle. Dex didn't want Uncle Kenny to accidentally bite his finger during a spasm," she explained.

"And he'll be okay?"

"I think so. It was a short seizure. That's not to say that a seizure is nothing. Sometimes it can require he go to the hospital, but I think this one will just make him really tired."

"How do you know so much about it?" Dahlia asked.

"My mother…had epilepsy," Kristin explained.

"What caused hers?" the child asked.

"I don't know. Sometimes…doctors don't know," she said softly.

"What happened to your mother?"

"She died…but not because of epilepsy. She was in a car accident with her best friend. They were both killed…and my sister died in it, too."

"How old were you?" Dahlia inquired.

"Your age," Kristin told her.

"Oh. That sucks."

"Yeah. Big time." Kristin smiled again.

———

Kenny opened his eyes and was momentarily confused. Slowly, it dawned on him that he had urinated and was wet, that his tongue hurt where he'd bitten it, and that Dex was talking to him. "You back with us, Bud?" he asked. Kenny nodded and tried to get up. "Woah, hold up, Ken. I got one good foot. Let Gordon and Mike get you up. You want me or Mike to help clean you up?"

"M… Mike," Kenny croaked out.

Dex picked up his crutch, pulled himself up off the floor, and limped out of the way. Mike and Gordon lifted Kenny to his unstable feet and helped him to the bathroom. As they got Kenny to the side of the tub, Mike turned to Gordon. "Would you go get him a pair of my underwear out of the top right drawer of the highboy in my room, and pajamas…bottom drawer? I'll get him out of these wet clothes," his brother said to the older man.

Kenny wanted the floor to swallow him, but he was so tired and confused that the embarrassment was secondary. He needed help. His brother turned on the tub faucet to let the water warm while he helped Kenny out of his soiled clothing. He soaped up and wet a washcloth, wiping Kenny's face and neck first.

"Just some spittle and a little blood. Did you bite your tongue?" Kenny nodded. "Ah, I'm sorry. That's going to hurt for a while. Look at me. Eyes on me, Ken." Mike cleaned Kenny as he spoke. Kenny knew what he was doing. It was a trick the nurses had used while he was hospitalized after…The idea was to distract him while bathing him, so he was less humiliated by needing someone else to clean him. It didn't work. But at least it was Mike. He felt a little better about his brother caring for him than the pretty nurse…a second lieutenant, he recalled…who had first tried the trick. Lydia…Lydia Yin. That was her name.

There was a knock on the door. Mike wrapped him in a giant towel and said, "Come in."

Gordon was outside the door with the requested clothing items. He opened the door and handed them to Mike, who thanked him.

When Gordon was gone, Mike dried Kenny off and helped him dress in the clean clothes. "Do you want to go to the doctor? Or do you just want to lie down?" he asked.

Kenny knew he was alright by this time. He was just post-ictal. All he wanted to do was sleep. He didn't even want to go home to do it. "Can…I…sleep in your room?" he asked drowsily.

"Of course you can. Anything I have is yours, Kenny," Mike told him. He didn't mean to, but Mike was making Kenny incredibly sad. He was trying so hard to pretend everything was normal, but they both knew that this wasn't how it was supposed to be.

As Mike helped him to his feet, he hugged his brother. Mike hugged him back, patting his back. "It's okay, Ken."

Kenny nodded and hugged Mike tighter.

Mike helped him into the bed and shut off the lights

before closing the door. There was the sweet smell of Lily of the Valley in the room. It was flowery but not overpowering. It was comforting. Kenny was asleep before the door latched.

———

Pam sat down in the chair next to Aunt Bertie. The old woman smiled and patted Pam's knee. "You need to let him go, Dear," she said, apparently oblivious to everything that had happened today.

"Aunt Bertie, he had a seizure…"

"I know. I was sitting right here," her aunt said.

"Aunt Bertie…"

"Oh, for heaven's sake, Child. It's Easter. Even if he lived in the apartments, he would be here today with you, and he would have had his seizure here. And if he had a seizure at the apartments, there would be health professionals like that young man to handle it…which he did far better than any of the rest of you, by the way," Aunt Bertie pointed out.

Pam was flabbergasted. But she was right. That old kook had a good argument.

"You're right. Okay," Pam acquiesced.

Jillian appeared at the entryway from the kitchen. "Dinner is ready," she announced somberly. "If anyone's in the mood to eat."

"I am," Aunt Bertie said cheerily. "I could eat a horse."

Jillian cracked a smile. "I'll get Mike to make you a plate," she offered.

She's a good girl, Pam thought. She liked her son's wife. She always had liked her. She had wanted Mike not to repeat the mistakes she had made. She had encouraged him to go to Ole Miss. She had never gone to the extent that Max had. If she had known what he was doing, she'd have put a stop to it. But she wasn't innocent in keeping the two of them apart, either.

Aunt Bertie patted her knee again and winked. "Don't live

in the past, Dear." How did her aunt always seem to know her thoughts?

"Didn't you know? I'm an old witch," Aunt Bertie cackled.

"Stop that. It's creepy," Pam chuckled.

They ate. Jillian and Kristin had prepared a feast...and on a minute's notice, apparently; ham, fresh biscuits, potato salad, macaroni salad, deviled eggs, spinach and artichoke stuffed mushrooms, cream peas, and strawberry pie. Pam started to feel less anxious.

The meal was good. Despite the seizures and anxiety, Kenny was generally happy. Mike was finally moving past his guilt over...well, everything. She could afford to step back just a bit.

Gordon smiled at her and winked.

Letting Kenny move into assisted living was going to be a good thing.

CHAPTER 17

The next morning, Mike arrived at work to find the box of evidence with the case file for Jacob Tilly's unexplained death on his desk as promised. He felt a chill run up his spine as he sat down and pulled the lid off the box. There wasn't much there. Jacob had been found naked, face down, in about 2 inches of water. His neck was broken, along with all his ribs, his cheek bones, his nose, both ocular sockets…as if he had landed face first.

Mike was confused. There were no clothes found at the scene. What had he worn to the gravel pit? Surely, he hadn't walked the 2 miles from his home to the scene naked. Mike looked through the crime scene photos. There didn't appear to be any abrasions on the child's feet. He double-checked that with the autopsy report. No abrasions were recorded. He was found in a gravel pit down a dirt lane. Had he walked 2 miles of blacktop and then ½ a mile of dirt and gravel barefoot, there would have been abrasions. This in no way looked like an accident. This looked like a body dump.

He read through the autopsy report. The medical examiner had checked for signs of sexual assault, given that he was naked. There were no signs of it.

His parents had said he'd gone to bed in Spider-Man pajamas. The pajamas were missing. His shoes, however, were all at home and accounted for.

There were 10 kids at the scene. Gordon Chisholm was the oldest, at age 17. He ran back to the house and called 911. Mike snorted, reminding himself this was 1989. He wouldn't have had a cell phone. Also, present were Jennifer Wade, age 16,

Pamela Poole, age 12, Richard Busic, age 11, James Hobert, age 12, Cameron Hobert, age 14, Lisa Kelly, age 12, Tanya Grummert, age 13, Lesley Corbin, age 15, and...Ned Tilly, age 16.

Each of them had been interviewed. Transcripts were in the file. It did not appear that officers ever asked if any of them had seen or taken the pajamas.

From start to finish, the investigation into Jacob Tilly's death had been horribly botched.

He set aside the file and leaned back. First, he had to locate the "witnesses." At least he had a head start and knew exactly where 4 of the 10 were.

A simple social media search led him to Richard Busic, who was residing in Williamsburg now, with his wife, Susan. He went by Dicky. He owned and operated a Goodyear store. Mike looked up the store's telephone number and called.

The phone rang twice. "Colonial Goodyear," a perky female voice answered.

"Hello. This is Deputy Michael Poole with the Westmoreland County Sheriff's Department. I need to speak with Mr. Richard Busic," Mike said into the phone.

"Hold, please," the voice countered happily.

"Hello?" Dicky answered the call.

"Mr. Busic?"

"Yes," came the reply.

"I'm Deputy Mike Poole, Westmoreland County. I think you may know my...mother...Pam Poole."

"Oh...God, yeah. Pam. I haven't heard that name in years. What can I do for you, Deputy?"

"I am reopening the investigation into the death of Jacob Tilly," Mike explained.

There was a long silence. Finally, the man let out a slow breath and said, "Yeah. That was a tough day, Deputy. And it was a long time ago. But I'll help any way I can."

"Thank you. I…I bought the Pruces' property a few weeks back. And I'm married to Jillian Chisholm, Gordon and Jenny's daughter…so, the case is kind of personal," Mike told him.

They spoke at length. Dicky was a nice guy. He told Mike that they had all worn clothing over their swimsuits and intended to jump into the gravel pit to swim. It was a dare type thing. There were plenty of places to swim; the Potomac, the pool at the State Park, Colonial Beach, Mattox Creek…heck, Lisa Kelly had a pool in her back yard. But the gravel pit was forbidden… for good reason. They had all gotten undressed, down to their swimsuits, but those were the only clothes Dicky had seen.

"The only thing that I ever thought was…off…was that Ned didn't show any emotion. I mean, I suppose he could have been in shock, but Jacob was his brother. You'd think he'd react a little."

Dicky told Mike that Tanya Grummert had married a man from Illinois and was living in Chicago, he thought. Her married name was Dwyer. Her husband's name was Rob or Bob. Lisa Kelly had died in 2017 from lung cancer. Jim Hobert lived in Fredericksburg now. His brother Cameron was in Denver. Les Corbin was still in Westmoreland, he thought. Mike thanked him for his help and disconnected.

––––––––

Kristin got out from behind the wheel of Dex's Galaxie. Joe pulled in behind them with the U-Haul truck. A woman emerged from the house they were in front of like a whirling dervish.

"Bitch! Who do you think you are? That's my cous's car. He don't let nobody drive it!" the woman yelled, rushing at Kristin with her nostrils flared, her shoulders back, her jaw protruded, pointing with an exaggerated thrust.

Dex calmly climbed out of the passenger seat, using his crutch to steady himself. "Chill, Lola. She's my girl."

The woman froze and lowered her arm. Her shoulders

relaxed, but she looked confused. "Dex?"

"Yeah," he laughed. "Kristin, this is my cousin, Lola Swift. Lola, this is my fiancée, Kristin Johnson, and her daughter, Dahlia." He nodded to the child sitting in the backseat. "And you remember Joe."

"Hey, Joe," Lola said to her cousin's best friend. "Fiancée?" she inquired, putting her hands on her hips. "Since when?"

"Last night," he answered.

Lola looked at the U-Haul. "You really movin' out?"

"Yeah. I told you. I got a new job. You're goin' to be fine," he assured her. "Lola's ex, Darius Walters, was harassin' her a year and a half ago. So, she and her kids, Marcus and George, moved in here with me and Pops. He's no longer an issue," he explained.

"I thought your grandfather was in assisted living?" Kristin asked.

"He is now. He made the choice to move in there with a group of his friends. He signed the house over to Lola."

"I told you that you didn't need to leave, even if the house is mine now," Lola said pleadingly.

"Nah, it's time. I bought a nice piece of land. I'm gonna put a house on it for me, Kristie, and that little lady in the backseat. In the meantime, I can stay at Kristin's. We got it all worked out. I'll pay rent until we get married. And we have a pre-nup. Her house is her house, whether she keeps it or sells it. She'll be added to the mortgage on my property, because that will be our home, and she'll deserve equal ownership."

Kristin smiled and extended her hand.

Lola shook it.

"I drove because it's hard to drive with a broken foot," she whispered, directing Lola's gaze toward Dex's booted foot and the crutch.

"What did you do?" Lola exclaimed, rushing around the

car to her cousin's side.

"Long story," he chuckled. "Suffice it to say, I'm not gonna be much help in loading stuff on and off that U-Haul. I was hopin' you and the boys would help."

Joe climbed out of the truck. "Jessup and Ryan are here to help, too," he pointed out.

Fortunately, Dex had been packing since accepting the new job. He had mostly packed all his things, at least those things that did not get used daily. Kristin set about packing his clothes into several boxes. His room, as expected of an ex-Marine, was spotless and well organized. His clothes were perfectly rolled. Kristin giggled as she opened his shirt drawer.

"What?" he asked, hobbling into the room.

"Nothing," she teased. "Nothing at all."

He dropped the crutch and grabbed her around the waist, pulling her close. She squealed as he tickled her. Then he lost his balance and they both fell onto his neatly made bed. "At least my aim is still good," he said before kissing her. She wrapped her arms around him and kissed him back.

"Yo! Packing. Not necking," Joe said from the doorway.

"You're one to talk," Dex retorted. "Every time I turn around, you're kissing Bethany."

"Bethany's not here. She's at work today," Joe said, winking.

They quickly had the U-Haul packed with Dex's furniture and boxes. His clothes and toiletries were packed into the Galaxie's trunk.

"You coming for lunch with Pops?" Dex asked his cousin.

She looked at Kristin, smiled, and shook her head. "Nah, I'll let you introduce your *fiancée* on your own," she replied. She kissed his cheek, and he got into the passenger side of the Galaxie.

———

Mike tracked down all the surviving "witnesses" from

his conversation with Dicky Busic. Each in turn answered his questions. None of them saw any clothes other than the group's. James Hobert said he noticed tire tracks inside the fence around the gravel pit and thought it was odd, since the gate was locked and they had squeezed inside. That was an interesting observation, but there was nothing about it in the original file. Mike checked the original transcripts, and sure enough, James had mentioned the tire tracks. Investigators dismissed them as belonging to either police or ambulance responders. Mike was sure they were wrong.

He searched through all the crime scene photos. Obviously, none were taken of the alleged tire tracks, but he found tire tracks in several of the photos, and one set, in a photo of James, did not appear to match treads on tires used by a full-sized vehicle…but more like those of a 4-wheeler. He took the negatives to the crime lab and asked for a blow-up of the tread portion of the photo.

God, he hated what he was thinking.

He dug through the file until he found the family information. He read, "Father: Curtis Tilly, age 47, manager at Ace Hardware in Colonial Beach. Mother: Ginger Tilly, age 39, second wife, mother to Edward, Jacob, and Quinton. Father's ex-wife: Rose Tilly, age 45, mother to half-sister Marilyn Tilly. Half-sister: Marilyn Tilly, age 24. Brother: Ned Tilly, age 16. Brother Quinton Tilly, age 1. Victim had been acting out lately, lying, stealing, jealous of the baby. No signs of abuse."

Mike sighed, reading Quinton's name. He was a piece of work. When approached yesterday evening by CPS, with Mr. Morgan in tow, he had flatly denied paternity. "I told her to get rid of the baby. Any child she had has nuthin' to do with me!" he had bellowed. Mr. Morgan procured his signature, relinquishing all parental rights. Arleen, his wife, hadn't even batted an eye.

"What a jerk," Mike muttered. But it would work out. Dahlia would be better off without him. The thought reminded him of something Ned Tilly had said to him about Big Billy. "Good riddance. I get you're just doin' your job, but my Chloe will be better off without that trash," Mike repeated. How exactly did Kierra get the keys to Curtis's old truck?

It wasn't difficult to connect Kierra and Ned. Rich and Ned were both members of the Moose, and Kierra was a member of the Moose Auxiliary. But beyond that, with what he had learned about Kierra when looking for Dahlia, Mike knew that Kierra was Ginger Tilly's childhood best friend's granddaughter. He'd found it suspicious that Kristin's daughter had ended up being adopted by someone with a cursory link to the baby's father.

Kierra had moved here around the time that Jillian had divorced Rich and was married to him suspiciously quickly. Jillian had confided she suspected Rich had been seeing Kierra before they split. Kierra had been living in Montgomery County, Maryland, just before moving here. But she had adopted Dahlia as an infant through the law firm of Morris, Blackstone, and Granger. They had represented Kierra, who had been a prominent interior designer in Philadelphia. Kristin had been represented by Oscar Jeeling, an old friend of her father's, it had turned out, though she had not known that at the time.

Shortly after the illegal adoption, Kierra had moved to Maryland from Pennsylvania with Dahlia. She had reestablished her interior design studio close to DC. Whatever the reason, the new studio failed. She then moved to Westmoreland and married Rich Lowe, becoming a housewife. What she saw in Big Billy, who knew?

Tom Palmer interrupted Mike's review of the case file. "How's it goin', Mike?" he asked.

"The investigation was completely botched, Tom," Mike responded, looking up at his boss. "This was a body dump…and Jacob Tilly…was murdered."

Tom nodded. "Yeah, I was afraid of that. I remember

thinking it was suspicious at the time. The old lock on the gate had been freshly oiled and looked like it had been recently used. But I had just joined the Sheriff's department. My suspicions were dismissed. I hadn't thought about this case in a long time. I…I have this for you. I was told that they were not pertinent and weren't needed. But I kept them." He set a file on Mike's desk. They were evidence photos. They included the tire tracks…and pictures of the "witnesses." Ned's was particularly interesting. He had scratch marks on his neck, like someone had scratched him.

Mike lunged at the box. DNA evidence had been collected from under Jacob's fingernails. "Oh, my God," Mike said. "He did it. He killed his brother… and I think…he might have helped Kierra kill your nephew."

"Really? Well…ain't that a kick in the pants?" Tom responded. "Can you prove it?"

"No. Not yet," Mike answered.

CHAPTER 18

Dahlia sat silently in the back seat. Kristin was driving. Dex took Tylenol out of the glove box and opened it. He took out two tablets, popped them into his mouth, and swallowed them with a gulp from his bottle of water.

"Foot hurt, Babe?" Kristin asked him.

"Hmmm. Yeah," he replied in a sort of groaning voice.

He seemed nice enough. He sure liked Kristin. And he hadn't said anything mean to Dahlia. In fact, he'd only been very friendly. That was so unlike the men Dahlia's mother...no Kierra...not mother...Kierra had dated. Rich mostly ignored her. Big Billy had never used her name. He had just called her "that snot-nosed brat." So far, Dex only referred to her by name.

"What happened to your foot?" Dahlia worked up the nerve to ask.

"Joe's dog ran it over with Joe's truck," Dex chuckled.

She laughed. She knew he was telling her the truth, but it was just...ridiculous. He knew it, and being a nice guy, he found the humor in it, even though his foot was obviously hurting.

"How does a dog run over somebody's foot with a truck?" she giggled.

"I know, right? And he didn't even have a driver's license, just a dog license," he retorted, laughing with her.

Kristin snorted, joining in the laughter.

"You snorted," he teased her. She blushed, and Dahlia, seeing her face in the rearview mirror, thought she was the prettiest woman she'd ever seen. She'd been very careful to not let those thoughts form so far, but after just one night and a few hours, it was getting harder to do. Kristin *was* beautiful. And so far, she had been kind and considerate of Dahlia's feelings.

After they had left Uncle Mike's last night, Kristin and Dex had taken Dahlia to her new home, Kristin's house. Kristin showed her to her new room. It was a guest room. But Kristin said she could redecorate it, even if they were going to build a new house soon. Kristin told her she could make this room her own for as long as they lived in the house, which wouldn't be long, Kristin hoped. Her father had bought it for her, and she wanted to sell it. She wanted to make her own home, too…with Dex…and Dahlia.

At first, the little girl was dubious, but Kristin had promised that while they were in Fredericksburg today, she would take her to Target and let her pick out whatever she wanted for her room. That promise had not yet been fulfilled, but the assisted living facility where Dex's pops lived was near Target, and Kristin promised they would go after they had lunch.

Kristin pulled up to the door to let Dex out, so he wouldn't have to walk too much. He got out, leaned his seat forward, and held his hand out to Dahlia. She was confused at first, but then she took his hand and climbed out of the back seat. He shut the door and hobbled to a bench. He patted the seat beside him. She sat.

"Looking forward to shopping?" he asked with a smile.

She shrugged.

"It's okay to like her, you know," he said, winking. "I do."

Dahlia shrugged again. But she was beginning to agree with him.

He handed her his phone. "Candy Crush is on there somewhere. It came on the phone. How come you don't have a tablet or something? I thought kids came with them attached at the fingers," he teased.

"Mama never got me one," she replied, shrugging again.

"She sometimes let me play with hers, but she said I didn't need one. She said I had a place to live, food to eat, and clothes to wear…and that stupid dog. That's what she called Muffy."

"Well, things like that aren't a need, that's true, but… harsh. And Muffy seems like a smart little dog. We'll get you one today. I'll add you to my family network."

"Okay," she said. Were they trying to buy her affection?

He sat there while she played Candy Crush for a minute. "We just want you to feel comfortable, Dahlia. We want you to feel like you belong. Because you do. I don't know how to do that, though. Kristin is better at it. She's a teacher, but I…I'm a Marine… and a nurse…more used to working with geriatric patients and military personnel than children. But I got a nephew…and I like kids. Just tell me what to do, and I'll try my best. Can you give us a chance? Especially your mother. She's been through a lot."

"Yeah, like what?" Dahlia asked.

"She told you her mother died?"

"Yeah. In a car accident, when she was 9," Dahlia replied, looking up from the phone.

"So was her older sister, Naomi, whom she named you for…and she was in the accident, too. She was in a coma for 7 weeks. She missed their funerals," he said sadly.

"She gave me the name Naomi? That's my middle name," Dahlia said.

Dex sighed. "Yes. Her father, Naomi's father, arranged for Kierra to adopt you. She thinks maybe he insisted Kierra at least keep it as your middle name."

"Oh. How old was Naomi?"

"12," he answered.

Kristin, having found a place to park, was walking toward them. She smiled and waved at them. He pulled himself up with his crutch. Dahlia handed him his phone, stood, and took Kristin by the hand. "Come on, Mom. Let's go meet Pops."

———

It was close to noon when Kenny awoke. He had no memory of how he'd ended up in his own bed. He was wearing Mike's pajamas, though, and he remembered the seizure, and the embarrassment, and sleeping off the seizure in Mike's room at Mike's house. He sat up and looked around the room.

"Pamb?" he called out. He still had a headache. But it wasn't as bad as the pain in his mouth. "Ow," he said, putting his hand to his mouth. "Dat hurs."

He heard Pam's footsteps on the stairs. Then his door opened. Pam came inside. She sat on the edge of his bed and hugged him. If he knew one thing, it was that Pam loved him. He had been raised to call her his sister, but she had always been his mother. He hugged her back.

"Feeling better, Baby?" she asked, rubbing his back.

"Otay. Mouf hurs. I bi ma tung," he muttered.

She released the hug and touched his face gently. "I know. Mike told me. You want a milkshake from the Pink Poodle? I'll send Gordon out for some."

Gordon? Gordon was here? He recalled Gordon helping him out of the car and up the stairs. Had he been here all night?

"Stawbewy," he said, nodding.

"I know," she teased. "Gordon, would you go get those shakes we talked about?" she yelled toward the still open door.

"You bet," Gordon replied from somewhere downstairs.

They sat and listened for the door to open and close. "You feel up to a shower?" she asked. "Do you need help?"

"Showa, es. Help, no," he responded, climbing out of bed. He was being stubborn, but he still pictured Roy and Charlie laughing at Pam putting a pillow behind his back in church yesterday. He could shower without his mommy helping him, and by-God, he would. Being stubborn was how he'd worked his way back to being able to walk and talk after being wounded.

He pushed himself to take one step after another, walking to his dresser and getting *his* clothes out to put on after the shower. He kept a hand on the wall as he walked to the bathroom alone. Pam watched, but she wouldn't interfere. He knew that. She would let him push himself that far, at least.

He showered and dressed himself. He made his way tenuously down the stairs. Pam and Gordon were sitting on the front porch, looking out over Monroe Bay just across the street. He walked outside and sat in a rocker. Pam passed him his milkshake. She was enjoying one herself, chocolate. Gordon was eating a banana split.

"I talked to Dex," Pam said between sucks on her straw. "I think you should move into Heritage Gardens."

He looked up, surprised. Pam had been so opposed to the idea. He thought the seizure would for certain kill any hope he had.

"Aunt Bertie pointed out that if you have a seizure at Heritage Gardens, there would be medical professionals to help you. Dex is taking over as the facility administrator. It's a little bit of a change in his career course, but he's excited to make the move. And with him there on top of the other benefits, I think it's a good idea," she explained, reading his mind.

He got up and hugged her again.

She laughed. "Okay. Okay. But you have to call me every day. I'm going to miss you like crazy," she said, choking up. "You can move this weekend. Mike says you can go through his and Jillian's extra furniture to furnish the apartment."

"Are ou oing ou tonight?" he asked.

"Yes. Jillian is bringing Missy over to stay with you tonight…not to take care of you…you can take care of yourself. Just to keep you company and to call somebody if you need help," Gordon answered.

Kenny nodded and gave Gordon a thumbs-up.

———

Jillian let Lily run around the yard while she hung the clean clothes on the clothesline. It was a gorgeous spring day with just a slight breeze. She was looking forward to folding the sheets just for that glorious smell of fresh air, line-dried linens. The sheets snapped in a sudden gust, and the shape of a child formed inside the billowing fabric. Jillian jumped and fell backwards. The sheet fell, and the shape stepped through it.

Lily didn't growl. She barked playfully and jumped around the boy like she did Missy.

It was the same child she'd seen in the basement. She was almost positive. But he looked very different. His eyes were normal. He was no longer wraithlike. He even had dimples. Most of all, he was dry and dressed. His jeans and T-shirt were timeless, even though the T-shirt featured the car from *The Dukes of Hazzard*. If it weren't for that...and the fact she could see through him and he had just walked through a sheet, she'd have thought him a living child. He looked about Missy's age.

Though startled, Jillian wasn't as afraid as she had been before. "Can you see me?" she asked the apparition.

The child nodded.

"You look different. You aren't...scary."

The boy smiled.

"Can you talk?" she asked.

He shrugged. He mimed by pointing at her, holding his hand up to his mouth, and mimicking a scream.

"Your voice is scary?" she asked.

He nodded.

"Oh. Okay. Well, thank you for not using it. Are you... Jacob Tilly?" she continued.

He nodded again.

"Why are you here?"

He shrugged and faded.

Jillian sat there on the ground for a moment. She hugged her knees to her chest. "I definitely have to believe Missy saw a boy in that barn," she pondered, thinking about how Missy had insisted a boy had been in the collapsed barn with her at Christmas. Next time she visited Bethany, she'd have to thank the ghost of Alec Gardner, the children claimed, who lived in the house on Ravens' Roost farm. He had died at age 18 in Vietnam. She had no idea how his spirit might have made its way home, but she couldn't explain spirits at all.

"Jacob, it's okay for you to be here," she said out loud before standing.

"You saw him?" her mother asked, appearing out of nowhere.

"Jesus! Mama! You scared the crap out of me! Where did you come from?" Jillian asked, clutching her hand to her chest.

"I came around the house," Jenny chuckled. "I just came from Clint Stevens'. I'm filing for divorce. I retained him."

"Oh. Sure, he's a good lawyer," Jillian said, catching her breath. "And yes, I saw Jacob Tilly... a couple of times. The first time was...terrifying. This time, not so much. He looked...more human."

"Yes. I saw that yesterday...after Mike told me that he would if I remembered the living child instead of the dead one. I wonder if that was the change," Jenny suggested. "I wanted to apologize, Jillian. I never meant to put you in harm's way. I...feel terrible. I...can't believe how blind I was."

"Mama...it's what it is. I know you love me. I know you wouldn't deliberately hurt me. I was hurt. You missed it. I don't love you any less," Jillian said, returning to hanging her laundry.

"But you don't forgive me," Jenny sighed.

"I'm not sure, and that's the truth. I don't hold it against you. Is that forgiving?"

"Partially, maybe. That's enough for now, I guess," she

said with a gentle smile.

"I think we need family counseling, to be honest," Jillian suggested.

"If that's what you want. I'm willing to do anything," Jenny told her.

Jillian picked up the empty laundry basket and walked toward the back door. "Good. Let's see what that does. You want to come in for some iced tea?"

"I'd like that," Jenny said haltingly. "Is your father here?"

Jillian laughed. "No. He stayed at Pam's last night, and he hasn't come back yet. He did call me from the Pink Poodle. He was getting ice cream for the three of them. He said he'd be home around 2 or so."

"Do you think they're serious?" Jenny asked, following her inside.

"I don't know, Mama. It's clear they like each other."

Jillian set the laundry basket on the stoop and entered the kitchen. She walked to the cabinet by the sink and took out two glasses. She filled them both with ice through the ice dispenser in the freezer door and set them on the table. She opened the fridge and took out a gallon pitcher of sweetened iced tea and poured tea into both glasses before returning the pitcher to the refrigerator. "Do you want lemon?" she asked.

"You know I do," her mother answered.

She grabbed a covered container from inside and set it on the table. Jenny peeled off the lid and took a wedge of the sliced lemon inside. She sat at the table and squeezed the wedge into one of the glasses, and then dropped it into the glass.

Jillian sat across from her and reached across, grabbing a wedge for her tea as well. She repeated her mother's procedure.

"Don't get me wrong; I want your father to be happy. And I've got nothing against Pam. It just…surprised me, I guess," Jenny said, taking a sip.

———————

Jessup Leroy Lawson, or Pops as he insisted Kristin call him, said he was tickled pink that his confirmed bachelor of a grandson had finally fallen head over heels. Kristin was a pretty little thing, he proclaimed in a jovial demeanor. Santa Claus, she thought. He was certainly rotund enough. He had a snow-white beard. He even had the spectacles. And Dahlia was as pretty as her name, he told the child.

"Is my name pretty?" Dahlia asked, clearly never having been told that before.

"A Dahlia is a beautiful flower," Pops told her.

But for all his friendliness, Kristin felt certain that Pops was disappointed. He liked Dahlia; that was genuine enough, but his congenial attitude toward her felt forced.

They offered to take him out to lunch. Pops refused, saying they were having spaghetti for lunch, and he liked the spaghetti. Dex made a face that told Kristin Pops did not like the spaghetti. But Dex arranged for them to eat with Pops in the dining hall.

"Suit yourself," Pops said.

At lunch, Pops announced, "Y'all know my grandson, Dexter. This is his girlfriend...Christine?"

"Kristin," she corrected him. "Kristin Johnson."

"I'm sorry, Dear. My mistake. I knew it was something like that," Pops said. "And this little lady is Dahlia. I remember that because it is a beautiful flower." He smiled kindly at her daughter. But there was no doubt now. His kindness to her was halfhearted.

Once they had eaten, they rose to leave. "I'll go get the car," Kristin said, feeling self-conscious. She hurriedly walked toward the door. Dex scowled at Pops. She saw. He hobbled quickly after her, catching her before she made it to the door.

"I'm sorry," she said tearfully. "I don't know what I did. He doesn't like me."

"I like you," Dex assured her. "I love you." He pulled her close.

"I love you, too," she sniffed.

"Yeah?" He pulled her closer, his mouth hovering so close to hers.

She felt breathless. All she could manage was a nod and a whisper of "Yeah."

He kissed her softly at first, then deeper, leaving them both breathless.

"He'll come around," Dex whispered. "He had his hopes on me gettin' with the granddaughter of one of his friends. But she has a boyfriend whom she loves very much, and I love you. So, he has no choice. Now. Let's go get your daughter some stuff for that room of hers." He smiled, and suddenly, she believed him. It would be all right.

———

Once Kristin had walked through the door, Dex reeled and confronted his grandfather. "Why would you do that?" he admonished, his voice slightly raised. "I love that girl. This is my life and my choice."

"You're makin' it hard on yourself, Son. You don't need to do that. There are plenty of women of color, even if you don't like Willow. You don't have to face the scrutiny and the heartache."

"Oh, for…Pops, Grandma was white."

"You think I forgot my own wife? When we got married in 1968, we had to leave the state, Boy. It didn't matter what Virginia vs. Loving said. A black man and a white woman is a different story. White men don't like it," Pops insisted. "And don't tell me times have changed. I know they have, but not that much. You both deserve better. A life without that struggle."

"Would you, if you could do it over, take a life without that struggle?" Dex asked, taking Dahlia's hand and limping out the door.

He had delivered the fatal blow. He'd won. Pops wouldn't behave that way again. He had meant well. He actually had no problems with Kristin. Seriously, who could? Kristin was amazing. Pops had just wanted him to not have to live through the hardships he had. But, in just a week's time, he knew beyond any doubt that he'd face any hardship to be with her.

Kristin had pulled the Galaxie up to the door. Dex opened the passenger side door and leaned the seat forward for Dahlia. The little girl smiled at him and got into the backseat. He returned the seat to its upright position and got in. He closed the door. Just as Kristin pushed the clutch to shift into gear, Pops knocked on Dex's window. Dex rolled down the window.

"Kristin. Forgive me. I…I have no excuse. I've lived a life where I struggled so that my children and grandchildren wouldn't have to. I forgot for a minute that was why I had done it. You are lovely. And I hope you'll give me another chance," the old man said, leaning in the window.

Kristin sniffed and smiled. She took a deep breath. "Of course, Mr. Lawson. You're Dex's grandfather. You're my family," she replied.

"Pops. It's Pops, not Mr. Lawson."

"Alright…Pops. Thank you."

CHAPTER 19

Gordon entered his grandparents' house...strike that...his daughter's house. She was not home. She had to go to work at 1:30, she'd told him. Missy was home alone, but at 13, she was old enough to be alone for half an hour, especially with Lily around. He called out to her as he came through the door.

"Missy Michelle!" he called.

She emerged from her bedroom with the dog. "Hi, Granddaddy. Is Uncle Kenny okay?"

"He'll be fine, Sweetheart," he assured her.

"How about Pam-ma? She was pretty upset," Missy continued.

"She's fine, too," he said. Pam had indeed been "pretty upset." She adored her boys. She was a good mother. He liked that about her. He found himself smiling at the thought of her. She may have seemed reserved, but that woman had a wild side. And he liked that, too...and everything in between. Once, he'd thought that was the most frustrating thing about her. That wild, independent streak was dangerous. He'd thought it was dangerous to her. Nope. He was the one in danger...of losing his heart to Pamela Jean.

First, she was drop-dead gorgeous. She always had been. As a child, she'd been a little doll. As a teen, she was every boy's dream...until she'd gotten pregnant. As a young woman, she had been stunning. And now...she was intoxicating. She knew it, too. The first thing he noticed was her legs. *ZZ Top* sang about those legs. Then there was her ass. God, that was a masterpiece. She worked hard to maintain that body. Now, it's true there were health benefits, but the way she worked to sculpt herself, she knew exactly what she was doing. Pam Poole liked sex. And that body, she hid under that conservative exterior, proved it. Well, that...and last night. Who needed young girls? Pam was a woman. She knew what she was doing and how to do it right.

"Granddaddy?" Missy interrupted his thoughts.

"Hmmm? Oh, sorry, Sweetheart, I was somewhere else. What did you say?" Gordon asked.

"I asked if you're hungry," his granddaughter giggled. "You like Pam-ma?"

"I do, indeed. And no. I've already eaten," he said with a smile and a touch on the end of her nose.

She went back to her room, and he sat down in the living room. He flipped on the television. The scent of Lily of the Valley filled the room. He didn't really believe in ghosts. He only joked about those things. But he believed in his grandma. He knew her scent. He knew the feel of her. He felt her here.

"I'm sorry, Grandma. I should have come home more. And I know you would hate that I sold the place, but I promise, I wouldn't have sold it to anybody but the right person...And the money isn't for me. I...I put it in trust for Missy... and any subsequent grandchildren, which I think won't be long coming. I miss you. Oh, and I hope I still make you proud."

He closed his eyes and let the feeling of warmth and love envelop him as the scent slowly faded.

———

Mike pulled into the driveway and stared at that big, ugly orange truck. He got out of the cruiser and walked toward the front door. He rang the bell. Ginger Tilly, now seventy, opened the door to him.

"Mrs. Tilly," Mike greeted her.

"Yes," she replied.

"Is Curtis around? I need to talk to you both," he said,

handing her his card.

She looked at it and said, "Yeah, he's watchin' *Judge Judy*. Come on in, Detective."

Mike nodded and followed her inside. He removed his hat and walked behind her down a hallway. The house could not have changed much since the eighties. The flowered wallpaper, the furniture, even the TV were straight out of a time lock.

She led him to a family room at the back of the house, an add-on from the mid-seventies. Curtis sat up straight as he entered.

"Mr. Tilly, Mrs. Tilly...there's been a development on your son's case. His death has been ruled a homicide. I've been assigned to investigate it," he said. He took out the court ruling and handed it to Curtis. "I know this is a long time coming. I hope I can get you some closure."

"We went through this thirty-five years ago...36 in August. There was no evidence," Ginger gasped, sitting beside her husband.

"Well, that's...not true. But I can't reveal the evidence. It would impede the investigation. But I am...very close to an arrest. I promise you that," Mike told them, smiling.

The phone rang. Another throwback to the 80s; it was a landline. Ginger excused herself to answer it. She returned moments later. "That was Quinton. He asked if you would wait a moment for him to get here, so you can explain this to him. Honestly, I think we need...help comprehending," she implored.

"I don't mind waiting. This was my last stop for the day. I'm just on my way home," he agreed. He accepted Ginger's offer of iced tea and peach cobbler. It was good cobbler.

Quinton Tilly arrived some 10 minutes later. He rushed in like a bull in a ring. "What the hell is going on?" he bellowed, coming through the door.

"We're back here," Curtis called to his youngest child.

He stormed into the family room. "You? Your bitch sister is the one trying to jack me up about her kid. She send you over here to torment my parents?"

"No. My sister, as you so astutely point out, is Kristin Johnson, but she's not trying to jack you up. You signed to relinquish your parental rights. She's happy with that. I'm here because your brother's cold case has been reopened, and I am notifying the family as required. Jacob's death has been officially ruled as murder. I'm close to an arrest," Mike calmly repeated.

"I don't believe you," Quinton protested.

"Why the pushback, Quinton? You were 1. It's not like you murdered Jacob," Mike said coyly. Quinton knew nothing. Mike knew that, but that guy really got his goat. He liked toying with him.

"Your father is…" Curtis started.

"Maxim Johnson," Mike finished.

"I never liked that guy," Curtis huffed.

"Me neither," Mike chuckled. "He's a dick. I know why I don't like him. He convinced my 15-year-old mother to sleep with him, resulting in my and my brother's births, then he spent our entire lives trying to cover it up. He did the same thing to my mother-in-law…and my wife. Why don't you like him?" Mike asked, smiling.

Curtis looked at him like he was crazy. The old man laughed…hard.

"It's a real question, Mr. Tilly. And believe it or not, it's pertinent," Mike said, leaning forward.

"No real reason. He leered at the neighbor girl a lot," Curtis said.

"My mother-in-law, his soon-to-be ex-wife," Mike affirmed.

"Yeah. I…His wife and kids got into a fatal car accident… and a year later, he marries one of the girls he…"

"Yeah, he's a piece of crap. I get it," Mike agreed. "But there's more to it. Isn't there?"

"Ned. Ned thought he hung the moon back then. I mean. I know that Max Johnson's desires leaned toward young girls, but he had a way with young teens in general. They loved him. All the kids in this neighborhood. I didn't like that Ned spent so much time across the street."

"Really? I don't remember anything like that," Quinton interjected.

"You were too young, Quinton. My father's window is 15- to 16-year-olds. He's like a Pied Piper. He got three teens to beat up my brother just a couple of days ago. Do you think he could have gotten Ned to…do things like that?"

"Sure. I think Ned would have done just about anything for him," Curtis replied.

"And Jacob?"

"Oh, no," Ginger said. "Jacob didn't like Maxim. At all. He was honestly a little afraid of him."

"Do you think your father…?" Quinton asked.

"No. Not at all. Max is a manipulator. But he's a coward. He wouldn't…kill someone…and not a child. If he could do that…he'd have killed me and Kenny when we were little, but I think a disturbed teen may have thought that it would please Max, and they took initiative," Mike told them.

"You mean a kid in the neighborhood? I see. Well, there were a few that seemed obsessed. Ned could tell you," Curtis offered.

"That would be helpful. Thank you. Let him know, I'd like to speak with him. Anyway. I have to get home. My father-in-law is going out on a date with my mother, and I need to take care of my daughter. Have him call me." He stood.

"Your mother is dating your father-in-law?" Quinton asked, shaking his head. "Man, that's messed up."

"Yeah. I'm not altogether on board," Mike agreed. He thanked them again and pointed to the back door. "Mind if I go out that door?"

"Oh, sure. Quinton will walk out with you," Curtis said.

Mike walked out, with Quinton behind him. He nodded at the truck as they rounded the house. "Hey, does your dad leave his keys in that old truck? It was used in another case, and I was just curious. I remembered when we walked past it."

"No. They're inside on the key hook thing by the back door you just went out," Quinton replied.

"Okay. Maybe it was hotwired. Thanks, Quinton." He held out his hand and shook Quinton's.

———

Pam emerged from the bathroom as Kenny shuffled downstairs. "Hey," she called to him.

He turned to look back up at her. "Yeah?" he asked.

"How do I look?" She was nervous, dammit. She knew Gordon liked her legs. He'd made that abundantly clear, so she chose a short, form-fitting cotton dress in a soft sage green. No matter what she wore, she knew all eyes would be on Helen Madison. But she'd at least like Gordon's eyes to be on her.

"The green looks pretty with your new hair color," he teased.

"Brat," she hurled at him. He knew that her hair color was honey blonde. The hair dye merely removed the few strands of gray.

"You should probably wear shoes, though," he continued.

"I'm going to wear shoes. I just haven't put them on yet," she retorted.

"The gold strappy ones...that show off your French vanilla pedicure," he continued, pointing at her toes.

"Really? The gold ones? With green?"

"That's money," he snickered. "Yes. The gold ones. And

that chunky gold chain choker, with plain gold hoop earrings. Nothing too flashy. You can't out flash Helen. I like the pastel coral tones in your makeup. You look very pretty."

"Thanks, Babe," she grinned. She hurried to her room and tried his suggestions in front of her full-length mirror.

Her hair was newly cut in a short bob wedge, with a natural curl to it. It was sassy. She had worried she wouldn't pull off sassy. But she had to admit, she liked the look. And Kenny was right about the shoes. They made her feet look great…not to mention her legs and ass. He was right about the jewelry, too. Exactly when had Kenny developed such a keen fashion sense? she wondered.

She was no stranger to dating. She couldn't explain why she was so nervous this time. She'd never noticed Kenny's ability to pair shoes and jewelry because she'd never asked him before. She'd never cared so much about how she looked. What was she doing?

She took a couple of deep breaths. She was suffering from spring fever, she concluded. Gordon was hot. That was all there was to it. Only she didn't believe herself. She had a lifetime of evidence that it was more than that.

CHAPTER 20

Dahlia was in her room, making it her own with all the new bedding and wall art they had bought at Target, not to mention the new clothes, shoes, and toys. They also bought Muffy a new doggie bed and new toys. Dex insisted on stopping at Verizon to add Kristin and Dahlia to his cell plan. He got Dahlia an iPad, too. Dahlia was in 7th heaven. Plus, she'd called Kristin "Mom" all afternoon.

Dex had collapsed on her sofa, on the chaise end, with his leg up. Joe had offered to store the majority of Dex's things in his new barn. Kristin had brought in his boxes of clothing and daily necessities…which included a box marked "Semper Fi" that she assumed contained mementos of his time in the Marines. She put away his clothes and toiletries where they had cleared out space for him, but she left that "Semper Fi" box for him, not wanting to invade his privacy.

She finally settled down in her office to finish grading some papers from before Easter break and to work on her lesson plans for the next day. She was obsessively organized, so her lesson plans came together quickly. Grading was not working out as well. She had one student who seemed to have a sudden big drop in her grades, and she was worried about what might be going on with her student. She spent extra time grading her work, trying to see some kind of pattern. But the only pattern she saw was an overall decline in the student's performance across the board. Her fear was bullying and cyberbullying. The girl's family was struggling financially. Her father was quite ill, and he was the main breadwinner.

The situation led her to scrap her lesson plan for the computer lab. She started over with a lesson on cyberbullying, how to recognize it, and what to do if it happened. Consequently, she lost track of time.

Dex knocked on her office door. She called for him to come in. She was on the floor on her hands and knees, digging through a ton of source material, looking for the right approach. He laughed.

"Shut up," she laughed back. "Would you happen to know anybody who is an expert in cyberbullying who can talk to 4th graders about it?" she asked, exasperated.

"Sure," he said. "When?"

"I was hoping for tomorrow," she laughed, realizing that would be impossible.

"Um…that might not be enough notice, but I have a Marine friend who works in that field now. He might be able to do it next week."

"So, I should just go with my original lesson plan, then?" she laughed.

"Yeah," he said, reaching his hand out to help her up.

"I guess I'm done then." She took his hand and stood. "I'm sometimes impetuous," she explained.

"Oh, you mean like agreeing to marry a guy you've known a week?" he chided.

"Yeah, like that," she chided back, kissing him.

They decided on a quick dinner of leftovers they'd brought home from Mike and Jillian's yesterday. The three of them sat around the dining room table while Muffy begged for and was given scraps.

Dahlia laughed when Kristin gave the dog a piece of ham. "Mama…I mean…Kierra…said dogs don't get people food," she explained.

"Well, Mom, that's me, says puppies are people too,"

Kristin cooed, giving the dog another small piece of ham. "But not too much, cutie patootie. It will make you sick if you eat too much."

A heavy fist banged on the front door. Dex didn't like it, he explained. A normal person would ring the bell. An angry person banged like a hammer. He motioned for Kristin and Dahlia to stay put and went to the door himself, limping on his broken foot.

He opened the door cautiously. "Who the hell are you?" a man demanded.

"Dexter Lawson. I live here. You?" he retorted.

"Quinton Tilly. I'm looking for Kristin Johnson. I thought this was her house."

"Kristie, Baby, you know a Quinton Tilly?" Dex called over his shoulder.

She sighed and rose from her seat. "Yeah. He's Dahlia's biological father," she replied, walking toward the door. She peered around Dex at the man she had once loved, until he broke her heart. "What do you want, Quinton? You signed. You said you want nothing to do with her."

"I'm not here about the kid. I'm here about your bastard of a brother," he said hastily. "Call him off."

"Call him off what?" she asked.

"He says he's about to make an arrest in Jacob's murder. My parents are distraught. They don't need his bullshit, Kristin. He's doing it because of you and that kid," Quinton demanded.

Kristin laughed. "If Mike said he's about to make an arrest, it's because he's about to make an arrest. I have nothing to do with it. Have a good night, Quinton." She nodded at Dex, and he closed the door.

"Dahlia, show me your room, Honey. Forget that nasty man," she said to her wide-eyed daughter. Dahlia smiled and ran to her, taking her hand and pulling her upstairs. Muffy followed them like a little white yapping cloud.

————

Pam opened the door. She could swear Gordon was dumbstruck. But he recovered quickly. He smiled.

"You're beautiful. Too pretty for a dark theater," he said.

He looked pretty good, too, she had to admit. He looked good in anything he put on, though. He was just wearing jeans and a button-down shirt under his black leather jacket. And, wow, he smelled good.

Missy tugged at his jacket, and he seemed to remember for the first time that she was with him. "Oh, right," he laughed. "Missy is here to keep Kenny company as promised."

"Hey, Sweetheart," Pam greeted her granddaughter, moving aside to let her in. "Kenny is in the living room, watching *Jumanji*."

"The Rock, or the old one?" she asked.

"The Rock," Pam said. "I ordered a pizza for y'all. I already paid on the app...including the tip."

"Okay," Missy replied with a smile.

Kenny called out for her. Her face beamed. Kids loved Kenny. Of course, he was kind of like a kid...but not really. She bounded off to the living room.

"Well, goodbye, then," Pam called to her retreating form.

"Bye," both she and Kenny called back.

Pam laughed. Gordon grinned. Pam straightened her dress, checked that she had her purse, and took Gordon's arm.

The Trans Am of his youth was long gone. Tonight, he was driving a Suburban. He opened the passenger side door for her, and she literally had to climb in, a task hindered by the pencil skirt of her dress. She heard him fight off a laugh as his hand landed firmly on her posterior, and he gave her a gentle shove. She laughed. "Well, that was graceful."

"I had a great view and didn't mind giving a helping

hand," he teased.

"I bet," she replied. He closed the door and ran around the front of the SUV to get in on his side.

As he pulled onto the road, she asked, "So, where are we going?"

He smiled. "Yeah, Beau called this afternoon. He wanted to know if we could skip the movie. A roadhouse in Stafford is having an 80s trivia night. I hope you don't mind."

"Of course not. 80s trivia is more conducive to conversation than a movie, anyway," she replied, settling into the seat.

He was quiet for a moment. "Jillian has told me some of what happened…with Kenny. I…I'm sorry. I've seen lots of wounded warriors over my lifetime. Some have even been close friends," he broached the subject.

"I'm sure you have. You served in the Navy for a long time. I don't mind talking about it. He's…doing really well now. He has anxiety. He does suffer from sudden anger and mood swings. I'm sure you've noticed," she explained. He nodded.

"It's not unusual. His scars…it was a fairly significant head wound?"

"Yeah. He has limited vision in his left eye and no peripheral vision on that side. He's also deaf in that ear. He still gets headaches. And then, there are the seizures. But the doctors at Walter Reed didn't expect him to be able to walk or talk again… and well, you can't get him to shut up," she laughed.

"He does like to talk," Gordon said, smiling. "How's his memory?"

"Oh, it's not too bad. He doesn't remember being wounded, which is a blessing. He has some short-term memory loss after a seizure, but it's not too bad… Though I think that's because he works hard to remember things. He has all kinds of memory tricks he uses. He's actually very bright. He always has been. He was an honor student, you know," she said proudly.

"Both your boys are good people, Pam. I don't blame you for being proud of them," he told her, squeezing her hand.

"Thanks. I am proud of them. I know I could have done better, but they turned out great anyway, despite me," she chuckled.

"You did great. You're a fantastic mother. Don't you ever think otherwise. We all just do the best we can, Pam. You were little more than a child yourself. Hell, so was I. Lord knows, I was no prize of a father. I was always…gone. Granted, some of that was because of the Navy, but I could have done better. I should have done better. I should have known…" he bemoaned.

It was her turn to squeeze his hand. "Jillian loves you. To her, you are the best father in the world, and hers is the only opinion that counts," she told him. He nodded again, fighting back tears.

"Hey, this is supposed to be a date. Let's talk about less serious things. Like, what's your favorite color?" he suggested.

"I take my colors very seriously," she teased.

"Oh, my apologies," he chuckled. "I guess you're right. Colors influence mood. They are serious." He was quiet for a few seconds. "I like green. Like the color of your dress."

"I made a good choice then?"

"Hmmm. I especially like it on the floor."

"Oh my God!" she roared in laughter.

———

Mike, instead of going home, drove back out to Oak Grove and pulled into the Stop In, where Jillian was working until 10 pm. He just wanted to see his wife for a minute, and it was a good time to fill the cruiser's gas tank.

He pulled up to the gas pump and got out. He filled up and turned to go inside when he noticed Caleb and Steve in a car with two other teen boys. He pretended not to see them and went into the store. He walked to the back wall of refrigerated sodas and grabbed a Coke. The teens had not moved, though they had parked in front of the store, so he perused the snack and candy aisle. They still had not moved. They were waiting for him to pay, he decided.

He walked up to his beautiful wife, smiled, and said, "Get down."

She looked at him, confused. But she ducked down behind the counter just as the bullets rained through the front window.

Mike was quick. He ran at the child about to come out of the candy aisle, with her father, tackling the father and pulling the girl back into the cover provided by the shelves.

He drew his weapon and returned fire.

Unfortunately for Steve, Caleb, and the two other boys, he knew how to shoot and didn't fire haphazardly. Only Caleb survived, and he was shot in the arm and leg and was bleeding profusely.

Mike lowered his weapon. The father and daughter peered out from behind the shelving. Jillian slowly stood up, shaking. "I...quit," she croaked.

"Okay, Baby. Is it okay if I keep working?" he teased, leaning against the counter as he tried to catch his breath.

"Oh my God, Mike, you'd better," she said, coming out from behind the counter and hugging him.

"It's broad daylight," the father mused, slowly standing. For the first time, Mike recognized him.

"Oh, hey. You're Blake West, Bethy's brother. Are y'all alright?" Mike asked him as he pulled Jillian closer.

"We are," Blake said, "thanks to you."

He released Jillian and quickly moved outside to cuff Caleb and check the other gunmen. He called dispatch on his radio as he went. "Officer involved shooting, Stop In, route 3, Oak Grove, 4 casualties, all perps, 3 deceased, 1 incapacitated, need an ambulance."

———

Gordon turned on the radio. It was a local station, one of those that broadcast national programming on a local transmitter. The news and advertising were local, though. The song was *Kiss of a Rose*. But before it ended, the local newscaster shut off the feed and interrupted with a news break.

"There has been an officer-involved shooting at the Stop-In in Oak Grove in Westmoreland County. Four gunmen opened fire on a Westmoreland County Deputy as he was paying for his gas. There are 4 casualties. This is a breaking story, and we will bring you more details as we get them," the radio said.

Gordon went pale and slammed on the brakes. "Jillian's at work!" he exclaimed.

"Mike's on duty," Pam added.

"Fuck!" Gordon said, making a U-turn. "Norstar, call Beau Madison."

The phone rang twice. "Hey, we were thinking Outback. What do y'all think?"

"Um, there's been a shooting at Stop-In…and Jillian's at work…and an officer was involved. Mike is on duty…and we're not going to make it. We're heading back to Oak Grove," Gordon explained quickly.

"Jesus. We understand. Let us know, okay?" Beau replied.

Gordon drove like a bat out of hell. But the intersection of Route 205 and Route 3 was completely shut down. A state trooper was stopping traffic and diverting it back toward Colonial Beach. As the trooper approached the Suburban, Gordon rolled down his window. "I need you folks to turn around," the trooper advised them.

"My daughter is the clerk at the Stop-in," Gordon said nervously. "Is my daughter okay?"

The trooper looked like he'd been struck.

"My son is Deputy Mike Poole," Pam added. "Is he there?"

The trooper nodded. "Yeah, Mike's there. Hold on." He walked away for a second. He spoke into his radio. Then he moved the barrier to let Gordon through. He replaced it as Gordon drove through and stopped the car behind them.

Gordon pulled into the parking lot and jumped out of the SUV. He ran around and opened Pam's door, literally lifting her out of the seat and setting her on the ground. He scanned the parking lot, searching for any sign of his daughter or her husband. He saw Mike first. He was talking to a state trooper and the sheriff. He pointed, and Pam ran to her son.

Then he saw Jillian. She was talking to another state trooper.

"Jillian!" he called and waved.

"That's my father," she told the trooper and waved him over.

He grabbed her and looked her over. She did indeed appear to be fine. He pulled her to him and hugged her tightly.

"Daddy, I can't breathe," she said after a moment.

————

Mike saw Pam coming and braced himself as she flung herself into his arms. "I'm fine," he said.

"I'm sorry, I thought you said the clerk is your wife," Trooper Yancey said to Mike as Pam covered his face in kisses.

"The clerk is his wife. This is his…" The sheriff leaned forward and whispered, "Sister, but not really. She's his mother."

"Well, his mother's not bad lookin'," the trooper whispered back.

"I can hear you," Mike said, pushing Pam back to arm's length. "Jesus, Mama, stop. Pam, I'm fine." Pam flung her arms back around his neck and hung on for dear life.

"You can't get wounded, too. I can't take it!" she cried.

"His brother was badly wounded in Afghanistan about 8 years ago," the sheriff explained. "Twin brother. Her hysteria is well-founded. Mike…uh…take care of Pam. We're done."

Mike grabbed Pam by the shoulders. "I'm okay. I promise. Not a mark on me."

Pam was breathing heavily. She nodded. But she was fighting tears.

"Mama, I swear," he said, trying to convince her. Usually, he called her Pam. But in intense moments, both he and Kenny had always called her "Mama." Now was surely one of those moments. He hugged her again. "Sorry about your date. You look pretty."

Pam laughed and kissed his cheek again.

The sheriff came back. "It's a clean shoot, Mike. It's all on the security camera. Caleb isn't talking, but the other three are his brother Steve, Bobby Furst, 14, and Ryan Taylor, 16. Caleb, Steve, and Bobby all lived in Westmoreland Shores. Ryan Taylor lives in Placid Bay."

"Max," Mike said, shaking his head. "I just said he wasn't a killer. Damn."

"We're getting a search warrant for his home," the sheriff added.

"You won't find anything. Jenny kicked him out yesterday. You'll need the warrant for his vehicle and apartment in Richmond…and his offices," Mike told him. "Sheriff…where in Placid Bay?"

"Um… 84 Mattox Avenue. Out by the civic center," the sheriff replied.

Mike smiled. "Right next door to 86 Mattox Avenue, home of Ned Tilly."

"Is that significant?"

"There was DNA under Jacob Tilly's fingernails. Tom Palmer gave me some photos that were not included in the evidence box, but he kept. Ned Tilly had scratches on his neck. At the time…they lived across the street from Max and Maddie

Johnson," Mike said. "I just left the Tillys, informing them of the updates on the case. I asked them to have Ned contact me."

"And not ten minutes later, you were being shot at by Ned's teenage neighbor. That's quite a coinkydink. We'll look into it. Go home. Take your wife. We'll let you know."

CHAPTER 21

Mike stared at what had been the gravel pit. It was grown over now. The pit was full of trees. Of course, it was still a pit. It was a very dangerous place. There were several places where the sides of the pit had given way and slid down the steep incline into the hole. He made his way around the perimeter cautiously.

He didn't know what he expected to find. Maybe he just needed to see the site of the murder. He'd repaired the fence first thing after buying the property, but he hadn't entered the fenced-off area. It was a blemish on his property that he wished did not exist.

One area where the earth had slid into the pit was near the gate. The slide had happened within the last two weeks because it had not been there when he'd repaired the fence. As he peered over the edge, about halfway down the slide, he saw it in the mud and clay…blue and red fabric. "Son of a bitch," he swore, taking out his phone and calling Tom Palmer. "Hey, Tom. I think a mudslide out at the pit has uncovered Jacob's missing clothes. Yeah. We're home. Yeah, we're both okay. Jill's had a scare, but we're okay. Thanks for asking."

He walked out of the gate, locked it, and walked leisurely back to the house. Lily was at his hip. He gave her a scratch behind her ears. She responded with a tail wag. As he neared the house, Gordon, who with Pam had gone back to his mother's townhouse…well, his…he rented it to her and Kenny at the cost of the mortgage… pulled into the driveway. They were bringing Missy back home after their aborted date. Mike felt kind of bad about that. Pam looked beautiful. It was obvious she had really been looking forward to it.

Kenny jumped out of the back seat and ran to him. Lily growled. "Heel," Mike told her. She sat. Kenny flung both arms around his brother. "I'm okay, Ken."

It was clear Kenny had been crying. So had Missy, and she flung her arms around her father's waist on the other side of him. Like he did with his mother, she sometimes called him by his name, having known him as Mike, and not as her father, for all of her life. But in the moment, he was "daddy."

"Daddy," she cried. "You could have been killed."

"I'm alright. It's scary, I know. But it is part of my job," he replied soothingly, but not wanting to hide the truth from her either. She needed to know that his job was very dangerous, but he didn't want her worrying needlessly. He wasn't quite sure where the balance lay. He decided honesty was the best course.

"You said that you'd never shot anyone in the line of duty!" she lamented.

"Well...I hadn't...until today. But if it makes you feel better, I am the only one in the county to have done so for 30 years," he replied.

"Why would that make me feel better?" Missy wailed, smacking his chest.

"I...I really don't know," he answered truthfully.

He lifted her onto his back, piggyback style, and carried her into the house, with Kenny right behind him.

Gordon and Pam followed. Inside, Bethany was sitting with Jillian. She and Joe had come over as soon as she had left her brother's. Joe stood across the room, by the piano. Their three kids sat on the floor, cross-legged and stunned. Mike let Missy slide off his back. "Really, y'all, we're okay," he said for the millionth time.

"Yeah, I know ya are," Joe said. "Bethany just needed to see for herself." He winked. "We just left Blake's. He's a nervous wreck, too."

"Thanks, Joe," he sighed.

———

Max stood on the doorstep of his daughter's house. He had done things he knew he should not have done. But that was his weakness. He had always loved his daughter. In fact, he had deeply loved her mother and her sister, as well, and had grieved their loss with Kristin. He had sat beside her bed while she was recovering, in a medically induced coma, praying for her to wake up. He knew he needed help. He'd known it for years, obviously. But he kept getting away with it.

As for Mike and Kenny, he truly never meant to harm them. He wanted to distance himself from them...and their mother, but he'd never truly hurt them. He hadn't told those boys to hurt Kenny. While it was true he'd never been a father to his sons, he had made certain that they were provided for. He'd settled a large amount of money on Pam after the affair. It had been paid to her father, as she was still a minor. He had no idea why that kid said he'd paid them.

He rang the bell.

Her new boyfriend opened the door. He knew he was there. It wasn't a surprise. His car was in her driveway. "Hello... Dex, is it?"

"Yes. Dex Lawson," he answered. Max offered his hand. Dex just looked at it.

"Is Kristin here? I need to talk to her," he pleaded.

"She's here, but whether she talks to you or not is her decision." With that declaration, he shut the door in Max's face. Max stood there, feeling indignant but with the realization that he probably deserved it. No, that he absolutely deserved it.

The door opened, and Kristin stood there. "What?" she asked.

"I never...I'm...sorry. I swear I wanted a good home for

Dahlia. I checked her out. I never thought…And I never should have…" he cried. He was stymied. He had no clue what to say. There was nothing he could say. She was entitled to hate him. He hated himself. "I guess…words just don't do it." He turned to walk away.

"Dad? Do you even love any of us?"

"In my way, I love you all. Especially you. I guess…I just loved myself more. I'm…not a very good person. But I swear, I'd never physically harm those boys. I wouldn't." God, he hoped she'd believe him.

That's when Tom Palmer pulled into her driveway. He got out of his police car and drew his weapon. "Maxim Johnson! I have a warrant for your arrest for the solicitation to murder Mike Poole and Jillian Poole. Put your hands on your head and kneel on the ground."

He did as he was told.

"I didn't, Kristin! I swear," he exclaimed as Tom cuffed him.

————

Aaron Muse was the deputy who showed up regarding the pajamas. It was clear to Jillian that Mike had expected Tom.

She watched as he and Joe walked outside to talk to Aaron. Aaron was a good deputy, Mike had told her, just young. The three men talked for a moment, then they all got into the police car and rode off down the old gravel pit road.

Her father and Pam walked out the back door and settled down at the picnic table to watch from a distance. She wondered what her father was thinking, having been there that day almost 36 years ago…but so had Pam…and her mother. There was something surreal in that realization.

She and Bethany followed them out and sat with them. The kids were drawn to the scene as well. Missy, Jessup, and Ryan, sat on the embankment down to the road in the grass with Lily.

Meghan, soon to be 5, sat with her mother. Bethany's expanding belly scraped against the tabletop.

The men were just barely visible at the top of the hill. They hooked a harness to Aaron and attached a line to the squad car. He walked through the gate with Joe and Mike. The three of them disappeared into the trees.

Jillian's phone rang. She looked at the caller ID. Kristin was calling. She answered the call. "Hey, Kristin. What? Yes, it's true. No, we're fine. Mike is…amazing. He saved everybody… except those kids." Jillian sniffed quietly into the phone. "What? Oh. They did? You believe him? How can you believe him? I see. Mike's at the gravel pit. I'm sure he's just not answering because he's in the middle of something. Give him 15 to 20 minutes. He'll call you back. Yeah. Love you, too. Yes." A tear dripped down her nose as she disconnected. Pam reached across the table and covered her hand with her own. Jillian smiled sadly. "Tom Palmer arrested Max half an hour ago. They found duplicate checks to all the kids in his office at the house," she told her mother-in-law and father.

"Well, that's good then, right?" Bethany asked.

Gordon lowered his head. "That bitch. Jesus."

Jillian laughed. "You see, Bethany…my mother is the only one who writes the checks. Max doesn't even have a checkbook. She signs his name. Max didn't do it. My mother did," Jillian sobbed.

———

Mike sat across from Kierra in the interrogation room. "Where'd you get the keys to Curtis's truck, Kierra?" he asked. It was the only question he had. The rest didn't matter.

"Why should I tell you?" she laughed maniacally. "I don't owe you shit."

"You owe me everything," Mike replied. "You owe Kristin and Dahlia…and even Rich. Hell, you even owe Max. You owe us all…Mama, Kenny, Missy, Jillian…but especially me. I believed you, Kierra. I tried to help you. And it was all a lie. Did Rich even hit you? Or was it Big Billy? Or maybe it was Jenny. Where'd you get the keys?"

She sat silently.

He stared her right in the eyes.

"I want my lawyer present," she said at last, when he was unmoved by her silence.

He nodded and sat back.

"Aren't you going to leave?" she asked, exasperated by his behavior.

"No. I'll wait right here with you for him to get here. He's in the building…so…" Mike said, taking out his phone and looking through his apps. He just sat there until Terry Roland joined them some 15 minutes later.

"I hope you didn't persist in questioning my client after she requested that I be present," Terry sneered.

"Nope, I looked at Facebook," Mike retorted with a grin. "You can check the footage if you want."

"Um…okay."

"Where'd you get Curtis's key to the truck, Kierra?" he asked again.

"Why is that important?" she sputtered.

"Because it tells me who was in on it, and you might get a deal," Mike said coolly.

She looked dumbly at her attorney. "What kind of deal?" he asked. The prosecutor entered. "She'll plead to murder 1. Because that is clearly what this crime was, she'll do the minimum 20 years and pay a fine of $100,000. She'll be eligible for parole in 17 years. She's not in a position to seek much more."

She leaned in and whispered to her attorney. He whispered back. "Yeah, okay," she said after a few minutes thought. "Ned gave me the keys the day before. He said he wanted Big Billy out of Chloe and Frannie's lives. He even paid me to do it…"

"He…paid you? To commit a crime you wanted to commit?" Mike sputtered. "How much?"

"$45,000," she answered. "I'll show you the transaction."

Mike walked away gratified but still somehow dumbfounded. He went directly to his father's cell.

Max jumped up from his seat on the cot when Mike approached. "I didn't, Son. I swear."

"You don't get to call me 'Son,' but I know. I know. Tell me the truth about Jenny," he said.

"What about her?" Max asked. "She's my wife."

Mike stared.

"Okay…She was the first…teenager. She flirted with me…and batted her eyes, and I…gave in to temptation. But I swear, she really did seduce me. I may have…later…but she awakened it in me. That's why…I married her after Maddie. As a penance," he told Mike. "I wouldn't physically hurt you or Kenny. I wouldn't."

"What about Jacob?"

"Who?"

"Jacob Tilly. The child Ned murdered…for you. His own brother."

"The kid across the street? No. I swear. He was a weird little kid, but I didn't do that. I didn't. I…I told that kid to forget that he saw me and Jenny together. I paid him $50. That's it. Ned killed him? Really?"

"Did Jenny know that he'd seen you together?" Mike persisted.

"Sure. She was the one who saw him lurking…Why?" Max asked.

Mike shook his head.

"When?" he asked.

"Um… about a week before he…died. God, I swear. I didn't!" Max repeated.

"Okay."

Mike turned and walked away. Ray was about to be arraigned. He was on his way to court. Hopefully, Mike could get there before he was called before the judge.

He made his way to the courtroom. Ray was still in the holding cell. Mike breathed a sigh of relief.

"Who asked you to do what you did to Kenny?" he asked. "I mean, the actual words came out of whose mouth?"

Ray was shaking. "Mrs. Johnson said that Dr. Johnson needed us to do a favor, and she gave us each a check for $200, but they were signed by him."

"Did you see him sign them?" Mike asked.

"No. They were already made out to us and signed."

"Okay…and who asked you to come into my home with a gun, Ray?" Mike asked.

"Well…it was Mrs. Johnson, again. Dr. Johnson was in Richmond."

"And the boys who shot up the Stop In? Do you know who asked them to do that?" Mike asked.

"No. I swear. I don't."

"Okay. Thanks."

Mike walked out of the building and got into his squad car. He stared at the steering wheel for a second. He was shaking. Tom Palmer opened the passenger side door and got in beside him. "Max says he didn't do it. Ray said Jenny gave them the checks. Jillian said Jenny is the only one who ever wrote checks and that she signs Maxim's name. Kristin concurred. And I…I never believed he was capable of actually trying to kill me. But I believe Jenny is," Mike said sadly. "I even think she manipulated Ned to kill his brother, Jacob."

"Why?"

"Jacob saw her with Maxim…after she was with Gordon, about a week before he died. She didn't want Gordon to find out and lose her status as Queen Bee at W&L."

"I got the DNA back. It's Ned's. He killed his brother. I guess we'll find out soon enough if Jenny had anything to do with it," Tom said before climbing out of the car and closing the door.

Jenny sat happily in her living room on her Mario Bellini sofa, like the Queen upon her throne. Jenny Johnson was at the pinnacle of society in Westmoreland County. Just as her husband's career was in freefall, she was escaping with the admiration of her peers and setting her sights on the next King, Clint Stevens, a prominent attorney, representing her in her divorce from her disgraced husband of 21 years. He was married, true, but so had Maxim been.

Clint sat across from her, all business, talking about joint assets.

She grinned like the Cheshire cat. Kristin was stubbornly falling in love with Joe's friend. She was no threat to Jenny's domain. Jillian had survived the shooting, as had Mike, but the blame had landed on Maxim. Jillian was easily controlled. And Jillian could control Mike. She wanted to get Missy, but that would happen. Missy would see the benefits of living with her once summer hit. She had the money, the pool, the big house. Even if the shooting hadn't gone to plan, it would still go her way.

She smiled seductively at Clint and feigned despair over the state of her life, wiping away imaginary tears. It was close to 4 pm now. All she had to do was keep him here until she could insist that he needed to stay for dinner. That's when the doorbell rang. She peered out the window to see Kristin, her boyfriend, and that child on her doorstep. Kristin pushed the doorbell again.

"Excuse me," she said to Clint. "That's Max's daughter." She rose gracefully from the sofa and made her way to the door.

"What is it, Dear? I'm in a meeting with my attorney," she cooed as she opened the door.

"I want my dollhouse," Kristin said happily. "I mean, Dahlia wants it. Would you mind? Dex borrowed Joe's truck to transport it." She pointed to the garish vehicle.

"Oh, um, I guess not. It is yours after all," Jenny said, trying not to grit her teeth. That dollhouse was quite valuable. But it had indeed been a Christmas gift to Kristin. She couldn't see a way out of releasing it to her. Clint smiled, and Jenny decided it was of little consequence. Let Kristin take it. She moved aside. Kristin ushered the child inside. The boyfriend hobbled in behind her. The sparkle on Kristin's finger caught Jenny's eye. Dear Lord, they were engaged. That was perfect. "Oh, congratulations, Sweetheart," she exclaimed, grabbing Kristin's hand. Then she leaned forward and whispered, "How did things go at school? You know…what with having a child out of wedlock 9 years ago and being engaged so quickly…to a man of color."

"Just fine, thank you," Kristin retorted, pulling her hand away. "Last room on the right, Dahlia, Honey."

"Oh, I seem to have upset her," Jenny pretended to lament.

The doorbell rang again. She was still standing there, so she opened it, somewhat thoughtlessly. She immediately shut it. Dear Lord, what was he doing here? She recomposed herself and said to Clint, "Excuse me, an old friend from school. I'll just see what he wants." She opened the door and shooed him back, stepping outside and closing the door behind her.

"What are you doing?" she hissed. "You can't be seen here."

"Mike Poole said he was close to an arrest for my brother's murder, you stupid cunt. I just want you to know that if I go down, you go down with me. You're the one who smothered him. I just held him down. But of course, I'm the one he scratched. It's my DNA on his body. So, you know, I'm the one he's after."

Ned Tilly hissed. "You said the kids would take care of it. Only he shot them all. He's even been asking my brother how Kierra might have gotten the keys to Dad's truck. So, he's lookin' at me for Big Billy's murder, too, when it was your money and your plan."

"Calm down. Just tell them it was Max. He told you it was for something else."

"Like what?"

"Do I have to think of everything? He told you Kierra needed to borrow the truck to move furniture...something like that. Whatever you do, do not tell them I was in any way involved. Do you understand me? Who do you think they'll believe? A stupid oaf like you, or me? Keep it to yourself that I smothered Jacob, and that I gave you the money for Kierra to kill Billy Walsh. He shouldn't have stolen from me."

Suddenly, there were police cars from every direction... State Police, Deputies, and even Colonial Beach police. They all emerged from their vehicles with their weapons drawn. Mike stepped out of his car and smiled.

"Good job, Ned. We got it loud and clear," he said.

CHAPTER 22

Mike awakened as Jillian gently kissed his mouth. He smiled and pulled her close. "Now that's the best way to wake up," he said huskily. She giggled, and he rolled her to her back and kissed her as she wrapped herself around him.

"What time is it?" he asked, remembering what day it was.

"7 am. There's plenty of time," she answered, bringing his attention back to her.

"Oh, good," he replied, kissing her again. She was right. There was plenty of time. And she was the most important thing in the world. He had wanted to show her that ever since their quickie wedding, but life had blown up, and they had barely been alone. They had had sex, of course…but moments of pure intimacy had been few. Right now, all he wanted was time alone with her. Instead of an overwhelming desire and ardent need, he wanted a slow burn.

That seemed to be what she wanted, too, as she responded with breathless anticipation. They were in their own world. No one existed but the two of them. Lily's barking was off in the distance. Missy's laughter from the living room was too far away to interrupt. Even the odd humming from the other room barely registered.

They spent two hours exploring each other, ignoring everything else.

As Jillian showered, he fell back asleep.

"Deputy Poole," Jacob Tilly said. They were out by the gravel pit. The overgrowth was all gone. Mike was in uniform. He turned to look at the living child. "Thank you. My parents came here for the first time in almost 36 years yesterday. Ned is in jail, being held without bond. Jenny will finally pay for what she's done. And I can finally rest. Nobody else cared enough to look at my death close enough. I'll never forget it."

Before Mike could speak, the boy faded away into nothing. Mike knew he was gone. He'd no longer haunt the old gravel pit road or his house that was built on it.

He was in his bedroom again, in his bed. A kindly old woman shook him awake. "Your beautiful wife is out of the shower, Dear, and your brother is waiting for you to bring him his furniture for his apartment. You need to wake up," she said, kindly. He sat up and looked at her, realizing he was fully awake, and she was transparent. She winked and turned to walk away. She walked through the closed door, humming.

He was dumbstruck. He didn't know how to react. So, he did what she said and got out of bed. Jillian opened the door and entered as he started to make the bed.

"I'll do that. Go shower. Kenny is waiting for you," she said, kissing him on the mouth with a contented smile.

He grabbed his clean clothes and headed off to shower.

———

Kenny stood in the middle of the living room of his very own apartment. It was empty at the moment, but it was his. There was his kitchen in front of him, his apartment door behind it. To his right was his bedroom. And to the left of the bedroom was his bathroom. He held his key to his apartment in his hand.

His mother was talking incessantly. But that was because she was anxious. He understood anxiety. "Pam, please stop talking," he said with a smile.

"Am I talking too much? I'm sorry. I'm just going to miss you," she sighed.

"I'm literally a mile away from you," he laughed. "I could walk it."

"But don't!" she exclaimed. "At least not alone. Your seizures."

"I know, Mama. I promise," he replied.

The intercom by the door buzzed. He clapped excitedly, making his mother laugh at his exuberance. She moved to press the button, but he gasped, so she stepped back, and he walked past her and pressed the button. "This is the residence of Kenneth Poole. How may I assist you?" he said in a grandiose voice.

"You can buzz open the door and open the apartment door so Gordon and I can put down this heavy ass sofa," his brother's mock irritated voice responded. Kenny could always tell when Mike was really irritated. He was just teasing. Kenny giggled and pushed the button to unlock the apartment building's lobby door.

He opened the apartment door and stepped into the hallway, looking toward the lobby. Three quarters down the corridor from the lobby, he bounced like a child on Christmas morning as Mike, on the backwards end of the sofa, backed into the building. Gordon on the other end said, "I'm clear. Turn." Missy followed them in, carrying a lamp.

"Hey, hold that door!" came Dex's voice, as he, on the backwards end of Kenny's dresser, his foot still in a boot, but no longer needing the crutch, appeared. Joe was attached at the forward end.

Before noon, Kenny's apartment was fully furnished. Kristin had put away his clothes. Jillian had filled his linen closet with clean sheets and towels. His mother had made his bed and put towels in the bathroom. Missy and Dahlia had filled his fridge. And he had hung all their framed photos on his wall.

Gordon collapsed onto the sofa. "Ug, I'm old," he laughed. Pam plopped beside him.

"Who do you think you're kidding? You have 5% body fat. You're cut like an Adonis. I've seen it."

"Okay. Please don't talk about my dad's naked body,"

Jillian said, making a face.

Everybody laughed, except Jillian, Missy, and Dahlia.

"I don't get it," Dahlia said to Missy.

"Me either," Missy replied.

"Missy, you and Dahlia go get Great Aunt Bertie. We're going out for Mexican, and she wants to come," Pam told the teen.

"Okay, Pam-ma," Missy replied. "Apartment 109, right?"

"Yes," Kenny's mother answered, resting her head on Gordon's shoulder as he took her hand and kissed it.

Joe was on the phone with Bethany. "Yes, of course, Mr. Morgan can come, Bethy. It's just tacos." He was laughing. He looked happier than Kenny could ever remember seeing him.

Dex had sat down on the recliner he'd donated to the furnishings, and Kristin had promptly sat in his lap. She kissed him on the mouth before hugging him. Kenny had to admit, Dex looked pretty darned happy, too.

And Mike had taken a beer out of the fridge and popped it open. Jillian took it and drank a full half of it in one swallow before handing it back to him. He burst out laughing and set it on the counter. He pulled her into an embrace and nibbled her neck.

Kenny grinned. Love was in the air. And that was the best he could have hoped for these people he loved so dearly. That and tacos sounded really good right now. It was a good day.

Lacynda Mathes is a graduate of Radford University in Radford, VA. She holds a B.A. in English.

She is originally from Oak Grove, VA, in Westmoreland County near Colonial Beach. She graduated from Washington and Lee High School, Montross, VA, in 1986. She attended Randolph-Macon College, studied abroad at Wroxton College in Oxfordshire, England, and ultimately transferred to Radford University, where she completed her degree.

She currently resides in Sterling, IL, with her husband. She is the mother to their teenage sons, the eldest with special needs, who has been diagnosed with Lennox Gestaut Syndrome, a catastrophic childhood epilepsy, and severe autism.

www.ingramcontent.com/pod-product-compliance
Lightning Source LLC
Chambersburg PA
CBHW050734180626
46814CB00002B/752